About the Aut

EBUN AKPOVETA is an IACP accredited Counsellor with a successful career as an Adult Guidance Counsellor and Career Coach with vast experience working with immigrants from over 70 different nationalities. Her debut into fiction is this evocative novel Trapped *Prison Without Walls* which also contains three original poems inspired by the characters in the book.

Akpoveta was born in Nigeria in 1970. She is from Okpe in Edo State and grew up in Benin City where she graduated with a B.Sc. in Microbiology. She started her working career in Lagos state and in 1999 she became the Administrative Secretary for the Nigerian Britain Association until 2002 before moving to Ireland. She has spent the last twelve years engaged in various roles including being the mother of two amazing boys who bring her breakfast when she can't stop writing; as a Training and Employment Officer at BITC Ireland; and postgraduate student of various programmes. At present, Ebun Akpoveta is a Ph.D. candidate at the UCD School of Social Justice.

Ms Akpoveta has a personal and professional interest in the experiences of immigrants and she has carried out research involving immigrant integration. She is the founder of The Unforgettable Women's Network—TUWN which advocates for the equal valuing of the female person; she is also a prolific motivational speaker interested in addressing critical issues affecting individuals' development and advocating for equality. Her core message is empowering people to actualise their full potential using life-changing principles to release their best self in society. She is a founding member of the African Women Writers Ireland, a Member of RTE Audience Council, and a Columnist for The African Voice Newspaper.

She was introduced to reading by her mum Lady Grace Arogundade who took her to the library from the age of eight to borrow and read four books a week and bought her books as treats and rewards instead of sweets! Ebun presently lives in Dublin with her family.

TRAPPED
PRISON
WITHOUT
WALLS

EBUN AKPOVETA

authorHOUSE®

AuthorHouse™ UK Ltd.
1663 Liberty Drive
Bloomington, IN 47403 USA
www.authorhouse.co.uk
Phone: 0800.197.4150

Published by AuthorHouse   08/22/2013

This novel is entirely a work of fiction. The names, characters and incidents portrayed in it are the work of the author's imagination. Any resemblance to actual person, living or dead, events or localities are entirely coincidental.

ISBN: 978-1-4918-0129-1 (sc)
ISBN: 978-1-4918-0128-4 (e)

Any people depicted in stock imagery provided by Thinkstock are models, and such images are being used for illustrative purposes only.
Certain stock imagery © Thinkstock.

For

For everyone who has been through or is going through . . .
To the light at the end of the tunnel
All those who make those tunnels lights possible . . .

TRAPPED
PRISON
WITHOUT
WALLS

"You are my wife and your body belongs to me ... you have a duty to satisfy me ..."

". . . I DON'T WANT TO DEJI, I am tired and I have a headache now." Ola pleaded as her heart dropped in panic. She could not pretend not to understand the intent in Deji's eyes.

"You are my wife and your body belongs to me. So whether you want to or not you have a duty to satisfy me. Now go upstairs and prepare for me."

"What do you mean . . . did you buy me?" Ola asked outraged at the audacity in Deji's words.

Deji moved closer to Ola, grabbing her by the jaw as their eyes locked in a clash of wills and power. Deji applied some pressure to her jaw as he spoke directly to her without blinking, with his eyes wide and his nose flaring like an enraged dragon.

"I didn't buy you but I paid your bride price and part of your duty is to satisfy my sexual needs, do you understand?"

PROLOGUE

LOOKING OUT THE KITCHEN WINDOW on a November day in Dublin, with gusty winds and biting cold that chilled to the bones of ones fingertips stood the lone figure of a curvy, beautiful woman. Her well groomed braids fell freely down her back hidden away with the hood of her padded outdoor jacket, the dark kitchen mirroring her mood and the cold floor tiles like talons of sadness snatching her dreams . . . Ola huddled against the window as a cold draft wafted across her flaring nostrils, drying away any last vestige of strength in her and her eyelids dropped shutting out the outside world.

"How did I get here . . . how did I become this . . . ? When did I become second best in my own home?"

Ola listlessly paced around the kitchen, taking note of every little thing as restless energy coursed through her body making her even more agitated. Ola had a funny taste in her mouth as she ran her hand over her head impatiently pushing off her hood ignoring the cold air. She knew that feeling so well because she had it all the time, it was her bed mate and her waking companion.

". . . when did I become this tightly wound ball of anger, constantly mad—angry mad . . . full of words but no voice, wanting to speak but no words, wanting to say but not able . . . scream, shout, cry for help . . .

. . . surrounded by darkness, with nowhere to turn, no one to talk to . . . no one who understands."

Taking a deep breath with her face pressed against the windowpane. Ola looked out at the dried leaves fallen on the pathway with a deep sense of detachment and loss as she struggled to find the word to capture her feelings.

. . . *Trapped, trapped, trapped*

The seven letters of the word danced before her eyes like a jigsaw puzzle moved around by invisible hands. . . . Bigger and bigger . . . clearer and brighter it became as the word grew louder in her head floating around her mind and settling heavily with a crashing sound, it found an easy home in her thoughts.

"That's it," Ola said grasping the niggling feeling she couldn't shake off. She was trapped but there were no doors . . . no keys . . . no way out.

". . . a prisoner in my own life."

"There was a time," Ola thought ". . . there was a time." Allowing her thoughts free reign, her mind trailed away to another time where she was free as the wind blowing where she wanted to go . . . full of dreams and life . . .

CHAPTER ONE

"... Woman that I am,
Woman that I have become ..."

"I AM GOING TO SILENCE all those gossips claiming to be my friends."

Ola Peters could not contain her excitement at the prospects of Deji, her husband joining her in Dublin after nearly one and a half years of love in absentia from across the sea. It had been really hard not to hear people sniggering behind her back. Some even referred to her as a single mother pretending to have a husband!

"Not any more" laughed Ola "not anymore!"

"I will show them . . . I will show them what a proper family is!" Ola promised herself as she turned her attention to her son whom she suddenly realised she was holding too tight.

"Hey Mikey baby, daddy is coming soon!" exclaimed Ola who was finding it hard to contain her excitement.

"We are going to be a family . . . a proper family," Ola's voice hardened as she emphasised her promise very loudly to Michael who was still smiling innocently at her.

"Amazing . . . ! . . . baby, just amazing."

Ola twirled Michael around again and gave him another free ride throwing him up in the air. Michael her eight month old baby whom she fondly called Mikey was a sport and always game for anything. Oblivious to the meaning of Ola's words, he enjoyed the air ride laughing and dribbling all over her head. Ola continued bouncing little

Michael around in the air, throwing him up again in excitement as her laughter bubbled over.

"I am so excited, I'm about to explode! . . . and you know why? . . . my sugar tops . . . your daddy is coming home," Ola carried on her one sided conversation with Michael.

"He is . . . ," she reiterated gurgling at Michael who had become her sole companion and talking buddy since his birth—that is if you could call his one toothed smile and squeals talking. It had been almost one year since Michael was born and his dad had not seen him. The immigration process into Europe had been really mad, Ola thought in her quirky way though she actually meant it was rigorous. It was almost unimaginable what some people had to do to make it to the Whiteman's land. But Ola was quite fortunate that she got a student's visa the first time she applied because she had a first class honours in her first degree at the University of Lagos in Nigeria where she studied Economics and statistics. She had really wanted to study for her Masters in International banking and Finance but just before she travelled, she found out she was pregnant with Michael. It was both a shock and excitement for her at the time. Ola blamed the visa office who took months to process her application and part of her fear was that if she deferred the course she would not be able to get another visa from them. Anyhow the flight was already booked and she had resigned her job with the bank where she had been employed for over three years, so there was really not much she could do. After long deliberations with Deji and her family, she decided to still travel and at least start the Masters and see how she got on. It had been a really difficult year for Ola but all that was about to change danced an exhilarated Ola twirling around with Michael.

"He'll be here in the morning . . . fingers crossed," Ola added quickly to avert any ill luck that might jinx her plans. She had made countless efforts to get to this day that doubts hit her again that Deji would actually succeed in getting into Dublin from Nigeria.

"I can't wait, I am so excited." Ola broke into singing as her thoughts wondered away.

"Three year ago, all of this was just a dream, but here I am today, living out my dream . . . all of my dreams . . . ," Ola whispered in amazement. She was scared at times as she kept thinking something might go wrong. She didn't believe she deserved to have this beautiful life . . . but she wanted it so much . . . , she had dreamt of it so often and she was going to hold on to it with both hands . . .

Ola had always had the desire to travel abroad and here she was now, living in the Whiteman's land. Many of her friends back home were just like her and wanted to come abroad, but she knew it would only remain a dream for most as the border control people were making it even more difficult to come to Europe from outside the EU. The good thing was that many had resorted to bringing the Western world to Africa by watching foreign TV and magazines and . . . yes the internet. It had definitely brought the world closer to Africa.

Moving to Dublin had been kind of bitter sweet for Ola but she was happy she made it to the elusive *'ilu Oyinbo* - the Whiteman's land as the Yoruba's from Nigeria called it. The icing on the cake for Ola was the birth of her beautiful son Michael. He was such a lovely baby with dimples and a smile that seemed to melt the heart of young and old women alike. At one time older Irish women used to stop them on the road, on the bus and just fuss over Michael. Some even went as far as giving him some loose change. It 'had been a common occurrence but Ola put a stop to it when a friend told her about Irelands history of collecting pennies for poor black babies. After that piece of information was delivered to Ola, she became hesitant about allowing such coin gifts to Michael. She was never sure after that if the women were just being generous or if they were looking at her son as the symbol of black penniless babies! Ola didn't want that stigma or spirit of always being the beneficiary to follow her son. She knew it was a loss especially for those who had genuinely good intention . . . but then, that was always the difficulty when groups are painted with the same brush . . . Though she knew some of her misgivings had come from very superstitious beliefs, she still thought it safer to err on the side of caution.

It had not all been smooth sailing for Ola as she remembered her struggles with loneliness being on her own in a new Country without familiar supports. It made her miss home . . .

"I really miss home . . . , my long standing friends . . . , my parents . . . , especially mum . . . oh how I miss her." Ola sighed. She thought about how much she couldn't wait to get rid of her mum and what she described as her *interfering bossiness!* . . . but now Ola would gladly have given anything to have her mum with her here. She missed her so much especially when she had her son. If her mum had been in Dublin then, she would have been with her in the hospital and made her the special Nigerian Pepersoup with fresh fish and peppery spices that she would have taken her time to prepare and clean." It was one of the few things women who just gave birth enjoyed. Ola's mouth began to water as nostalgia for the soup made the aroma stored in her memory waft up her nostrils. That wasn't all Ola was missing, in fact the all over body massage was top of the list for her. The older women around the new mother would give her a bath with a soaked hot cloth. How those women were able to put their hands in water that hot and squeeze the soaking towel was truly beyond her but they did it so well. This kind of body massage was common place back home where Ola saw countless numbers of young women being bathed and massaged when she was growing up. By now, Ola's mum would have massaged her tummy and inner thighs with this hot boiling cloth as the old wives tales claimed it hastened the healing process of a new mom's body. Ola had missed that . . .

She laughed as she remembered being nicknamed a social crawler during her university days in Lagos. Ola was a people's person and having friends had always been really important to her . . . but lack of strong friendships was making life in Dublin very difficult for her. However, Ola was starting to develop some really good ones but many of them were questionable and anyway it was not the same thing as people one had known for years. People living in Dublin all seemed to have their own lives and struggles to take care of.

". . . Oh . . . but all that is going to change for me real soon," laughed Ola who was too excited to go to sleep because Deji . . . , her very own man would be coming to Dublin in the morning! After all the escapades, ups and downs, Deji had finally been granted a two year student visa—at least that was something. Ola didn't even want to think about what it took them to arrange that visa for him, the family favours they had called on to get the money together to pay Deji's international student fees just for him to get the visa.

". . . oh well, it will all be worth it at the end because all that is going to change now."

Pulling herself together, Ola gave the two bedroom apartment she would be sharing with Deji from the next day a quick once over to make sure all her wifely duties were done. Ola hadn't thought of the responsibilities that went with the title in her earlier excitement. She had to start doing wifey! And it was not just about sitting and looking pretty. In most of Africa at least definitely in Nigeria it was still seen as a woman's duty to clean, cook and care. The three C's of marriage no one talked about. Some days she really thought they should change the wedding vows for women to include those words.

". . . I Blah blah . . . blah . . . promise *to honour, cherish and love you* becomes *I promise to cook, clean and care for you*," Ola laughed at her own joke.

"There will probably be less conflict in marriages at least then the terms of the contract would be spelled out clearly," she reasoned. "Even those bra burners or feminists as they call themselves who claim equality, when they get home they still have to do the major share of the work. It is still seen as their automatic responsibility as the woman in the relationship to take care of the home! What kind of equality is that?" questioned Ola making a weary face. Ola was not expecting much as she knew that kind of equality still eluded many women especially those from the developing world, unless of course they were so rich they could afford to pay for help.

"If you want to keep your African man, you have to do the three C's. Me I want to keep my man and as they say, a girl's got to do what a girl's got to do.

"So this is me doing what I have to do."

House tidy . . . check, food in the fridge . . . check, drinks available . . . check, and finally, sexy lingerie . . . check. Ola was worried about how Deji would interpret her smalls wondering if he would think of her as a *wicked* woman. But the truth was that after almost a year and a half of being apart she definitely had plans for his body. Sixteen whole months Ola had not felt the loving arms of her husband around her, she had not felt the heat of passion between her thighs.

"I have had to suppress my desires and longing on many cold nights or some of those funny nights where you cannot account for it but you want something."

"Oh my!" exclaimed Ola, "I hope to get me some action tomorrow," she thought as her whole body was flushed through with heat and she almost would have blushed—that is if it was possible for her dark skin to change colour! Ola's mind strayed back to the really sexy nightdress she bought that plunged all the way to the waist at the back. The pictures in her mind coloured her thoughts in ways that made her burn. The well rounded bra cup pushed the cleavage up accentuating her burst line. Ola's plan was to show off her body to Deji and serve him with it so that he would never want any other woman.

". . . he is in for a definite treat tomorrow! I will show off my man and find a way to satisfy sixteen months of unreleased passion," thought Ola.

"Okay . . . ! Before I burn through my clothes I am going to get some sleep. After all, tomorrow will be here soon enough . . ." she wisely decided.

Sleep eluded Ola as she lay awake watching the clock, tick tock . . . tick, tock . . . turning restlessly in bed. Her eyes strayed to the clock hanging over the door, the long hand had just crawled past four while the short hand seemed determined to stay on six. The last time she had looked the long hand was just going past the six o'clock hour mark.

"Whoever said a watched kettle never boils has probably never seen a watched clock," Ola grumbled as she plumped her pillow into a more comfortable position.

The clock suddenly seemed to sound so loud as Ola counted the ticking of the clock.

"All that sleep, tossing and turning and only twenty minutes has gone by!" Ola grumbled as she heard a baby crying.

The sound of Michael crying was a welcome distraction for once. She was usually frustrated by the early morning cries which signified his request for food but today was different. Ola needed anything to keep her distracted from her anxiety because Deji was flying into Dublin at ten in the morning . . .

Michael's insistent cries broke into her thoughts again as he seemed to increase the sound an octave or so to make his seriousness known.

"I'm coming, I'm coming," Ola called back to him.

"Maybe I should just connect a pump to my breast attached to your mouth Michael," she joked. Ola tried to feed her son exclusive breast milk from birth but she didn't seem to be able to keep up with his demands. Some of the other African mothers said that boys were like that, they sucked more and needed more feeds but Ola could not keep up. It was one of her disappointments with herself . . . not being able to do what her own mother did for her. Her mother fed them breast milk exclusively for one year while Ola only lasted three days with her son. She often wondered if it was the loneliness or the lack of support but she just realised she was too drained and didn't have the energy to feed herself after feeding Michael with his on the hour demand for milk! It made her feel like a cow at one time and Ola chastised herself for such an un-motherly emotion. It was one of those thoughts which she had never been able to voice to anyone for fear of being seen as a bad woman.

It made Ola wonder if she really was a bad mother for not being a natural with child rearing as people said women were supposed to be. The way it was, she had two choices, either to keep trudging along like most of her friends until the day she got found out as a fraud or hopefully she'd learn on the job and become really good at it.

"It's just amazing the number of things people expect us to know automatically," thought Ola as she laughed at herself when she remembered her earlier struggles with being the perfect mother.

"Probably by the time I perfect it I will be a grandmother!" . . . but all is good reasoned Ola as she realised she was not crying as much as she used to when Michael was born. Some of those days had been really crazy and hard.

"Oh my . . . ," exclaimed Ola as she remembered when Michael was three weeks old, she was so hungry yet so tired and sleepy, because Michael was feeding continuously and her breasts were sore and heavy.

Her tummy was empty from hunger because she was too tired to get up from bed to go and cook. She felt so drained, she lay in bed crying and every time Michael cried, she would pull him close and connect her nipple to his mouth. That was the only thing that stopped the tears but it left her feeling so exhausted from not eating that she could not get up from bed. That was definitely one of the worst times of her life in Dublin . . .

Ola had never in all of her life known tiredness like that. It scared her so much that she thought she was going to die. The image of people finding her bare chest and dead in bed for three days with Michael still sucking milk from her dead breast came back vividly to her mind. That's what had given her the energy to get up from the bed to take care of herself. The sad thing was that no one in the country had been looking for her . . . no one had cared. No family to call her own. No one came knocking on her door to see if she was okay. Of course she had received calls from Nigeria but she couldn't tell anyone the truth about her situation. At the time of Michael's birth, she had just moved out of a flat in Summerhill which she had been sharing with four other students near the City Centre. So all the people she knew were her new church friends who only saw each other in the church once a week or when they passed each other at the shops.

"I am definitely better now," thought Ola as she wiped a lone tear from her face. "It's all going to be okay now."

Ola knew people thought she was mad putting so much hope in Deji, but they had not been lonely like she had been, with no one to call her own . . . coming back home to herself and her little baby. She had perfected the art of speaking baby babble being starved of adult conversation, it had been almost unbearable sometimes.

". . . Mm . . . mm," sighing, Ola continued with a cynical laugh as she thought of all the calls she got from Nigeria from people who just wanted to come and live abroad. She wondered what they would say if they knew half of what people endured in the name of living abroad.

Ola grimaced as she remembered the day she got scared by three lads, the oldest was probably twelve . . . maybe, thirteen years old. They wouldn't dare approach her back home in Nigeria, but like they said, this was not her country so anything she saw she had learnt to accept it. That day she was walking down the street, with two big shopping bags just after she got off the bus. She had just bought a few items for her baby in preparation for going to the hospital when the three lads rounded the corner and it was too late for her to do anything.

"Hey . . . !"

The tallest of the three shouted pointing in her direction. Keeping her head down, Ola pretended she didn't see them as if they were not talking to her. She increased her pace as much as she could waddle with her bulging stomach. She had seen a movie where a woman's stomach was cut open by a mentally ill woman who wanted to steal her baby that her mind went into over drive. She wasn't even thinking that they were just kids, she was so scared that it annoyed her. Ola was disgusted with herself as she felt her hands shaking with fear.

"Black bitch, I am talking to you. Do you want some more," he jeered as his mates egged him on. From the corner of her eyes Ola saw this young boy grab himself and do a pumping grind in her direction.

Ola felt defiled but she swallowed the feeling as her heart rate accelerated, maybe from fear or rage she wasn't sure. The one thing she was sure of was the urgency to get out of there fast!

"I have to get out of here unhurt." She knew things like this could very easily escalate especially when one was trying to prove their rights. Discretion they say is the better part of judgement or as the English say, he who fights and runs away lives to fight another day. Deciding to pick and choose her fights, Ola doubled her steps saying nothing as she tried to move away. There were people passing by saying nothing, two ladies in fact crossed over to the other side of the road probably to avoid the fracas. She remembered placing her hand over her bulging stomach as if to protect her unborn child from the insults.

"This too shall pass," Ola encouraged herself ignoring the lads who disappeared as she rounded the corner and there were two Garda officers patrolling the street.

"I know I might look like a silly woman waiting for my husband to come and join me, but I have been without and I know how horrible it is."

Ola realising she was getting carried away in thoughts pulled herself together as a well feed and burped Michael immediately fell back to sleep which had become part of his morning routine.

Food, burp and sleep . . . that should be the title of his first essay in college laughed Ola.

"Oh no . . . , I am going to be late to pick up Deji." She cried as she rushed around crashing her hip into the kitchen table as she noticed that the slow clock had decided to speed up the minute she took her eyes off it!

"Typical," she moaned throwing her hands up in the air feeling overwhelmed. Ola rushed into the shower for a quick wash.

"I don't want any funny things wafting to Deji's nose," Ola wrinkled her nose as she still made the time to laugh about her situation.

Ola was a truly odd mixture of a woman. She was deeply philosophical and at the same time she had this weird sense of humour that she could find something to laugh about in everything. She could rightly be described as an oddball or more accurately a nut case!

Grrhh . . . grrhhh . . . , the persistent ringing of the doorbell interrupted Ola's shower.

"Who is that now?" Ola wondered, deciding to ignore the person she carried on rinsing the soap off her body. She scrubbed her body so hard under the shower you would almost think she was washing the bottom of a burnt jollof rice pot!

"Okay, I really have to get on with it," Ola urged herself.

"Come on, come on . . . , I have to pick Deji from the airport and at this rate I am going to be late."

Ola felt bad that she hadn't told any of her friends about Deji's impending trip or that he was in fact due to arrive that morning! She wanted to surprise them, but more than that, she was worried in case he didn't make it.

"People who can just get up and go, decide they want to live in another country and all they have to do is pay the air fare . . . don't understand the stress others have to go through. Relocating to Ireland was a big deal for Ola, it meant her mum could not just get on a plane and visit her to help her even when she is stressed out of herself. It meant her immediate family could not just get on a plane to attend her child's naming ceremony, special birthdays . . . nothing spontaneous could happen especially where cross border visits were concerned.

"No, I didn't tell any of my new friends because I don't want my humiliation to be publicly shared if anything goes wrong." This way she wouldn't need to explain to anyone else if things didn't go as planned.

Ola wasn't expecting anyone but it seemed the person at the door was not going away! She stomped her feet in mild annoyance as the caller at the door seemed to permanently leave their finger on the door bell.

"Go away," Ola shouted at the closed bedroom door.

"Oh all right, all right," Ola cried as she came out of the shower. She grabbed a black dressing gown lying on the chair quickly pulling it on. She was a bit worried as she was not used to getting early morning visitors. Ireland was not like back home in Nigeria where people just arrived at your house to visit at any time of the day.

Most African people had become very westernised here and they hardly dropped by unannounced anymore.

It suddenly dawned on Ola that maybe something was wrong with Deji's trip.

"Oh my God, please Lord, anything but this, anything but this . . . ," Ola prayed as the muscles in her tummy began to twinge. Grabbing her stomach Ola wasn't sure which one she should attend to first.

". . . Loo or door?" Ola questioned as she wavered between the two.

"I have heard of anxiety provoked pooh but this is a first for me," she laughed.

The door won over as it seemed whoever it was had no plans to leave unless they were attended to.

"Maybe something is wrong with Deji . . . , maybe his flight has had an accident, oh my God! Maybe it's the police . . . did Deji get in trouble?" Ola's thoughts went completely wild.

"Oh please God," Ola offered up a silent prayer as she didn't know what to expect. She finally hastened her steps and ran to the door with her heart pounding and her stomach continuing its somersault.

CHAPTER TWO

"WHO IS IT?" OLA ASKED looking through the peephole at the door.

". . . Me," a very gruff voice answered hesitantly.

"Me who?" Ola snapped back impatiently at the closed door.

". . . Open up woman!" the voice behind the door replied firmly. It sounded like a male trying to disguise his voice. Ola could hear a hint of laughter in the voice and she concluded it must be a friend. Ola's suspicions were beginning to be aroused as she again tried to decipher who the person was through the peephole. One can't be too careful she told herself. The height was suspiciously familiar but Ola had not seen Deji in over a year.

"Deji . . . ?" Ola asked inaudibly beneath her breath. "Could it be him at my door?" She wondered her anxiety slowly changing to excitement.

Ola turned off the door alarm which was giving out its warning beeps. She had gotten used to leaving the alarm on at night for extra protection being a woman living alone in the house with only a baby for company.

"Give me a proper view of your face," Ola insisted leaning closer to the door for a clearer view. As Ola took one more look, she came eye to eye with a face she had only seen in pictures in the past year and a half.

". . . Deji!" Ola exclaimed audibly this time. She saw that beautiful face that she has come to love so much, a face that had been nothing but a distant memory, one she only saw in her dreams.

As reality hit her, Ola's heart began to thump, her hands became shaky and unsteady as she mentally took stock of how she was looking. She quickly ran her fingers through her hair to bring some order to it.

"Oh my . . . ! I really wanted to look nice today," a flustered Ola thought of the time she'd spent at the saloon getting her hair and nails fixed the day before.

"Now I don't even have the chance to have it all set up as good as I should look. I can't believe it . . . Deji is at the door . . . oh my world how did this happen?" A myriad of thoughts flooded Ola's mind disorienting her actions and thoughts as she took stock of her clothes. Gone was the well planned sexy nightdress and undies firmly tucked away in the cupboard for the evening! All she had on was her well-worn old dressing gown.

"Oh well I'll have to do," she consoled herself. "He will just have to understand. That's what he gets for surprising me—a half dressed grumpy woman!"

"Come on woman, I am freezing here . . . ," snapped Deji, but the laughter in his voice took any sting away from the hardness of his tone.

The timbre of his voice was enough to move Ola as she quickly snapped out of her reverie. Still with shaky hands but barely concealed excitement, Ola opened the door and there was Deji, her six foot two inches tall husband . . . her love . . . her darling, her lover had come to complete her. Ola was so happy she felt she could die. With outstretched arms, Ola rushed into the arms of her lover as he grabbed her lifting her off her feet swinging her around. Deji had always been big and strong. He lifted Ola up so easily it felt really good she felt like a baby again guessing it was one of the reasons many Nigerian women were encouraged to call their husbands daddy, especially those from Yoruba land. Ola was so happy at that moment she would have happily called him anything. She had missed the feeling of being in Deji's arms, his strong firm muscles around her well rounded hips . . . , the closeness of being with her own husband, not just having wet dreams at night but the real Deji being in her arms.

Ola suddenly felt shy and nervous as he allowed her body to slide down his firm torso. He put her down holding her close . . . , so close in fact that she could feel the hardness of his manhood pressing against her. It felt strange and exciting all at the same time.

"Oh God I feel alive again," Ola cried silently "so alive"

Ola kept looking at Deji as if to commit every part of his face to memory. One million questions she was bursting to ask flew through her mind like a mighty wind going in opposite direction to an express train. How did he get here, he was supposed to arrive in three hours' time?

"Let me look at you babe," said Deji

Deji was a good kisser and kissing him was definitely high on Ola's agenda at that moment. Ola hesitated as she wasn't sure if she could take the lead but Deji bailed her out as he placed his hand under her chin and angled her face to his. Ola knew that in romantic novels they claim the earth stands still from a simple kiss, well . . . , just looking into Deji's eyes did it for her. Ola for the first time in her life felt herself go dizzy for a few seconds. As they stared into each other's eyes and the un-communicated words flowed between them, all of Ola's dreams seemed to come true in one breathe. Maybe it was being apart for almost a year and a half or the expectation she had built up. At that moment Ola didn't really care, she just wanted the pressure in the lower part of her pelvis to ease.

". . . my family all together and me in the loving arms of my own fella . . ." That was the last coherent thought Ola had just as Deji moved the last few inches between them and their lips locked hungrily, one minute, two . . . or ten minutes, Ola wasn't sure how long they stayed locked in each other's arms as they tried to satisfy their hunger. All she knew was that . . . em . . . em, yeah, feeling so happy . . .

Ola and Deji walked hand in hand into the adjoining room, this time it was Ola who had a surprise for him. Ola urged Deji into the room where little Michael slept . . . her little bundle of joy. Deji hesitated for a minute as he saw the baby wrapped in a sky blue baby blanket. He was sleeping so soundly with his mouth slightly open and his tiny fists clenched on either side of his head. The sight of Michael sleeping was so lovely that sometimes, Ola would take pictures of him as he slept. It seemed Deji was also not immune to Michael's charms even in his sleep state. The reaction of 36 years old Deji's first sight of his son was an image Ola would cherish for a long time as she looked at him in amazement. She knew the awe of being a parent . . . , of producing a whole human being could be quite humbling sometimes and not just for women as Ola had assumed. Deji took a few hesitant steps closer to the cot as Ola nudged him forward. She watched the play of emotions flowing across his face as he looked down at his son. She saw Deji's chest swell with the pride of a father who was priding himself for doing well.

"Thank you," he said as he pulled Ola closer, tucking her firmly at his side. Deji's words of appreciation gave her some insight into the value he placed on having a child, especially a male child. His voice was so low and tender she actually almost didn't hear him. Ola could not believe how the sight of his son . . . our son brought out that amount of gentleness in him.

She figured it was typical especially for many African men. Deji's actions just showed that he was no different as most would commonly measure their manhood by being able to have a male child. The banter and back slapping that went on at the birth of a male child you'd almost think they did the whole work themselves or that their personal efforts affected the gender of the child, mm . . . mm . . . One strong argument they mainly gave in their own defence when they were accused of not valuing female children equally as the males, was that boys were the ones who made the family name continue as girls marry and quickly take on their husbands' names.

"I guess, with the way many African women take on our husbands' names once we are married, many Nigerian women do it automatically no questions asked . . . the joys of being an M.R.S . . ." thought Ola. It made many parents worry if they didn't have male children or heirs as they thought of them, though both sexes worried for different reasons.

Ola remembered growing up in a family being the second of three girls. It had been hell for her mum who used to cry when she thought the children were asleep. Many nights Ola heard her mom plead with dad to be patient and that they should keep trying for a son. After the birth of the third daughter her dad went out and had an affair and when the woman produced a male child for him he married her as his second wife. That fear hung over so many families so much so that women had this pressure to produce male children so that they could be assured their partners wouldn't have an excuse for having another wife or kids outside marriage just to prove their manhood. She wished they understood the science of X and Y chromosomes and that it didn't make them less of a man having female kids. Maybe some women could have a bit more peace within the marital relationship Ola punctuated her thoughts with a long drawn out hiss at the injustice and pressure this placed on women even when the fault is not theirs.

"Look at me!" Ola caught herself quickly. "Can you imagine, that I a woman, I am thinking that having female children is a fault! Then how can it end, when can it end, who is going to make it end?" She scolded herself strongly.

Ola could not understand why she was thinking all those crazy thoughts at that moment of all times when her excitement should be over flowing. After all it was not a problem she would have, as Michael her first child had answered her prayers so no pressure for her in that regard.

"Come honey, you must be tired after travelling all night, come and have a shower and let me prepare you something to eat and you can have some rest now that Michael is still sleeping." Ola turned her attention to enjoying the moment with Deji.

"I have missed your caring nature Ola . . . I have really missed you."

"Me too . . . ," holding onto his hands they walked towards the room that she would be sharing with a man for the first time.

"This is a really nice place, how did you manage to do that?"

"I survive . . . My visa allowed me to work and I was also minding kids especially in the evenings for parents who were either working long shifts so that helped pay a lot of the bills. The sad thing though was that I barely completed the first year of the Masters as my due date coincided with a lot of the essays but they have allowed me to defer it till next year. The only problem is that I have to pay fees for another year and it is high, really high because I still have to pay international students' fees even as my visa has been converted to stamp 4 visa because of Michael."

"Come here my industrious woman, I have been thinking of only one thing coming here."

An unexpected feeling of shyness suddenly seemed to overcome Ola as her eyes widened in bashful excitement as she got the meaning of what he wanted.

"Oh my . . ." tingles went through Ola's body and she felt her insides shake and her womb tighten as her excitement increased ". . . maybe after you get some rest and had something to eat" she suggested coyly

"I can't wait, it's been over a year since I was with you . . . come here and stop talking."

Excitement at his manly take charge nature coursed through Ola as she walked into his open arms.

Deji made Ola his woman again and as she lay beneath him with his laboured breathing that seemed to increase with each hard trust he made into her body. Ola seemed to have forgotten what love making or sex with Deji was like. He always had this tendency of going for certain body parts without any preamble but she had always been too shy to mention it to him or to even ask him to slow down . . . and as the hands on her breasts squeezed tighter bringing pain . . . Ola thought maybe she should have said something . . .

"I don't know . . . but I am a woman . . . an African woman . . . we don't talk about things like that to our spouses, we just don't. He'll think I am a slapper." Ola wasn't sure if all women didn't talk about sex, what pleased them or even how they wanted their bodies to be pleasured but she knew most of her friends didn't. They spoke to each other about what wasn't working or what they didn't like while the main culprit was left in the dark. Ola tensed as she too fell into that same mould with Deji,

"Is that good, honey . . . , is that good . . . ?" Deji asked between panting thrusts into her body for reassurance.

"Yeah it is good."

Ola's mouth said yes as her heart cried out *nooo* . . . , she didn't say it though . . . , she couldn't say it to Deji. She thought he was such a proud man, who believed in his sexual prowess. She didn't want to embarrass him and hoped that since it had been a while it would get better.

"I think . . . I hope" she prayed silently.

"I can't tell him I was disappointed, I just can't. Ola stayed still as she listened to his laboured breath and the deep guttural sound of his cry of release. She held onto his shoulders with her thighs tightly wrapped around his hips in the hope that she could assuage some of the tension in her loins that seemed to hold her just on the edge. . . . maybe, she tried to move around a bit but Deji finally collapsed on top of her as he found his release.

"You are so special babe, you are the best," he said giving Ola a kiss as he rolled away.

Ola lay there with a mixture of feelings, physical pain and the pressure of being on the brink of release, aroused but unfulfilled. She bunched up her body to try and release the tension.

"I am not sure which was the bigger pain," Ola thought saddened by the unrequited desire in her that had her wound up like a fully coiled spring ready to snap and the physical pain of the thrust that seemed to reach the back of her womb. Ola ran one hand close to her breast . . . she wanted to touch it the way she felt it should be caressed but she didn't . . . she couldn't. She just held the ache in her body and lay still in the foetal position till the desire slowly ebbed away. There began her new journey of pretending. She felt she had been brought up like that and besides she had to protect his ego and self-esteem because he was her man. She was taught that she had to make him feel special and like a king in his home, yet something in her was crying "what about me . . . , what about me . . ."

CHAPTER THREE

OLA DID NOT KNOW HOW much she wanted to be seen as the good wife until Deji's arrival. She quickly settled into the routine and chores that came with the role, while her excitement could easily be seen by how much she was willing to do to make the relationship an enviable one!

"I want a perfect home and anything I need to do to make Deji happy at home I am going to keep doing because *a* good woman builds her home, and I will build mine," Ola vowed.

She did not envisage any troubles as she was confident of her capabilities. She was certain that if there were difficulties in between, it would not be due to her because she was going to love him to submission she promised herself.

Ola started with the basics as she remembered the popular saying that *the way to a man's heart is through his stomach.* So making perfect meals was her entrée into being the dutiful wife. She made sure Deji's food was always well laid out, he got the best part of the cooked meat, chicken or fish. Meals were proper food not just some dried bread slapped with a bit of butter—none of those make shift foods was good enough for her Deji. Ola frequented the African shops for all the delicacies in fact it was like Nigeria in Dublin when it came to meal times at their home.

Ola spent her days attending to the three C's which she reckoned sustained any good relationship. She didn't expect much help from Deji in that department neither did she receive any! "That's the way it is with these men" thought Ola as she tried to rationalise Deji's behaviour at home especially when it came to what he called women's jobs. Ola smiled as she mimicked the disparaging look on his face when he talked about such chores. She didn't mind all of that at all, what she found odd was Deji expected her to take pride in doing them because somehow or other she was supposedly pre-wired for it. As if she should feel less of a woman for not doing it. . . . Maybe some women get off on it Ola thought but she was sure very many women would easily survive without having to do such chores if they were sure it wouldn't be waiting for them when they got back home!

Ola tried to understand how such beliefs came to be prevalent . . . if women just took it on or there were some unwritten rules somewhere that dictated the ascription of such roles. Ola could not understand how a lot of the world seemed to have changed in many areas but when it came to things like this particularly when it concerned women, there seemed to be constant fights to resist any small change tooth and nail!

"Seriously," thought Ola as she went about putting the bedding and towels in the washing machine.

Ola smiled as she entered into that weird mood where she got very philosophical, unfortunately most of the thoughts and ideas she had were kept to herself.

She marvelled at the double standards sometimes where on one hand they said it is not African culture for men to do house work and cook, but they are very willing to accept technological advancement and fly in the air like the birds even if it was in a metal bird called the aeroplane. Ola laughed at her own analogy. Seriously though, human beings were meant to either walk on their feet, run or climb to get from one place to the other Ola reasoned in that quirky way of hers that made her such a funny character to be near sometimes. . . . but a few people decided they wanted to make men fly in the air like birds and today many of us enjoy the aeroplane.

"You would have been seen as an *'air force'* . . . and not in a good way if you could fly in the air." Ola thought of the Nigerian vernacular way of saying someone was a witch!

"Meanwhile, today we all pay to fly in the air. How come African's who fly in planes are not called the Whiteman's witch or wizard. . . . But when women decide they want the men to share in the house work they are said to have been destroyed by imbibing the Whiteman's culture."

She smirked at how tradition, religion and culture conveniently accepted riding in a car, using a telephone or flying in the sky as she brought out the ironing board and iron to begin straightening Deji's work clothes for the week and the children's uniforms and play clothes.

Ola knew that the assignment of cooking, cleaning and caring duties in the home was not unique to African women, otherwise there would not still be a need for Western women to push their agenda for gender equality

". . . pffffffffftttt," Ola pursed her lips drawing out a slow and long hiss. Ola saw this life as her fate . . . the price she had to pay for being a Mrs Somebody as if she was nobody before she fumed.

With a big yawn she stretched out her body, throwing her arms out slowly in the air, twisting from side to side to ease her aching back.

"I didn't chose this life . . . it chose me from the day I was born a woman, on the other side of the continent," Ola thought as her mind drifted to her parents and her home when she was growing up. She could not remember seeing her dad pick up even a brush to clean the floor, never . . . , not even once. Yet she remembered her dad's room being the cleanest part of the house, his bathroom was the cleanest at home, his bed was always spotless and well laid with clean sheets. She remembered her Dad even having this special chair, special drinking cup, dinner dishes and crockery! It was so unreal but at the time, no one questioned it. They all did it, from mum to the kids. They all did their share to maintain dads 'kingship' at home. Incredible as it was all dad's things were always kept spotlessly clean and tidy and no one dared touch them.

Stopping mid-way through her ironing, the veracity of Ola's situation seemed to hit her as she saw the parallels between her parent's relationship and hers.

"I have made Deji my king! umh mm . . . hum . . . hum." Ola shook her head vigorously from left to right.

She realised she had married into the very same kind of relationship her parents had, or maybe she was just acting out her parents relationship in her own marriage.

Ola wondered why she was grumbling after all she was simply reproducing exactly what her mother did. She briefly entertained the idea of blaming her mum for not showing her another way of being but she laughed at herself as it dawned on her that Deji was an advancement on her dad in the negative direction!

At least her dad hung up his own clothes when he took them off but her Deji was a serious case. Ola didn't complain about it but it irritated her to see him step out of his clothes and leave them there till she came and sorted them out . . . She was grateful for small mercies that she didn't have to manually wash clothes any more.

"I think I will actually do a little jig and dance the day Deji puts his own clothes in the washing machine or even take his dirty dishes to the sink himself! Sometimes it feels as if I have two sons," thought Ola, "Deji and Michael . . . maybe three soon she added hesitantly as she put her hands over her tummy, rubbing it in a circular motion lost in thoughts . . . thinking of her missed menstrual period.

The sound of Michael crying broke into Ola's thoughts and she quickly jumped to sooth him.

"Can you take care of that child woman? I am trying to sleep here!" snapped Deji from the bedroom where he was.

"Yes honey, I'm on it, shhh . . . ," Ola cooed at Michael as she tried to settle him down.

Deji couldn't stand Michael crying especially when he is having a nap and Ola couldn't blame him reasoning that he worked really hard to try and provide for the family.

He didn't really consider what Ola did at home as work, some days she just wanted to remind him of how much she would have been earning if she was doing these seven day shifts she did at home outside the home as paid employment.

"Providing care, personal development for the child, feeding one adult and child, bathing one child, cleaning a two bedroomed apartment daily and maintaining all health and safety procedures in the home.

Ha . . . ha . . . ha . . . ," Ola laughed softly as she mentally prepared her curriculum Vitae.

"I guess some people would say I was doing it for myself after all they are my family and the child I am taking care of is my own son. Maybe it is time people begin to see that having a child is not just satisfying ones maternal need but as ultimately providing a service to society!" Huffed an irate Ola. This was a sore point for her as she listened all the time to the way parenting was seen simply from the point of meeting individual needs. She wondered if the day would ever come where parenting would be valued the same way as qualifying as a doctor. Ola knew it was the kind of radical thinking which she had come to like but she wondered how radical it would be if women were to boycott giving the gift of children to society!

"How does one explain that a person studies medicine and becomes a doctor and we all appreciate them by paying them huge amounts from the States resources? They conveniently forget that if mothers did not allow their bodies, their lives and homes to be taken over by babies the doctors would soon have no work because there would be no human beings to treat!"

Ola was very particular about this and she wished people would see giving a child to the world as a gift women allowed their bodies to bring to the earth and not simply a duty or chore which they performed! Ola knew that the possibility that she could be pregnant was probably making her more sentimental about this . . . To her, these children were the little humans the earth needed to be the future workers, tax payers or simply those who populate the earth with continuous life flow.

"Yes we enjoy the reward for being mothers—well some of us," Ola laughed as she remembered some days when she wondered what she was doing having children after long hours of tedious work punctuated with constant crying, exploding bottoms and smelly nappies!

Ola could not get away from the thought as the plot thickened about a society suffering from human shortages. She knew society had never really given proper thought to the role of women which many took for granted. She imagined a world where women became selfish with their bodies like many professionals who gained their wealth and were unwilling to share and charged exorbitantly for their services.

"The Earth could so easily wake up one day and the world would be empty, full of 80 and 90 year olds with no one to bury the dead, care for or even serve the living. Chiefs would have no one to rule, kings with no kingdoms, graduate doctors and surgeons with no one to operate on and politicians with no one to lie to. Ha . . . ha . . . ha . . . ," Ola laughed aloud again as the plot grew in her mind as she pictured a city full of leaders and no one to lead.

Ola's inner world could be mad sometimes with the kind of impossible thoughts she entertained.

"What is that country . . . ?" Ola racked her brain as she tried to remember the report talking about a country whose population was ageing. There was even another place where younger women were refusing to have children because they felt it would limit their chances of having a career.

"That might just serve the world right," Ola laughed enjoying her thoughts.

Ola lost the fun in her thoughts as she saw the difficulty of being placed in situations where women needed to choose.

"Mm . . . mm . . . ," Ola laughed again, this time giving off a more cynical sound as she thought of the night time duties that women were automatically expected to do, not for fun or their own pleasure but a duty they performed. Ola didn't know if it was the same for every woman. She wondered if other women were more daring when it came to sex or if she was just timid. It was something she thought about a lot but never really found anyone to really voice her worries to.

"With Deji, sex is on demand-whenever and however he wants it and for peace sake, I just do it and the worst part is that I never . . . you know . . . I just never . . ."

Feeling herself welling up, Ola placed Michael in his bouncy chair in front of the telly with a few colourful shapes to distract him. She moved into the kitchen to start preparing dinner while keeping the door open so she could keep an eye on him. Ola was appalled that she could not freely use the word . . . orgasm even in her own private thoughts. It felt as if she was doing something wrong.

". . . I am not supposed to talk about things like that anyway. I am not supposed to want to enjoy sex as if my body was just an object for another's pleasure or a baby factory. It is un-African, some say—unladylike." Ola thought it was hypocritical to be expected to be doing ladylike things with someone who saw her without any clothes on! Unfortunately, her friends and even her sisters who were married said the same things. It felt like a hopeless life sentence with no way out. Yap, yap, yap . . . they all went. A good woman is supposed to build her home that means clean, cook, care, provide sex.

"Who takes care of the good woman?" Ola asked ". . . because after almost one year of being a full time wife and carer for Deji this one is stressed, tired and really, really exhausted . . ."

In all fairness, it had not been all bad as there had been some perks for having a husband especially within the African community—at least now people were referring to her as madam. They invited her for traditional group meetings called 'kparakpo. Even in church she seemed to have more recognition from the pastors and the members, particularly other married women who were worried before that she was a single woman who was there to tempt and steal their husbands. Ola cringed as she thought about the attitude many of the women had given her before Deji came. She wondered why women were more antagonistic and suspicious of each other.

"Married with benefits that should be the title of my blog or book if I ever indulge my creativity," Ola shook her head. She knew she was bolder in her thoughts than in person but she wished she could verbalise even half of the things she thought about. She knew she would probably have a more fulfilled life . . . she might respect herself more.

Ola was happy that the more established women in her local church invited her more regularly for programmes, they even stopped and chatted with her more, whereas before they treated her like a leprous single woman who had something that could be contagious. Ola snorted as she thought about Joshua's mum in particular. Ola had concluded she was the most suspicious woman in the whole place. If anyone so much as spoke to her husband for more than one second she would be beside them asking for their phone number and name. Ola suspected she was one of those women who checked their husband's phones and pockets for messages from other women.

". . . ughhhh, disgusting . . . , I will never do a thing like that, . . . I can never be so insecure and jobless," Ola criticised harshly "I know things are bad but I pray they never get that bad. . . . I will never reduce myself to such gimmicks . . ."

Chapter Four

PREGNANT!

The doctor just confirmed what Ola already knew. She was nine weeks pregnant! It had been a year since Deji and Ola were reunited and it seemed all the nightly escapades between them had paid off as Ola was definitely pregnant and hopefully would have another little one soon . . . She kept it quite for a while as traditionally in many African settings, you did not have to announce the obvious. She would wait till the evidence of what she had done in secret or under the covers of darkness became apparent when the tummy bulged! Anyway, many people worried about announcing their pregnancies too early in case telling the wrong person who was not happy about their having a baby would bring a jinx into it. Superstitious maybe, but it was always better to be safe than sorry, as they said you never know who is happy for you or what people are wishing for you.

The first person Ola told apart from Deji of course was her sister Janet because she was worried about her ability to cope and she needed to offload her worries on someone. Connecting with Janet over the phone she broke the news to her.

"I think I am pregnant—no, I am pregnant," Ola corrected her evasive omission.

"Whoa . . . , for definite?" asked Janet,

"Hmm mm," mumbled Ola as she nodded at the phone

"That is a good thing isn't it?"

"Yes I suppose it is, I have wanted another child since Deji came."

". . . So why the sadness in your voice?"

"It's hard . . . , it's really hard doing everything at home. I feel used now like a housemaid in my own home and I don't think I can cope with extra responsibility."

"What about Deji?"

"Oh you know the way these men are, he doesn't seem to be able to do anything at all."

"You can't continue to do everything in the house darling, especially with a young child and you being pregnant. You know at home in Nigeria it is a bit different as there is a lot of help from cousins, sisters, parents even poor relatives who are only too willing to help in exchange for bed and board or school fees."

"I know Janet . . . , I know. But I think I made the mistake already and it is really difficult now to change things and ask Deji to assist me at home."

"Remember you are just a woman not a super woman."

"Yeah I'll bear that in mind though sometimes I wished I was supper woman or Cat woman," laughed Ola as the call ended.

"Maybe it's not too late," Ola thought as she reflected on her conversation with Janet. "Maybe I can start gradually before the baby is born to ask Deji to support me and just do some bits and pieces in the house . . . yes, maybe that's what I will do." Ola resolved.

Armed with her new found strength Ola waited for an opportune moment to try out her plans on Deji. Fifteen weeks into her pregnancy, Ola found that her previous experience of having a baby counted for nothing as she was overwhelmed with constant morning sickness and lethargy that she didn't experience when she was pregnant with Michael. Still, she had not been able to summon the courage to ask Deji to help around the house, even with cleaning up after himself. The conversation with Janet left a lasting impression on her as sometimes she had to remind herself that she was suffering from a condition that took two to create and two of them would benefit and enjoy. She wondered why she was carrying it all on her own.

Looking around the bedroom and the pile of washing, Ola took the bull by the horns and decided that there was no time like the present.

"I have to ask for help," Ola repeated to herself to fortify her resolve. This was usually the point where she chickened out and decided that maybe she could manage for that moment. *"I'll see how I feel tomorrow"* was her usual exit line! But her situation was changing and so she knew she had to take action now. "I have to do it now because things are not getting better . . . ," she repeated to herself over and over.

"Honey please can you help me hoover the house as I am trying to sort out the washing while Michael is asleep?"

"Sorry?"

Taking in a deep, breath, Ola almost retracted her words as the dark look that accompanied Deji's solitary word requesting her to repeat herself almost intimidated Ola from speaking. She knew he'd heard her as she sighed feeling frustrated at Deji's silent tactics daring her to repeat what he thought was an audacious statement. He did that all the time, as if giving a recalcitrant child the time to rethink something! Ola silenced her inner fear as her resolve hardened.

"I . . . , I am not feeling too well that's all," Ola finally stammered watching Deji purposely climb up the stairs towards her.

"So I was wondering if you can help me with the cleaning of the house so I don't have to carry the hoover up and down the stairs."

"Oh . . . , oh . . . , oh . . . I see, so this is the reason you were so desperate to have me come to Dublin. You want a houseboy . . . You think I am to be your house husband. I have heard about you women that when you come abroad, you forget your African values. Now you can actually open your mouth and ask me to clean the house. Unbelievable . . . when did that start? That you can talk to me in that manner Ola, answer me!"

"I am sorry Deji . . . I didn't mean anything like that, I just said it would be nice if you can help out in the house since I am sorting out the washing and cooking. And honestly, I am not feeling too well. You know I wouldn't say anything like this otherwise. *Me oh ron yin nishe* - I am not sending you on an errand. You must understand that," said Ola as she appealed for Deji's understanding.

"You still have the audacity to say I should clean the house eh, you silly woman. I have told you to cut off contact with all those single women with loose morals whom you've been hanging with but you have chosen to defy me"

"Ah ah Deji, relax," Ola teased gently as she tried to make him see reason. "What is wrong if I said that any way, I am tired of cleaning up after you too. After all you are an adult and you don't even wash your own plate when you finish eating, you act as if it's a big deal for you to take your dishes to the kitchen. Come on now, Deji . . . , me too I am not your house girl. You are my husband not my owner, do I look like your propertyyyy . . . ?"

Whack . . . the imprint of Deji's fingers on Ola's face and the sound of it in her ears cut off her words midway. When people say they *'saw red'*, with the force of that slap, Ola understood what the expression meant because she saw red immediately.

"So now you can talk back to me? You can argue with me? You think I am your mate now you stupid woman? You show me no respect in my home! I tell you if you will not learn how to behave well willingly I will make you learn it by force." Deji shouted at Ola at the top of his voice, ending each word that came out of his mouth with a punch that landed anywhere his fist could find on Ola's body.

"Deji, please stop, you are hurting me, you will hurt the baby, please Deji . . ."

Deciding which part of her body was the most vulnerable . . . her face or her tummy was an easy choice for Ola, as she quickly held up her hands over her tummy to protect her unborn child. That meant her face and head was open to the blows Deji forcefully directed at her. In fear Ola tried to back away, but she panicked as she felt the back of her legs hit against an obstacle as Deji lunged at her.

"Dejiiiii!" Ola screamed in fear for her baby as she felt herself losing her balance, she barely managed to turn sideways to avoid the full weight of his body as he fell towards her. As if in slow motion Ola felt herself falling slowly but it was just a split second that seemed like an eternity. She gingerly reached a hand behind her, to try and break her fall.

"Oh my God . . . ," Ola chanted over and over as she had only one thought in her mind,

. . . my baby . . . my baby

Luckily for Ola, it was a soft thud. She landed on a play mattress she had left on the floor for Michael but her joy was short lived as Deji didn't seem to be done with her.

"I will teach you never in your life to talk to me that way. I am the man in this house you hear me? There can only be one person wearing the trousers in the house. You are my wife and your job is to submit to my needs and desires. Whether I want food at three am or sex at midnight you provide it. You hear me, you provide it or you are dead, you hear me dead . . ." Grabbing her face, Deji shook it from side to side shouting at her at the same time.

"I am sorry honey, I am sorry . . . ," Ola cried over and over, and she was truly sorry as her body ached all over from the punches.

At this point, Deji was past hearing, he wasn't listening to Ola any more. Ola watched in dread as Deji pulled down his pants and turned towards her where she was trapped between his legs as she lay on the mattress.

What happened next in Ola's mind was the scariest thing that had ever happened to her in all her life and to believe that it happened in her home, with her own husband, Deji . . . the man she loves . . . , loved . . . , she corrected herself, the same person who promised to love and cherish her in sickness and in health . . . where did all those promises go. She didn't want to believe he meant to do it . . . maybe it was him towering over her watching her lying helplessly on the mattress that gave him the idea because suddenly, Deji began unbuckling his trousers!

"Wh . . . , what are you doing Deji?" Ola stammered as she interpreted Deji's intention.

"You should count yourself lucky to have a man. There are many women out there who have none. Many women who are willing to do anything for me and you try and disrespect me?"

"Please Deji stop, not like this, you will hurt the baby."

"Shut up . . . , you are still telling me what to do?" Deji screamed at Ola even harder, his eyes red with rage. Ola had never seen him like that. If he had not been home all day she might have thought he had taken some strong drink or smoked something, but Deji didn't do drugs and he didn't drink more than two pints of beer on any day.

As his eyes darkened whether with rage or desire Ola wasn't sure but she was not prepared to wait to find out as she pulled her weight up and tried to crawl through to the other side of the mattress. Deji being physically stronger than her reached out with his right hand and he easily grabbed one of her feet pulling Ola back to the edge of the mattress. Holding her down with one hand, he yanked open her dressing gown and in one fell swoop he had her undergarments off.

"Not like this Deji . . . please, not like this . . . , I am sorry, so sorry." Ola cried over and over. She tried to struggle thrashing around but all her efforts seemed to be futile as Deji easily held her body down to the makeshift bed with his weight. He grabbed first one hand and then the other pulling them over the top of her head putting a stop to Ola's feeble attempts to punch his back.

"You are not sorry enough but you will be by the time I am done with you. I will teach you a lesson that will make you think twice before you go against my wishes again or try to control me."

Realising the futility of her resistance and efforts, Ola decided to stop struggling and give in as she finally just lay there and took it.

Yes, she did! She lay there and just took it, everything . . . whatever he wanted she did. It was easier that way as his hands began to meander over her body. He bit her breast at one point bringing pain to her eyes as he thrust into her harder and harder. All Ola could hear was Deji saying over and over . . . ,

"I am the man in this house . . . I am the man in my own home . . . no Jezebel with a controlling spirit will stay in my home no way . . ."

As he pulled out of her body which was wracked with pain, Ola felt too physically drained to even lift her hands to investigate the state of her bruised lips. She could feel her lips swollen and the taste of blood in her mouth. With her ears still ringing from the blows . . . , Ola finally curled up to try and hold her emotions in. She was scared of falling apart. She kept telling herself she had to hold it together. Ola didn't know what had come over Deji . . . but he had never . . . ever hit her before. There had been words and he had even called her names but never had he physically hit her! Ola starred at Deji in shock.

"That will teach you. In your life, you are never to answer me back. You hear me, when I speak you listen, is that clear . . . is that clear?" he shouted even louder at her

"Yes, I am sorry . . . , Deji, I am sorry . . ."

Ola just wanted to get away. She felt defiled, she felt dirty. She just needed to wash herself . . . , to wash his seed away from her body. She wanted to wash the feel of his callous hands away from her skin . . . She finally pulled herself together and got up off the mattress in a blind haste to separate herself from what had just happened. Ola moved groggily around the room with tears blinding her eyes as her head began to spin. She reached out to break her fall but this time she wasn't as lucky as she must have come out of the room onto the landing instead of into the bathroom as she thought in her haste to move away from Deji.

"Ooooh God, help meee!" thought Ola as she screamed "My babbbbyyyy . . . !"

Unfortunately, Ola's hands didn't find anything to break her fall this time.

She rolled down the stairs bumping against the wall in an ungainly manner, confused about whether to protect her tummy and the baby or cover her head to reduce the risk of injury. "Help me oh God, help me . . ." cried Ola as more pain wracked every part of her body. The last thing she was conscious of was Deji's voice from a long way up . . . maybe the top of the stairs screaming "Stop you silly woman do you want to dieeee?"

"What's her name?" Ola heard fuzzy voices that seemed to be coming from a long way off, echoing inside her head.

"Ola," that was Deji, Ola realised as she was able to pick out his voice in the commotion around.

"Ola . . . , Ola . . . can you hear me?"

The voices were still very faint to Ola as she tried to move her body but it felt as if every part of her body was glued to the floor where she lay.

"We have to take her in . . ."

"How did this happen?"

"She fell down the stairs" that was Deji's now, his voice was the only one Ola could pick out clearly as the other voices sounded strange, they sounded foreign like Irish voices. Ola slowly opened her eyes as she tried to lift her hands to her head as the banging inside her head increased.

"Don't try and move Ola, you seem to have had a nasty fall . . . , can you hear me?"

"Yes . . . ," Ola moaned in a weak voice laced with pain closing her eyes again as the painful sensation seemed to increase with light shining into her eyes.

"We are going to take you into the hospital to give you a proper check"

"The baby . . . ?" Ola whispered her fear to the attendant at the same time noticing one of them was an African.

"Just my luck," Ola thought, "only I would be unlucky enough to get a Nigerian as an ambulance attendant. What are the odds of that ehn . . . , how unlucky am I . . . how unlucky can I get?" Ola's distress seemed to increase visibly as she prayed silently that he was not someone she knew or from her cycle as she feared her news going all over Dublin like wildfire.

"Don't try and talk, we'll take you into the hospital now as fast as we can," he said as he noticed Ola's feeble attempts to speak.

"No . . . ," she insisted, reaching for her tummy. "My baby . . ."

"Are you pregnant madam?"

"Yes . . . three . . . almost four months."

"We'll have you checked out . . . can you tell me where you are feeling any pain?" Ola could hear the urgency in his voice. She prayed silently as she listened to the conversation between the two men.

"Let's move, this lady needs to get to the hospital and fast." The activity seemed to start again as there was a lot of buzz it seemed or maybe it was people moving really fast. Ola couldn't be sure as she closed her eyes with a single tear rolling down her face.

In her hazy pained condition, Ola heard Deji say "I'll come with you."

"No!" cried Ola mustering all her strength making her voice come out much sharper than she intended.

"No . . . ," Ola repeated a little gentler, "you stay with Michael . . . , take care of Michael," Ola told Deji firmly as she became conscious of the wailing baby in the background. He was still in his room ". . . oh my poor baby." Ola cried becoming even more upset.

"Okay I will . . . you fell, Ola . . . , okay? . . . but you'll be fine, it was a nasty fall . . ."

Ola looked at him silently questioning how he could know that . . . , how anybody could know. She turned away from Deji suddenly becoming conscious of her body soaking with hot liquid between her thighs as it began rolling down her legs.

"Oh no, please help me . . . I think I am bleeding . . . , I am losing my baby . . . ," Ola screamed in panic grabbing the nearest attendant in a death grip.

The two ambulance attendants proceeded to carry Ola out of the house on a stretcher, the same time she became aware of the blaring siren from the ambulance outside the house. Embarrassed Ola wondered what the neighbours would say . . . as she noticed small crowds of people gathered at different doors on the street. How was she to have known it would turn out to be the least of her worries . . .

—————ινν∾⌒⍟⌒⊙⌒⍟⌒∾ννι—————

Being in the hospital gave Ola time to think. She thought about what she was going to say to them . . . , all those caring people who wanted to help her. She wondered if she should tell them her husband beat her up . . . , forced himself on her . . . or if she should say he raped her? She asked herself if a married woman could claim her husband . . . her own husband had raped her, and told herself no. Men didn't rape their wives, worse still African men didn't rape their wives. She told herself they would say she was frigid if the news got out. It was just sex and her duty to supply it. What could she say really . . . ? That she was crying and fainted from the pain and then fell down the stairs . . . but to what end? He'd go to jail, the father of her child . . . , only one now as her poor unborn child had been a bigger casualty than herself. The little life snuffed out before she had a chance to enter this world. Ola lay still on the bed with tears rolling down her face as she cried for the daughter that was not to be . . . , killed so needlessly . . . a miscarriage . . . spontaneous abortion they called it.

"Did my three month old baby not have rights? Who will take up the fight for her . . . , Me?" asked Ola mockingly in derision of her weakness.

"Hm . . . hm . . . I am too weak to preserve even my own life how am I going to get the strength or . . . the resources to preserve another human being. He wins all the time. He always wins . . . ," Ola turned over on the bed and gave herself over to more tears.

"Hi Ola." Shock coursed through Ola's body as she heard his voice. She noticed that her heart suddenly began to beat too fast that it scared her. She felt her body freeze up as if she had been placed in a bathtub full of ice.

"Deji . . . ! He's here, why . . . , how dare you . . . how dare you . . . ?" Ola fumed silently as her heart beat accelerated further and her head started pounding with renewed intensity. Ola kept her face turned away and her eyes firmly shut. She couldn't bear to look at him . . . , she couldn't bear to talk to him . . . not now, just not now. Ola felt still too raw, like an open sore.

"Ola? Are you sleeping?"

Ola refused to turn around as she continued to keep her eyes shut.

"If you can hear me Ola . . . , I just want to say I am sorry . . . , I didn't mean for you to get hurt," Deji said in an apologetic voice which seemed to break on the last word.

A fresh bout of tears rolled down Ola's face as the pain was rekindled in her heart. She could feel Deji standing beside her hospital bed for so long it felt like an eternity but in reality it was only about twenty minutes—but it was twenty minutes too long as far as Ola was concerned.

She just couldn't face him . . . , she couldn't talk to him . . . not now . . . maybe not ever. But then where would she go, where would she start from? It was all too much for her to take in now.

"I am just going to lie here and be dead." Ola decided. "That's what you have done to my daughter, that's what you could have done to me.

So enjoy the silent, unresponsive me," thought a resolute Ola silently as she let her actions speak for her.

Deji must have finally grown tired of standing beside her silent body. She held her breath as she heard the patter of his shoes moving away from the bed. Ola waited a few minutes before she opened her eyes and turned around. Her face hardened as she noticed Deji had left a bunch of flowers and a card on the bedside table. Reaching for the bell, she called the nurse for assistance.

"Do you want a vase for these lovely flowers?" asked the nurse

"No thank you. Can you please find a nice home for them? I am allergic to flowers." Ola fibbed to cover her real intention.

"Okay . . . they are very beautiful," said the helpful looking nurse

"I don't want them . . . ," Ola said snappishly, giving vent to her anger. She couldn't stand any more reminders of Deji right now. She had the pain from the bruises all over her body and the emptiness of her womb to remind her . . . so no thank you, Ola decided she didn't need any more reminders of Deji.

"See how good a liar I am becoming as well . . . , heaven help me . . . heaven help me," cried Ola in self-recrimination. She was embarrassed because she was sure the nurses knew what had happened to her. She could see the pitying looks from them as they came to tend to her wounds. They all seemed to know she was lying that all her bruises were not from falling down the stairs . . . No doubt they had heard variations of this story from silly women like her . . . but there was not much they could do without her cooperation . . . She knew it was difficult to take in but she felt there wasn't much she could do as well. She had to think about the implications for her family. She'd be eaten alive by the family back home in Nigeria and even her friends here would never understand if he got arrested for hitting her.

"Hitting me indeed . . . ," laughed Ola. "If I say it that way, it is the Oyinbo man's way of describing what Deji did to me. No . . . ," thought Ola, "he beat me! . . . the way a master beats something he owns that has no rights.

"That's what Deji did. He beat me. No . . . , I have nothing to say to him . . . , not now, hopefully not ever . . ."

———∾∾⬳⬲⬳∾∾———

After two days in the hospital there was not much else the hospital could do for Ola, so she was being discharged with her head still all over the place, uncertain what to do. Deji was still the closest person to family she had in Dublin and she had to leave the hospital. So any way she looked at it she was stuck. Ola exhaled deeply

Picking up her mobile phone from the bedside locker, Ola released her frustration on the phone by punching the buttons with more force than was necessary as she concluded she had to call him . . . , she had to go back to him . . .

"Can you come and pick me from the hospital? I am being discharged," Ola spoke briskly to Deji.

"Okay, I will be there in forty five minutes or so. How are y . . . ?"

Ola cut the line off with Deji's question and attempt to show he cared hanging mid-sentence. She didn't want to hear it . . . , she didn't want a conversation with him. She actually didn't want to see him not ever again. But what could she do . . . what . . . ? The tears were free falling across her face again as she was overwhelmed with feelings of helplessness. She seemed to cry so easily these days.

"I am sorry about the baby . . . , but you'll have another one. Maybe she wasn't meant to stay . . . ," Deji said as he helped her into the car.

"Murderer, murderer . . . , you killed her . . . you killed her!" Ola shouted but the words hung in her throat. She raged that even now she couldn't say what she really wanted to say. Ola was not going to blame herself this time as she had no fight in her, and felt so, so drained.

Yes they had another daughter four years later, Alicia . . . her sweet angel. She came and took Ola's pain away. They gave her a Yoruba name, Dayo, the full name being Ekundayo, meaning, he turned my sorrow to joy.

Deji and Ola never talked about that incident after that. In fact Ola realised that they never really talked again after the miscarriage. They became two strangers fulfilling their duties as husband and wife. Died at thirty, buried at sixty was no longer a proverb that made her laugh, it had become her story. She was living the proverb. Maybe her tombstone would read died at twenty eight buried whenever the body gave up on her . . .

CROUCHED IN TREMBLING FEAR
Poem inspired by the pain of the character Ola Peters

Woman that I am . . .
Woman that I have become . . .
Made to feel responsible . . .
For . . .
The Abusers abuse
The Tyrant's tyranny
The Bully's low self esteem
The Rapist lack of control
The Sluggards dirt
The Miserly' meanness
The Brutes' force
The Controlling's temper

You have raped my Mind, my Body, my Emotions . . .
I have become what you have made me
Hard . . . brittle and dry!

I have become what you have called me
Dependent, needy and weak
Though alive, I walk around going through the motions

Till the day I find myself . . . to be tormented no more!
Till the day the Rapist is sent down to rape no more
Till the Bully is cowered to intimidate no more
Till the Brute is snarled to beat no more
Till the Abuser is hushed to wound no more

I remain crouched in fear . . . a trembling fear
Controlled by *society*
To perform as the *Perfect* woman . . .

BY EBUN AKPOVETA

CHAPTER FIVE

"You have raped my Mind, my Body, my Emotions . . .
I have become what you have made me . . ."

"HELLO . . . , HELLLLOOOO . . . ," OLA'S INSISTENT CALL into the phone was meet with a deafening silence. She cradled the phone against her shoulder for a few seconds willing the caller to speak. She contemplated her best course of action for a few more minutes but finally gave up as the disengaged beep sounded in her ear.

Ola had been getting these worrying strange phone calls on the main house phone and when she answered the caller didn't say anything. The worrying thing was that the line connected sometimes for as long as two minutes with no sound then it was clicked off. Ola was worried because it wasn't the first time it had happened. Even as her thoughts strayed to the last telephone incident in the house and all the palaver it had caused, the sound of the ringing phone began to echo round the house again. Ola offered a silent prayer that her intuition would be wrong but she couldn't stop her body from reacting. By the fourth ring, Ola's heart beat had increased and she could feel it racing as if in competition with the sound of the ringing phone.

"I know it is silly," thought Ola, "but I am afraid . . . I know the signs and it usually means a season of trouble for me and my family. Please, not again . . ." she silently prayed.

"I know what it means . . . unless I want to deceive myself," Ola mumbled wearily as her voice echoed in the house.

"It means Deji is at it again and the truth is that I am so tired I can't go through this. Not now . . . I am too exhausted for this." With her resolve firmly in place, Ola walked away from the phone, shaking her head as she gave the phone one last warning scowl.

"I am just going to let the phone ring till the caller gets tired," she said . . . and finally there was some quiet in the house as the sound died out.

The last ten years had seen Deji and Ola going from one crisis to the other that had left her disillusioned about her marriage. Her dreams of the ideal, enviable home were in shreds. . . . But in spite of the major upheavals in their relationship, they always seemed to find a way to mend things and stay together.

" . . . because that's what we do," Ola answered the critical voice in her head in resignation. Ola had always believed that marriage was for life and even if she didn't anymore, she wasn't going to make the children live separate lives from their parents.

"Even if things are a bit difficult with Deji, we have to stay together, at least for the children's sake," Ola told herself as she silenced the questioning voice of reason inside her head. Michael was now a lanky twelve year old going on twenty who fed on chips and sausages—apparently all the African cuisine was lost on him. Alicia was six and had turned into a right little madam, a real princess into all the pinks and frills popular with girls. The good thing for Ola was that Alicia was her daddy's pet and he didn't mind taking care of her as he always said yes to whatever she wanted. Seeing Alicia with Deji sometimes made Ola wish she could ask her for the secret to getting his love as Ola still longed to improve her relationship with Deji. They were in a much better financial situation as Deji had gotten a really good job as an accountant after completing his training while Ola remained at home for the kids since they were still young. She fleetingly toyed with the idea of returning to her plans of building her own career as they had planned but she immediately abandoned the idea as she remembered previous conversations with Deji on the issue. He always told her not to forget that her minimum wage earnings would always be less than the childcare costs they would incur not to mention the running around getting the kids to a minder. He usually added what he considered his winning argument of why she had to continue as a stay at home mum which was that both parents would be too tired to supervise the kids' homework and failure to do that would nullify the essence of working if they could not give the children quality life and support. Ola usually found herself floored by Deji's argument which could sometimes go on and on until Ola agreed with his view. Her one big regret was not returning to complete her Master's programme after Michael was born. Anyhow, there was no way as Deji insisted they couldn't afford to pay two international students' fees at the same time. She wished she had at least insisted on taking a job then in spite of his arguments. That would have given her some economic base, unlike now where she was as dependent on Deji as the kids and he knew it and wielded his power well.

Ola heaved a sigh of relief . . . finally some peace and quiet as the phone remained silent. Her joy was however short lived as a few minutes later the phone began to ring again. This time Ola felt a kind of magnetic pull to the phone. Like someone in a trance, she found herself walking slowly in the direction of the ringing phone, as gently as she could muster as if not to scare away the person on the other end of the line, Ola slowly reached for the phone.

"Mm . . . mm" Ola took another deep breath. She was doing this so often that it was almost becoming her signature tune! Ola nestled the cold surface of the phone against her ears as she decided not to speak first.

"I will give this useless caller a taste of their own medicine. Let's see how they like a silent line!" She plotted against her *silent caller*. Ola pressed in closer to the phone as if doing that would bring the caller's voice through the phone. She was certain there was someone on the other side because she could hear a faint sound in the background. As she waited and waited . . . , her patience seemed to be wearing thin and still nothing . . . no one spoke. Ola suddenly felt confused as she could not understand the intention of the caller or as she had come to call them—the *silent caller*. Ola was annoyed at the sheer patience which the caller exhibited because she couldn't hold herself much longer. She knew she definitely wasn't going to get any marks for patience. "Come on!" Ola raged gritting her teeth to stop herself from speaking. Hers urge to say something to this person on the other side of the phone seemed to be getting the better part of her as she indulged herself in her thoughts in calling them all kinds of unprintable names!

"Come on" Ola screamed inside, she really wanted to scream and curse at the phone but she held herself back with her last shred of patience.

Bang . . . , bang . . . , bang . . . , Ola could feel her heart beating erratically. She could feel herself perspiring and a sour taste in her mouth—maybe from fear, maybe from anger she wasn't sure but one thing she was sure of was her increasing frustration. Ola was breathing so hard her nose was almost flaring like a dragon breathing fire. She was at the end of her tether and wanted to give in and satisfy herself and just scream, but she choose to count to ten instead as she lost this round and said in the calmest voice she could muster.

"Hello", there seemed to be some hesitation from the other side of the phone.

"Hello?" Ola said again in a slightly louder voice laced with impatience. Click . . . and the phone went dead in her ears.

"Why, why, why . . ." she raged. Every particle in Ola's body rose up in protest at the thought of another woman having the effrontery to call her home.

"It can't be anyone else," Ola told herself "it has to be another woman on the line because it has happened before." Two years before precisely when there had been a big bust up in her family, Deji promised it wouldn't happen again. Ola knew then as she could see now that it was only a matter of time. "Please make this go away, please . . . ," she prayed hoping for any type of help at all.

"Is it that Deji doesn't love me . . . is it that he disrespects me? Does he think there is nothing I can do? Is that why he allows another woman to call his home phone?" Ola seethed silently feeling more distraught by the minute.

Ola's shrug of indifference was contradicted by the muddled thoughts raging back and forth in her mind.

"I don't know what to do or how to address this now."

The last time a mystery woman phoned the house Deji promised it was a colleague of his at work who was being mischievous. Even Ola felt it sounded lame then but she wanted to believe him so much and avoid arguments that she accepted his explanation. Ola wondered where he came up with such a ridiculous story claiming that his colleague had taken the house number off his phone when she borrowed his mobile to make a quick call. Ola laughed mockingly at her gullibility for believing him.

She knew what she didn't want to believe . . . what she refused to see. Even when it sometimes looked like paranoia, she was certain it was another woman . . . It had to be. All the signs were there. The thought was beginning to aggravate Ola as her heart began to beat too fast and loud it was almost as if it had added external sound systems.

Caught in the paradoxical dilemma, Ola concluded that Deji was having an affair but her dilemma was that she really didn't want to know.

"I don't want to find out" cried Ola even as she began to hatch the plan of how to catch him.

"Oh help me God, I am scared of catching him. Why . . . , why . . . can't Deji be like other men" Ola wondered. "Why couldn't he keep his affairs as affairs and leave them out there . . . , why must they come to my home with him." Ola remembered that when she was growing up, affairs were common place in the society considering that men were actually allowed and even expected to have more than one wife, partner or concubine. At least then enlightened men in Nigeria used to have affairs but they made sure the woman at home or wife number one as she was referred to never found out. They always made it a well-kept secret but not her Deji," thought Ola. "Trust him to rub it in my face."

Ola knew what she was going to have to do, she was going to have it out with him. "I am a woman and not a door mat where Deji can just clean any rubbish he likes."

She waited and waited after she put Alicia to bed and sent Michael up to his room. She resolved to trash out the matter once and for all as it seemed anything swept under the bed had a funny way of rearing its ugly head. Finally, a little after 10pm Ola heard the rattling of the door handle which signalled Deji's return. She watched as the door swung back on its hinges and Deji walked in looking really tired. Ola's mind went into overdrive as she couldn't help imagining all that Deji might have been up to, . . . who he had been with . . . what he had done . . . with whom. Looking at his hands brought all kinds of torturous imaginations to Ola about where his hands could have been and what he might have done with them. ". . . ughhhh" She shivered as anger and revulsion passed through her body. Though all that was going on between them, Ola had instinctively given herself a quick once over to make sure she was looking attractive and presentable for Deji.

"Pathetic isn't it?" Ola questioned herself in self-recrimination as she took in her slinky peach coloured nightdress with its dipped front neckline that showed off her well rounded breasts. Ola had heard it said so many times that a man only strayed from the home when his wife didn't make herself attractive or let herself go after childbirth. Maybe if she gave Deji more sex . . . maybe he would not be tempted by other women out there Ola remonstrated with herself. Maybe . . . , maybe . . . , maybe . . . , just so many maybe's.

Despite Ola's tiredness—and she was truly tired, she still found time to square her shoulders and paste a welcoming smile on her face.

"Hi Babe" Ola smiled at Deji as he walked into the room. She grabbed the black work case Deji liked to take with him to work and then reached up and planted a kiss on his lips. When people said women multitasked, Ola's way of doing that was in her head as she had this really vibrant life inside where she was able to carry on parallel conversations!

"I just have to make myself more attractive and make him want me more. I need to show him he is the man of the house and I am a desirable woman" Ola told herself again and again, with all her initial anger melted and gone—maybe not really gone . . . , just bottled-up.

"Why don't you go up and have a quick shower to unwind while I prepare your dinner." She asked lovingly.

"Yeah okay, I am kind of tired."

"You guys were at work late today, hope everything is okay." Ola carried on conversationally.

"Yeah, the guys from work wanted to go out for drinks. You know the culture of after work drinks, so I just stayed with them and nursed my glass of coke all night since I was driving."

"Liar! Liar!" Ola again reverted to self-talk as the scream was only resounding inside her head. This was one of her biggest frustrations as she wished she could boldly voice her real thoughts.

"I don't believe you," said Ola in a voice that was only audible to her since its volume appeared as always to be on mute outside 'World Ola!' As she retreated into her thoughts, she knew she really wanted to tell him she didn't believe him, but she couldn't. She had learnt over the years to hold herself back to avoid a backhanded slap for daring to be forward as Deji called it. Ola had become scared of saying such words . . . , even thinking them made her feel like she had violated her part of the relationship even when Deji had no qualms about showering her with derogatory remarks. Ola was scared of challenging Deji and he knew it. He maintained his edge over her with just a hint of what could happen if she crossed him and it seemed to work to keep her silenced. She was intimidated by the fear of the full blast of Deji's anger being directed at her.

"I can't handle his anger now" she decided as she reconsidered mentioning her suspicion about the phone calls. Worse still, Ola was reluctant to bring everything out in the open when in fact she really wanted to know—but told herself she didn't want to . . . not really. Okay . . . , she admitted shaking her head as if to clear it from all the confusion. She wanted to know but not that he was cheating . . . but rather that he wasn't! Ola huffed as she tabled out her predicament.

"What if I ask and he admits to having an affair, what then ehn . . . ? Then what? Do I leave my man for another woman who was not there when we suffered together? Do I get angry and fight with him . . . to what end?" she asked embittered by her limited choices.

"If I leave him then I'll have no man and I'll become 'Ola no man', back to being a single mother, then the whole world will say I could not satisfy my man." Ola was upset at how weak she sounded but she couldn't help it right now she admitted in resignation.

Still feeling hazy, Ola mechanically went about heating up Deji's dinner just the way he liked it, a bowl of his favourite vegetable soup mixed with roast turkey and well spiced chicken pieces and pounded yam which Ola described as sticky mashed potatoes.

Chapter Six

The game Spot the Difference popped into Ola's mind as she sat down opposite Deji watching him work his way through his dinner. She mentally ticked off the difference between the picture of her present life with Deji and what she'd hoped it would be when she romanticised the idea of marriage-the cure for loneliness!

Deji didn't bother asking if she had eaten . . . he didn't ask if she was okay or even if she wanted anything, no romantic exchange of food, kisses, or desirous looks . . . nothing. Ola wished he would reach across the table and offer her a piece of meat. Not because she was hungry as she had her dinner with the kids but as an act of love and sharing. She imagined him putting a piece of chicken half way in his mouth and enticing her to take the other half from him. The romantic in Ola went into over drive as she imagined the playful banter and struggle for the piece of food turn serious as sexual tension develops between them and they end up making love on the dining room table happy that the kids had gone to bed already!

Ola lifted her head startled by the sound of Deji's teeth clamping on his meal with single minded attention, munching away and the futility of her daydreaming hit her. Her fantasy turned to anger and the difference between her inner picture and her real life with Deji took her from zero to mad. Ola became plagued with renewed anger at the thought that Deji might be having an affair when she remembered the silent caller. She wished she was treated with more consideration as she simmered slowly feeling unappreciated. Maybe she wanted too much, maybe she was too idealistic she wasn't sure. All she knew was that there was no joy . . . , no excitement in her life.

Ola was deeply flustered at her inability to have easy conversation with Deji instead of holding it in. They were the picture of an old married couple sitting across the dinner table in stony silence which wasn't Ola's idea of fun. She wanted to joke and make small talk but uncertainty about Deji's reaction deterred her and her self-talk was not helping her build a better relationship with him. She decided on a safe topic—the children, realising it was the only thing they seemed to have in common now. She asked herself how they had become that way

Saying the first thing that popped into her head, Ola used the kids as an ice breaker with Deji. "The teacher sent a letter with the kids about the fees for books." Deji looked up from his meal at her with a blank stare for a minute that Ola innocently assumed he didn't understand what she said.

"Why don't you jump inside my pockets and take everything there since that is all you are good for." Deji answered snappishly.

"What is the meaning of that Deji?"

"You are just a leech . . . you take . . . and you take . . . and you take," said Deji with so much force each word dropped heavily on Ola's heart as if laced with scorn. It sounded as if he had been waiting for her to say something.

"Why the insults Deji, what did I say that was wrong now?" asked a baffled Ola. She began doubting herself and her ability as she wondered what she could have said or how she could have said it any differently.

Ignoring her bewildered look, Deji ranted on "You sit on your fat arse asking for one thing or the other. What do you do and you call yourself a woman? Just the school books you can't even handle that. I pay for everything . . . , everything! Look at yourself, you are nothing but a drain pipe and then you wonder why I don't come straight back home. Tell me how does that work? Just looking at you reminds me of running water in a basket. You know what . . . , if you cannot sort out their school books then let them stay at home."

Ola sat for a few minutes with her mouth wide open bereft of words.

"Where is all this coming from . . . ? Deji, Deji!" Ola just kept calling his name to stem the flow of vile words. She quickly became teary as the shock wore off. She couldn't recognise herself in the tirade of words which Deji spewed at her.

"Are you done? What have I said that warrants all these insults Deji? What have I said . . . ? I don't understand all this. You asked me to stop working so we could save on childcare costs. You wanted me to be here for the kids when they came back from school. Is this the way you choose to reward me Deji? What have we come to . . . what have we become . . . ? Can't we even have a conversation and discuss how expensive things have become?" Ola's eyes overflowed with tears streaming slowly down her face.

". . . you asked me Deji, you asked me . . ." Ola continued as she seemed unable to contain her disappointment at how the conversation had gone.

". . . I stopped attending college because you said we could not afford to pay my fees and our childcare costs. Deji! You said you would complete your conversion programme in college before I could go and complete my Masters. Is this the reward you have for me making as if I am a lazy person who can't go to school, ah . . . Deji?" Ola cried even louder and harder.

Deji's response to Ola's litany of words was to move his thumb and four fingers together mimicking a yapping motion throwing it all back in her face.

"Yap . . . , yap . . . , yap . . . , that's all you are good for isn't it?" he asked after she had stopped talking

"What are you saying? Why are you saying these vile words to me, Deji . . . ? I stopped college and gave up all my savings to pay for your college fees when you came to make a way for you."

"Oh stop those crocodile tears you . . . , they are as false as you are. I have seen them so many times I am not moved any more. I let you keep the children's allowance, where is it? What are you doing with it?"

"But you know I have to buy things for the children and when there are no groceries I replace them with that money I buy school shoes and pay for school trips as well."

"Same difference Ola, same difference, with you it's one bill after the other. What do you offer me, nothing, absolutely nothing! What do you do to make me feel okay?" Deji shouted. Reaching out his hands, he grabbed her shoulders so hard Ola thought he was going to crack her joints. Deji upped the game and began to shake her back and forth so hard she could feel her teeth rattling in her jaw.

"Deji you are hurting me."

"Oh get off!" He screamed giving her one final push causing Ola to hit her knee as she fell back into the chair. Ola sat stunned, taking in deep breaths propelled by rage unable to defend herself as the things she had done and endured to make Deji feel comfortable raced through her mind. She could not even find the words to defend herself any more.

"I don't want to fight with you Deji. Please not now." Ola tried to reason with him. She knew she had to calm down and speak gently or she ran the risk of aggravating him. The last incident was still vivid in her mind and she didn't want to enrage him because at least that way the physical pain and bruises would be less. Thoughts of the children upstairs in bed were enough to make Ola back down. She realised that scrapping with Deji would wake them up. She took a deep breath and forcefully calmed herself down suppressing her own feelings and anger . . .

"I will go and talk to the school and see if they can allow us pay it in instalments and we can break it up over four months." Ola conceded for peace sake.

Deji at this stage had gone back to eating his meal as if nothing had happened. Finally out of steam, Ola went silent and watched Deji till he finished eating. Uncertain of what was to come. Ola felt Deji's eyes fixed on her making her look up. He was staring at her with a frown on his face as if he was looking at the most ignorant of fools he had ever seen. The unwavering intensity on Deji face gave Ola a hint that something other than their recent conversation was on his mind. Finally Deji curled his lips while waving his fingers at Ola making the motion of someone washing their hands.

Ola jumped up immediately as she got the message—she didn't bring him the bowl of water for him to wash his hands after eating. Ola was indignant that Deji had cleaned his hands on her shoulders when he shook her earlier. The image of him wiping his hands close to her eyes just to make sure she didn't forget again flashed through her mind and it was enough to move her into action.

If it wasn't so annoying Ola would have found it funny.

Walking into the kitchen as quickly as she could a tumult of thoughts flowed through her. Ola was saddened by her situation as it seemed never ending with no way out. This was one of those times when she really felt small . . . , so small that she thought she could fit in the small space between a thumb and fore finger. Ola felt pressure mounting so she did what helped her most of the time—put her back against the door and counted backwards from three. It upset her that this was how most of her conversations—if she could call them that . . . , this was how most of her chats with Deji went, it had become her familiar story. Ola allowed fresh warm water to run from the tap into the bowl, enjoying the calming sound of the flowing water. She knew she could not stay in her private respite for too long if she didn't want Deji breathing fire down her neck. She quickly squeezed some liquid soap in the bowl of water and grabbed the green pastel napkin for him to dry his hands.

"I better go quickly before my lord and master gets cranky," Ola teased as she hastily made her way to Deji with the bowl of water.

Just as it always happened, Deji her husband of thirteen years was still sitting at the table waiting for Ola to bring in the water for him to wash his hands. As each step brought her closer to him, she considered slowly pouring the bowl of water over Deji from the top of his head down his small goatee. A slight giggle escaped her as she replayed the picture in her mind.

After all, if he wanted to behave like a self-proclaimed paraplegic who can't get up to go and get his hands washed Ola thought she might just help him all the way by giving him a full bed bath—or maybe a *chair bath* would be more appropriate Ola smiled at her private joke.

Ola seriously considered the consequences of speaking her mind.

What if she were to ask him to get up and go to the kitchen to wash his hands . . . ?

What if she refused to bring him the bowl of water . . . ?

What if she really poured the water over him . . . ?

"Spill it over me why don't you . . ." Ola snapped out of her bold daydreaming as Deji's voice rapped sharply into her ears.

"Sorry," Ola replied like a robot.

"You are so clumsy . . . with no style. Just water to wash my hands you have to wait for me to remind you. You are a waste of space Ola, honestly. Look at you . . . just look at you. You have to think about your life and see what you can do with it."

"I'm sorry," Ola repeated as quickly as she could get the words out as her private smile was immediately replaced with dread. She placed the bowl in front of Deji and watched him take his time washing his hands and drying them with his gaze fixed on her. He flung the napkin back on the table, pushing back his chair noisily making a scrapping sound against the tiled floor. He got up slowly with exaggerated energy giving Ola a final disparaging look from her head to toe then walked away.

Ola remained standing where Deji had left her with arms on her waist. She was just tired, even more tired as she looked at all the dishes and mess on the table.

"You are welcome" Ola mouthed silently to the non-existent thank you from Deji's disappearing back. She knew she would have to wait forever to get a thank you from Deji for anything she did for him because to him, everything she did was her duty! How do you thank someone for doing their duty Ola stated rhetorically? She could not understand Deji's duplicity where he went out, paid for his meals with his hard earned money and ended up thanking the staff and even clearing his own table. Yet in his own home, he offered nothing but took her service and compliance as his right.

Ola asked what she got from him . . . not even a thank you, not even a 'nice meal Hon . . .' nothing . . . Ola thought feeling dispirited.

"Hm mm . . . hm mm . . ." laughed Ola in her usual self recriminatory way. "Maybe the honey as an endearment is asking for too much but it would make the service I give him as my husband worthwhile. It would make me feel valued or wanted like a human being not a thing or a property at another's beck and call!"

The words *Modern day slavery* popped into her thoughts but she dared not call it that because it would mean that she was not grateful. Many interpreted such thoughts as the ideas of a non-submissive wife and worse still she would not fit the criteria of a good wife. To expect and demand gratitude and respect was to want recognition for something that was a duty.

Ola wondered if Martin Luther King had been a woman and had thought to add that to his *'I had a dream speech'* that one day men and women would be treated equally in and outside the home . . . What a difference it would have made to women. . . . ah but that was Ola's secret desire and dream while she endured a life of not being respected or valued.

Ola was slowly working herself into a depressed state again but she could not help the thoughts that seemed to catapult into her mind from one thing to the other. She hated it when she got philosophical like that because she felt it would have been good if she could express them but it only burned a hole in her heart leaving her feeling low and weepy.

She wondered about what she was becoming . . . this darkness and its possible end. She despaired at how she could escape it as a picture of a black hole with no end in sight danced before her eyes depicting her future.

"What have I done to deserve this? Am I so unworthy of respect . . . or maybe I am truly just a waste of space . . . of no use to anyone?" Ola wondered if that was the case. She thought there had to be something about her that made Deji feel it was okay to treat her the way he did. Her mind strayed to her friend Rita and the last time they had gotten back home from shopping. Rita's husband had come back from work, he'd picked up the children from the minder, made dinner and completed homework with the kids. As if that was not enough shock for Ola, he hadn't been mad, he wasn't giving them the evil eye when they came in. To top it all he had prepared dinner for Rita! Ola was so shocked she was speechless. She had thought it was a Nigerian thing or a macho African man thing that made Deji unwilling to do anything in the house. Rita's husband Ugo proved otherwise. He was a Nigerian and he didn't seem embarrassed to be making dinner in front of his wife's friend.

Such instances usually made Ola feel she had to be the problem as she threw her weight into the chair Deji had just vacated. She looked around the dining area and it seemed so much had happened but as her eyes fell on the wall clock sitting on the glass cabinet she realised it had just been slightly over an hour since Deji walked into the house. It was only eleven fifteen, nearly midnight anyway and she still had a load of dishes to clear and wash.

Letting out a deep sigh the tears Ola held back all evening slowly flowed down her face as she settled into the sorry state her life had become. She knew how unproductive these silly pity parties were as she called them because she was usually the only one in attendance. . . . but looking over her life's circumstances and situation always did that to her. Even when she knew crying over the wrongs in her life was not a solution . . . she somehow still found some form of release from it because for a few minutes the feeling of doing something was satisfying even if unproductive. With her eyes blinded by tears, Ola shuffled to her feet and began to clear the dishes from the table. She emptied the chewed up pieces of bones from the chicken and turkey into the bin and completed the washing up. Ola had formed the habit of leaving the kitchen clean at night as it made it easier to come into the next day. Anyway, she realised, if she left it untidy, there was no dish fairy who was going to come in at night to clean up for her so at least she would have one less thing to worry about, one thing she could control.

Ola stood by the living room door and watched Deji sprawled on the couch watching the telly. She watched him for some time before deciding not to stay in his presence any longer. . . . Not really because she didn't want to but because they didn't seem to have anything productive to say to each other. On second thoughts Ola decided to sit down for a while in the living room thinking that after all the house belonged to both of them.

"Are you still watching that programme? I would like to see this movie coming up." Ola asked as the TV reminder for a programme she set earlier came up.

Without saying a word, Deji picked up the remote control and hit the backup button cancelling the reminder. Ola's first instinct was to jump at him and grab the remote control off his hand, but she could not find the energy to move. She sat transfixed for a few minutes as she admitted there was no fight left in her. She knew any way that there was no way she was going to win the fight. It was better to go to sleep.

"Goodnight, I am off to bed." She said quietly to Deji as she grabbed her phone to go upstairs.

"Mm mm . . ." the sound of Deji's offhand dismissal served as the goad that pushed her overboard.

'You know I really wanted to see that movie. I have been home all day and I programmed it to watch. Even if you want to watch something else at least acknowledge me and even explain that you want to see something else . . . !' Ola screamed at Deji . . .

Oh no . . . , no, no . . . ! Ola couldn't say any of that. It was what she wished to say. Those words raged inside her but she'd learnt to suppress them so there could be some peace at home.

Many of Ola's friends regularly advised her that not talking back was the only way not to aggravate trouble situations at home. As her heart swelled with hurt, those words were the ones that came to quell her storm. She wondered if that wasn't also saying it was okay for her to be aggravated. What was that thing, that lady said on the radio—*don't complain about what you permit*? Did such actions not make it okay for Deji to continue to treat her this way she wondered?

If ever there was a catch 22 in marriage, this was it Ola laughed—get hit or stay repressed! A true lose—lose situation, be hit physically by another person or hit yourself internally through repression. She knew that either way she was the only one who got hurt. Ola hated feeling this way, she hated that even some dogs and cats got treated better than she was. She'd seen animals which people called pets get more consideration than herself. Ola grumbled as she stomped noisily up the stairs. She had learnt how to grit her teeth and bear as a way of avoiding being hit. She was becoming an expert at suppressing but the price—had a mental tag. Once again she would be taking her pent-up anger to bed and true to form she knew it was bound to keep her awake for the best part of the night till she became weary and dropped off to a fitful sleep.

Ola looked in on the kids on her way to bed, her pride and joy that made the lonely days worthwhile. She went into her son's room first and stood just looking at him. Michael was such a loving child and he had always been overly protective of Ola. He was always watching out for her and even managed to sneak her a hug and kiss when no one was watching, especially his friends as he didn't want to be uncool. Ola pulled the covers over him and went to Alicia's room.

"I love you my little angel" she kissed Alicia on the head and turning off the bedside lamp as she exited the room. Moments like these helped Ola ignore some of the sad times in her relationship with Deji.

Ola told herself tomorrow would be better as she dropped off to sleep. She could hear the distant ringing of the phone but it stopped immediately. Ola put it down to her imagination . . . as she waited for more buzzing but nothing. She didn't share her earlier worries about the phone calls with Deji, thinking maybe tomorrow . . . maybe tomorrow . . .

Chapter Seven

THE UNCOMFORTABLE FEELING IN OLA'S bladder as it expanded to bursting point woke her up. Instinctively she stretched out her hand to the other side of the bed and it was still cold from not being slept in. Ola rolled over with her back bones cricking from being so tired the previous day and noticed from the bedside clock it had just gone past 2am. She sighed remembering how tired Deji had been earlier when he came back from work and wondered why he had not come to bed yet. He had most likely fallen asleep downstairs she thought. He did that most nights and she sometimes had to go and wake him to come upstairs. Ola thanked God for small mercies—at least sharing the same room and bed was still something they tried to do as husband and wife. It made quarrelling and not talking to each other that bit more difficult.

Slipping her feet into fluffy bedroom slippers she got for her birthday the year before from one of her closest besimates as they jokingly referred to each other, Ola made her way groggily to the bathroom and spent longer than she would have wanted. She focused briefly on the slippers which were actually one of her nice bedroom comforts . . . , she enjoyed their warmth from their fluffiness.

Ola knew going to bed too tired obviously took its toil as having to move around for any reason felt like a big task.

"Mm mm . . ." she moaned standing at the top of the stairs contemplating leaving Deji to sleep on the sofa to wake up with a crick in his neck by morning from sleeping in an uncomfortable position. Her smile deepened as she relished the thought of revenge, even if it would be a small one. That would serve him right . . .

"Oh . . ." she muttered wishing she sometimes could be hard, mean and wicked and not have a conscience to condemn her. She really wished she could as she made her way down the stairs protesting vehemently . . .

. . . Ola slowed down becoming suspicious as she heard muffled voices and laughter. At first she thought it was the television . . .

Nah . . . Ola realised as she took in the scene in the living room. Deji was wide awake and sprawled on the sofa with his laptop across his broad chest. He had his ear phones on and didn't hear her come in. He was looking very cheerful and relaxed talking away at the computer . . . Ola stretched and looked over his shoulders to see what was so exciting on the screen.

"Hah!" Ola's shocked gasp didn't seem to alert Deji to her presence. There on his computer screen was a nearly half naked dark skinned woman with everything hanging out on display.

"Oh my God" Ola clamped her hand over her mouth to stifle her shocked exclamation. Contrary to her naïve thoughts, Deji had not fallen asleep on the sofa. In fact if he had a crick in his neck it wouldn't be from sleeping on the sofa, it would be from trying to follow all the demonstrations of the girl on the screen! An incensed Ola could not contain her shock that Deji was up till the wee hours of the morning chatting with another woman on the computer in their home while she was in the same house.

"Oh no . . . ! What has my life become?" she cried in despair. She must have made a sound as Deji suddenly became aware of her presence. . . . Maybe it was her shadow which fell across the computer blocking out the light as she moved closer to see if she recognised the lady on the screen, Ola was uncertain. Deji immediately moved into action and slammed the computer shut with a loud thud, cutting off the connection.

Ola could feel her blood begin to boil and her heart rate accelerating in fury . . .

"Who were you talking to Deji . . . ?"

"What do you mean?"

"What do you mean what do I mean?" Ola responded, piqued at Deji's deliberate attempt to evade the question.

"Who was that half naked woman you were talking to on the computer? So this is what you are doing again in my house," thundered an infuriated Ola.

"What did you just say . . . , oh . . . , oh . . . , oh, so . . . because I let you live here you think to open your mouth and say this is your house? Are you the one paying the mortgage for the past three years?" Deji barked at her with a snarl which he ended with that condescending laugh which enraged Ola even more if that were possible in her present state of fury.

"Hah . . . ha, you are a joker."

"I won't be side tracked Deji, you were chatting with a half-naked woman in our home, what is that all about? How can you after all we have been through, after all the promises you made that it wouldn't happen again? Deji you are doing this again, even in our home."

"You are just barking because I don't know what you are talking about"

"Oh really, you want to tell me you don't know what I am talking about?

Ola lunged for the laptop as she was at this time past reason. Reading her intension clearly, Deji quickly moved the laptop out of her reach. Ola knew that without hard evidence Deji would deny he was chatting to any woman. She went for a counterattack refusing to be deterred by Deji's interception. Finally grabbing the laptop, they both struggled for it for a few minutes. The tussle ended in the only way possible considering Deji's size and sheer strength. He pried her fingers loose from the laptop and gave her a gentle push which was enough to topple an already shaky Ola onto the sofa.

That was only enough to stop her for a few minutes as the wind went out of her. Ola immediately jumped back up in a frenzy propelled by her thoughts. She had been through this kind of situation with Deji the year before and he had promised and even swore on his children's lives that there was nothing going on and here he was again.

". . . No way!" Ola screamed even louder.

"I am not taking this from you Deji, you cannot be having an affair in this house, you hear me . . . you cannot do it! It will not happen here."

"You dare to tell me what I can or cannot do in my own house? Hah . . . ? Now I see that you have grown so much that you can raise your voice at me. Maybe these people who are talking to you, maybe when I leave you maybe they can marry you. You want to be out there like those silly women with no husbands' ehn, that's all right. You keep talking to me that way and you are on your way out"

"I don't care Deji, I don't care. Anything is better than this."

"You said it, you will get it. So you don't have to worry about who I was talking to as I am a free agent now . . ." Deji stopped for a while, as if waiting for effects . . . for his words to sink in then he added in a gentler voice as if reasoning with a child.

". . . unless off course you want to calm down and let your home work, remember it is up to you to build your home. You make it what you want it to be. If you want it broken you can have it. If you want to go out there and be a single mother all well good for you. There are many people even those so called friends of yours and advisers you have out there who are begging to have me. If you like, act like a silly woman and I will be gone so fast and you will be on your own. You think any man wants a liability . . . , a woman with no skills, no economic value? Think about it, you have no work experience, where will you go? . . . Social welfare? Ha . . . ha . . . ha . . . , you should see what they do to silly women like you. They will dump you in a homeless shelter with drug addicts and junkies and you see your daughter, Alicia . . . ? They will so abuse her in those hostels . . . you will have only yourself to blame."

"I . . . , I . . ."

"Go on shout . . . , scream . . . and see what will happen to you."

". . . then who were you talking to?" Ola asked calmly trying to contain herself.

"I wasn't talking to anyone . . ."

"I . . ."

"Let me finish!" Deji said authoritatively as he seemed to see Ola's fight gone. He'd gained the upper hand and he knew it.

"I was preparing a proposal document for a new business idea and I was carrying out an internet research but some of these sites have what are called pop-up windows and there are different offers that come up. Sometimes its phones and sometimes girls' faces, maybe one of those faces came up when you got here. That must have been what you saw. I said nothing like this will happen in our home and it isn't. You have to wipe any suspicion from your mind."

Ola didn't believe a word he said. It was obvious to even a two year old that the story was false but at least Deji was trying to cover it up. She reasoned that he cared enough to attempt to lie about it. If he were to tell her he was having an affair there was nothing she could do Ola rationalised over her inner turmoil. At this point Ola was emotionally drained with no argument or fight left.

"So open the site you were on let me see what you were researching," she added one last feeble attempt to prove her point.

"You have to learn to trust me. That's what you have to do. You cannot dump all your insecurities on me or on this relationship, it's too much. It's not my fault if you are feeling insecure. You have to help yourself there."

Deji reached out for Ola with his right hand and with his other hand he gently pushed the laptop away under the sofa behind him while Ola pretended not to see that as she allowed him pull her into his embrace.

"Then who is the woman who has been phoning the house and saying nothing?" Immediately the words left her mouth, Ola knew she had made a mistake. She blamed herself for not letting it rest . . . , for not letting things go for the moment and enjoy the peace they had.

Deji turned her to face him fully and at the same time his gentle hold on her shoulder becoming a hard squeeze.

"Tell me about these calls you are talking about" he said in an ominously quiet voice.

"It's nothing" Ola denied with a quiver in her voice

"It's not . . . nothing. Obviously it was important enough for you to notice it and mention it and in fact it seems you have made connections between the calls and your accusations this morning. So tell me about it."

"Look, it is nothing really, just that for the past one week, I have been getting phone calls and the person says nothing and it is usually in the evenings. She says nothing and when I say hello, hello, she drops the phone."

". . . If the person said nothing, then how do you know it's a woman?"

"I just know," said Ola with her eyes blazing defiantly even as she feared Deji's calm response.

"So that's why you decided to come and check up on me tonight isn't it? You wanted to catch me cheating on you? You see how evil your mind is? Instead of sleeping, you were crawling down the stairs to catch me . . ."

"That's not true Deji and you know it, I thought you fell asleep and I wanted to come and wake you up to come to bed."

"You know if you were able to satisfy me I would not be looking outside. If you were half the woman I need you would not have any reason to be suspicious. But you know that you are lousy in bed and that any normal man would need more than your weak attempts to satisfy him. Hah . . . , so you want some of what according to your suspicious mind I am supposed to be giving to those women out there that you have created? Okay . . . go upstairs and prepare for me" Deji said in a commanding tone that did not leave room for negotiation.

"I don't want to Deji, I am tired and I have a headache now." Ola pleaded as her heart dropped in panic. She could not pretend not to understand the intent in Deji's eyes.

"You are my wife and your body belongs to me. So whether you want to or not you have a duty to satisfy me. Now go upstairs and prepare for me."

"What do you mean . . . did you buy me?" Ola asked outraged at the audacity in Deji's words.

Deji moved closer to Ola and grabbed her by the jaw. As their eyes locked in a clash of wills and power, Deji applied some pressure to her jaw as he spoke directly to her without blinking, with his eyes wide and his nose flaring like an enraged dragon.

"I didn't buy you but I paid your bride price and part of your duty is to satisfy my sexual needs, do you understand?"

"Deji, look I am really tired, it's nearly 4am, and I don't want this, please." Ola knew that force with Deji didn't usually work, so she changed her tactics and tried to appeal to his sense of reasoning.

"Now you know the time, when you tried to sneak up on me you didn't check to see the time. I said go upstairs now and prepare for me or you want me to take you here . . . ?"

The strength in his words made Ola jump as she looked at the door . . . any of the kids could wake up and just walk in.

"No . . ." she said and she rushed upstairs dreading what was to come.

CHAPTER EIGHT

A BEWILDERED OLA ASKED HERSELF how she could dread having sex with her own husband. She wanted to call it making love but she also knew they were not going to be making anything. Deji was just going to come and take from her emotionlessly. Ola quickly climbed into the bed as she heard Deji coming up the stairs. She decided to feign deep sleep hoping that Deji would be considerate and leave her alone. She turned her back towards Deji's side of the bed with her heart pounding in her chest. Ola kept her eyes tightly shut as she heard his loud steps on the stairs. She could almost picture his actions as he moved around the room. She heard the snap of his slacks as they came off, followed by the sound of the elastic of his boxers as he ran his fingers around it and allowed it snap back against his waist. Ola heard him snap the elastic again and this time she heard the swish as he seemed to be pulling the boxers down.

"My God," cried Ola inwardly wanting to be excited but lay huddled on her side of the bed. Ola felt the bed sag behind her as Deji dropped his weight on the bed. She knew there was no escape when she didn't hear Deji pull any clothes on.

"Turn around," Deji said as his voice broke the silence in the room
Ola didn't move a muscle pretending to be asleep.
"Ola, I know you are awake, turn around. You know what happens when you start making trouble and start a fight. I can't go to sleep

without releasing the stress from my body. You know that and I warn you all the time but you still choose to provoke me."

"I am sorry . . . ," she said as she turned on her back. "It won't happen again."

"I think you like it . . . you little minx. I think it is your own shy way of saying you want me. I have told you all you have to do is ask and I am ready to oblige. You don't have to create a fictitious phone call or accusations . . . , eh . . . , I am your husband and I have told you I will take care of you. Do you understand . . . ?"

"Hmm" mumbled Ola in acquiescence.

"Now come over here and say hello to Jerry, you woke him up so you have to make him okay so he can go to sleep."

Ola hated it when he referred to his penis by name, but decided not to dwell on that as she pulled her nightdress over her head and moved closer to Deji. Waiting . . . waiting . . .

"Go ahead, he won't bite you," Deji said encouragingly. Losing patience, he grabbed Ola's hand and forcefully splayed her fingers over himself. "Now rub and say nice words to him. Tell him how good he is . . . , move closer Ola!" With an impatient sigh Deji pulled her smack against his own body that she could feel the heat of his body almost permeating into her.

"Kiss Mr Jerry and tell him how strong he is" said Deji as he tried to cajole her into cooperating.

"I am sorry Deji, I don't really want to."

"Do it now!" he screamed in a no nonsense voice that was hard as steel. Ola recognised that tone when Deji used it. She knew him so well and knew there was no point in resisting at that point. This was the side of Deji that left Ola very bewildered. He didn't joke around when he wanted something and he got whatever he wanted, however he wanted it and worse still whenever he wanted it!

Ola was lost in her thoughts and did not notice Deji move having lost the patience to wait for her to increase the tempo of her touch and voluntarily participate. He grabbed Ola by the neck and pulled her head down on himself, holding her down.

"Kiss me now . . . kiss me faster . . . faster . . . rrr," he said in a low growl as his hands began to tense. Ola could feel more pressure at the back of her neck where Deji held her head in place—as if she would dare to stop! She went on till he pulled her back and in one quick motion he had her flat on her back. Deji moved his hands up and down her body, squeezing every part of her body his hands could go round. Angry tears were burning in Ola's eyes as Deji squeezed her nipples very hard.

"Ouch!" exclaimed Ola, "that hurt."

"Hah . . . , you like it don't you? Don't pretend to be shy, I know you like it. Move your body around, move faster!" his command came out as a guttural groan.

With his other hand he felt his way inside her body. Unable to hold in her emotions any longer, Ola turned her face away from Deji . . . her love . . . her husband, the one who was to love, honour and protect her. Her eyes brimmed over and the tears rolled from her eyes down her face soaking into the pillow. Though Ola's body was smarting with pain, she could not stop him. She wanted to meet all his sexual demands hoping it would stop him from needing other women. Ola squirmed in shock as suddenly Deji adjusted his body and in one powerful swoop he was inside her.

"Call my name . . . , come on, call my name"

"Deji stop please you are hurting me . . . , please, Deji . . ." Deji's strong shoulders posed too much resistance to Ola's puny efforts to push his body away from her as she tried to ease the pressure in her womb. Deji ignored her efforts as he continued to pound into her body with sweat pouring from his shoulders over Ola's body, running down between her breasts.

"Make some sound for me Ola, come on . . . , talk to me."

Deji's hands moved from Ola's breasts to the nape of her neck and then he moved them round the front and splayed his fingers under her jaw around her neck. He seemed to be testing the size of his hands against the size of her neck, but suddenly, he began to apply pressure.

"Uhm mm . . . !" Ola gasped in panic as her air waves began to close up. She lifted up her hands and tried to pry Deji's hands loose from around her neck. Agitated, Ola began to thrash around, she tried to scream but they came out as little moans as she struggled to breathe. The more she thrashed around struggling for breath, the more Deji seemed to get excited. Ola was shocked to see him moving faster and faster hitting at all the corners of her body in his heightened state of excitement.

"Oh my God, I'm going to die" were the words in Ola's mind as she cried in fear imagining herself being found in the morning on the bed naked and dead. People had died from less pressure than this she knew. Just a little more pressure and she could be dead. Breathing became even more difficult for her as Deji's hands tightened even more cutting off her air supply. Mustering all her strength, Ola tried to cry out to get his attention.

"Deji, Deji . . . you are hurting me" she croaked as loud as her voice could carry.

Ola moved frantically in her struggle to get some air,

"Oh God help me," she cried thinking of all the women who had died sudden unexplained deaths in their homes.

"Please God," she prayed "just save me this once and I will take action to stay safe. Please God Ola," prayed harder.

Some people say fear is a great aphrodisiac, well it seemed to have that effect on Deji who seemed to be getting more excited watching the rise and fall of her breasts. Ola was saddened as Deji seemed to enjoy watching her fear. Deji went for one last frenzied plunge into her body tightening his hand even further on her throat. Finally Ola realised there was no way out, she was going to die. Her eyelids dropped, her hands fell away from Deji's arms in surrender to the pressure in her chest from lack of oxygen . . . Suddenly her air waves opened as Deji released his hold from her neck, pulled out of her and sprayed his juice all over Ola's body.

"That was good for you wasn't it? See what you can do to my body. See what a good wife can do to keep her man."

"Urgh, urgh," Ola coughed continuously gasping for breath. She struggled to take in deep breaths to replenish the emptiness in her lungs. Her body hurt and for the first time she didn't know which pain was worse, the one within or the physical pain in her body.

"Good girl, good girl," Deji crooned at her oblivious of her pain. Rolling over to the other side of the bed, he smacked her across the bottom. "Good girl . . . you can be a good girl sometimes!" Ola fixed her gaze wishing she could do something, anything at all to wipe the satisfied smirk off his face. Ola heard him move around in the bathroom and then the next minute he was back in bed and fast asleep.

Ola was still shaken. Needing to get some air different from the one Deji was breathing she rolled out of bed and went to the bathroom. She knew she would have to massage her body with a hot towel or a hot bath to ease her discomfort. She didn't relish the idea of not being able to walk properly in the morning but first she needed to talk to someone. She needed to ground herself that she was still alive. Ola grabbed her phone as she went into the bathroom. She crouched on the floor beside the toilet with her feet against the door as tremors built slowly from the centre of her stomach all over her body into a visible shake. Tears from fear, shame and disgust flowed freely as she covered her mouth to muffle the sobs that wracked her body.

Ola needed to hear another human voice but it was almost 5am. She couldn't call her sister Beatrice because she would simply tell her to deal with it and Janet was away on business and may not be reachable. Women and men had different needs and roles Beatrice claimed and that a woman's job was to satisfy her man. That was one of the reasons Ola stayed on the bed and allowed Deji do unimaginable things to her body, even make her kiss him in places she never thought she would allow her mouth to go. What if she'd died that night Ola wondered in fear. What if Deji hadn't stopped on time, she sobbed as images of Alicia and Michael flashed by her mind with no mother or worse still with a step mother who maltreated them.

"O God," cried Ola "what am I doing to myself? What am I doing to my kids?" she sniffed noisily . . . , blew her nose and hoped that her friend Rita would understand as she dialled her number. Ola needed to hear someone's voice. She was so sure she was dead and needed a voice to remind her she was still on the same side with the living.

"Hello, hello . . ." Ola heard panic rising in Rita's voice as she didn't answer her first groggy response.

"Hello Rita, I am so sorry to wake you up. I am sorry . . ."

"Are you okay . . . ?"

"I am so sorry Rita, I am so sorry . . ." sobbed Ola unable to speak coherently about her feelings.

"Are you okay . . . talk to me . . . , are you at home . . . ? Please talk to me Ola, I am scared now . . . ," said Rita with her pitch rising.

". . . I am sorry Rita, I didn't mean to scare you. I am oo . . . okay," Ola stammered as she tried to keep the tears out of her voice so as not to frighten her more.

"Have you been crying, what happened? Ola, talk to me" Rita bombarded Ola with multiple questions

Silence and hesitation,

"Ola!"

"I can't really talk, I just wanted to feel your presence just for a few minutes please, I am so sorry to wake you up. I had no one else to call"

"Shhhhh . . . , it's okay, sshhh . . . , it's okay . . . , I am here now, shh . . ." Rita's gentle voice hummed to Ola over and over. It felt like an hour but it was just a few minutes.

"Thank you Rita, I feel better now, thanks, I will talk to you tomorrow. Please apologise to your husband for me"

"Let us talk tomorrow okay, please."

"Yeah . . . , yeah we will." Click and the line went dead.

Ola saw Rita as her own special angel. She was always there, never asking questions. She had been such a huge support for Ola these past years that Ola called her an angel specially sent to Dublin to help her.

"Who was that?" asked Ugo, Rita's husband who was also woken up by the ringing phone.

"It's Ola, I am so worried about her, but there's not much I can do. I wish I can just throw caution to the wind and tell her what I really think." Rita thumped the pillow to vent her frustration as she moved closer to Ugo who cuddled her comfortingly in his arms.

"Come here, love." Ugo said running the tips of his fingers down the side of her face.

"I am afraid he is going to kill her one day. I am afraid one day I will get a call and I will have to go and identify her body."

"I am sure it's not that bad."

"I am scared Ugo . . . , I really am because sometimes we don't know the half of it and I think sometimes she can't even tell me the whole story, I mean like tonight. She didn't say anything but I could feel real fear across the line".

"Here, now, now . . . , we can't have that can we, come and let me drive all your fears away."

"No can do, I have to work tomorrow, in fact I have to be up in the next two hours . . . ," groaned Rita light heartedly as she turned fully into Ugo's arms.

"Come and work on me . . ." said Ugo in the most seductive voice he could muster.

"Just hold me tight. . . . please, that's all I need right now." Kissing her along the nape of her neck, Ugo gathered Rita close to his warm chest and wrapped her in the protective circle of his arms. Even after Ugo settled back to regular breathing in sleep, Rita still lay awake, her mind troubled about Ola. She had never heard Ola sound so distraught even when she didn't say much. She wondered what had happened . . . , how Ola was really doing . . .

Chapter Nine

Two days on Ola was still walking with a slight limp from pains all over her body especially in her groin area.

"Mum are you okay? You are walking funny," Michael her twelve year old son asked innocently.

"I am fine love. I slipped on the stairs when I was going to the toilet at night and I seem to have sprained my ankle," Ola lied to cover her embarrassment. She tried to make the limp which her son described as funny look like it was coming from her ankle rather than her groin area.

"Go and get ready for school Michael . . . , where is your sister? I woke her up already."

"In here mum," cried her sweet small voice which seemed to be muffled

". . . I am brushing my teeth."

"Great darling . . . , great . . ."

Ola quickly worked her way through the daily routine, shower, lunch bags packed and the children rushed into the car.

"Come on guys, I think we are going to be late again today." Their school was a five minutes' drive usually but at 8:40 am with so many parents trying to get kids to school and workers on the road the traffic at some of the junctions could be quite long, taking up to 15 minutes. Most times Ola would walk to get some exercise and also to avoid the hold ups but she had not been her best in the last few days. Driving up to the school gate, they made it just in time it.

"Have a good day in school and I'll pick you up myself," said Ola exchanging kisses and an exaggerated bone crushing hug with Alicia.

". . . love you mum"

". . . love you too honey"

"Uh . . . , see you later," Michael said as he made a quick escape in case Ola tried to hug him in front of his mates. Ola was amazed that the little boy she held in her arms was almost a teenager and was now too old for public show of affection. She was troubled as she pondered about how much her relationship with Deji was affecting him considering that he never saw his Dad show her any affection. She knew she couldn't blame him because children more easily learnt by what they saw rather than what was said to them. She just hoped that he would not grow up dysfunctional as the Irish people described children from problem families. She was worried he might take on the belief that being mature meant not showing affection.

As usual, Ola was greeted with more chores as she returned home. She started by picking up all the stuff from the floor right from the door as she walked back in. Deji's jacket had to be put back on the coats hanger, the kids' toys were strewn all over the floor, the dining table still messed up with the kids' breakfast bowls and cereal boxes. Deji's left over from the breakfast she made for him before he went to work were all still sitting on the table waiting for the glorified cleaner. One hour later, Ola put finishing touches to the final tidying of the house and the place was back in shape—spick and span.

A slight humming sound coming from the living room around the sofa distracted Ola from her plan to have a quick rest. She groggily followed the sound but it was a very muffled hum. She moved the cushions from the sofa onto the floor, nothing . . . then the sound stopped. About a minute later it started again. Ola suspected it to be Michael's phone which he would have thrown down the back of the sofa. She was tired of Michael's carelessness with his things. He was in the habit of throwing his stuff all over the place. Screams and screams, cajoling and even threats—nothing seemed to work with him . . . Many other parents with children his age told her it was the same thing with most teens. It amazed Ola that the only group that no one made excuses or allowances for was woman. She could not understand how they could say it was just being a teenager and that was why he stepped out of his clothes and left them on the floor.

". . . oh heck," Ola exclaimed exasperated as she cautiously went down on one knee following the sound of the ringing phone. Ola looked under the Chair and there it was . . . a black touch screen mobile phone. She was sure it couldn't be Michael's because she didn't recognise it. By this time she got to it, the phone had stopped ringing.

Flipping the phone over in her hand, Ola tried to operate the phone. It showed two missed calls with the name Jennifer. She knew it had to be Deji's phone . . . maybe he forgot it at home or it may have fallen when he was watching telly the night before. It surprised her that she didn't recognise the phone. Ola was aware of Deji's other two phones so a third phone was a surprise. Ola carefully unlocked the phone which didn't seem to ask for a pin. It was one of those new smart phones which unlocked when you press the lock icon and slid it across the screen. Ola had a bad premonition about it as she imagined every reason possible why Deji would have a fully functioning phone that was a secret possession. The presence of the missed calls from a number stored under the name Jennifer did not help matters.

"Hah! Settle down girl," Ola laughed self-consciously, irritated by how quickly she jumped to conclusions where Deji was concerned, yet she couldn't seem to contain her feeing of dread. Ola could not deny she knew her husband—Deji, having a secret phone if he thought he would get away with it was exactly the kind of thing he would do - no half measures for anything!

Ola began to scroll through the numbers and names from the outgoing and incoming calls. She noticed some of the calls were quite late at night with three constant callers. Ola didn't know what to expect but she was sure that it wouldn't be good. That would be out of character for Deji. Ola was up to date with Deji's other phone. She hated to admit it to anyone but she had formed the habit of regularly checking Deji's phones for strange numbers or suspicious messages. She needed to know if anything was going on she interjected her thoughts trying to justify reading the text messages on the phone.

Ola needed to sit down at the exchange of sweet nothings between Deji and different women.

"Oh no . . . ," she exclaimed in shock as the tightness in her chest increased. The messages told their own story between Deji and a Jennifer, Jen sometimes . . . sweetheart . . . I love you . . . I miss you . . . when are you coming home . . .

"Oh . . . ," cried Ola as the dates Deji went on a seminar or supposed training for work coincided with . . . a great holiday this Jen woman referred to in her message!

"Oh . . . ," cried Ola again, sitting transfixed with her mouth agape.

The energy from the shock coursing through Ola was so much she needed to take some action. She jumped back up on her feet and began pacing around like a wounded Sahara tigress. Ola just wanted answers.

"Oh God help me, what am I going to do?" Ola asked the empty room.

She was infuriated by the thought of Deji carrying on with another woman—women in fact. The texts and voice messages spoke for themselves. . . . Favour, Kefilwe, Beata, Jen or Jennifer was a definite one which seemed to be a full blown affair. The thought that Deji was able to build relationships with other women and most likely he had to have spent money wooing them was the worst. She remembered how he almost killed her for asking for money for the kids' school books.

Ola had finally reached her breaking point. She resolved not to be Deji's fool any more. She swore not to let him treat her like shit anymore.

"I won't let him," she declared fervently. "Oh I will disgrace Deji in front of her. I will disgrace him in this Dublin. I will make him ashamed," Ola swore vehemently.

"Hell! I will make him pay . . . ! If Deji thinks he can make a fool of me and my generosity to him in this city he has another think coming." Ola's body began to shake as she considered everything she had borne to make their relationship a good and enviable one.

"I have been a fool for Deji, I have apologised just to make peace and now this is how he repays me. I will give him fire for fire," Ola promised herself slapping her hands together in a fast rhythm.

"I will make Dublin too small for both of us."

"Hahhhhh . . . !" screamed Ola frantically waving her fists in the air over her head.

"He has touched the tiger's tail . . . that's it. No more Mr nice guy . . . no more fool for all." Ola screamed hysterically throwing the cushions from the sofa onto the floor and messing up the sitting room she just took pride in cleaning. Life with Deji did not cease supplying, Ola whose emotional state could easily go from zero to mad in the space of seconds', opportunities to lose control.

She knew that crying wasn't going to solve this latest development. She needed a plan that would make Deji pay, one that hurt him as much as he had hurt her. She remembered the saying *you have murdered sleep and you will sleep no more.* Well it is true because Deji had murdered sleep—his and hers and she was determined to make sure he never slept again!

Ola wanted to meet the woman, she couldn't help herself but she wanted to meet this Jennifer person. She wanted to see what she was like, what was so special about her that Deji had to choose her over his own wife . . .

Ola's anger turned from Deji to the women. She was mad that this Jenifer woman thought it was easy to raise two kids and look good for a man.

"Well she can come and try raising these two and then live on nothing. Let me see how loving she will be to him," Ola stomped her feet as she cursed at Deji and the women.

"The idiot . . . ! She won't go get her own man she wants to steal mine from me. I won't let her. I will not let her . . . I will not let anyone break up my home."

Ola needed someone to blame in her desperation to ease the pain and pressure building up inside her chest.

"I will not let . . . , I will not . . . I have invested too much to allow one chinch come and take my man from me. All these useless girls that throw themselves at any man, so desperate to have a man they are willing to do anything. Well she has met her match in me." She was thankful the children were not there to witness her crazy display. She sat down again to gather her thoughts together as the threads of a plan began forming in her mind.

"Deji will be so sorry he messed with me. I will disgrace him in this town. In fact we will all disgrace ourselves," Ola promised.

"Argh . . . ," she shouted as her anger erupted again. Ola needed a way to vent her anger. Her body was tense with unexpressed emotions. She was like a tightly wound turbo spring charged and ready to explode.

"As if I don't have enough problems to contend with in my life," Ola thought feeling drained.

Ola was excited but scared about her plan for revenge but there was no going back now as she clicked send on the text message. Meet me for lunch at three pm at the BlueCrown pub. I'll wait for you at the entrance D. Ola's plan was to draw Jennifer out so she pretended to be Deji and replied Jenifer's text. Ola couldn't help herself, she really wanted to meet Jennifer. She wanted to see what kind of person Deji was attracted to. She needed to know what the attraction was. Why she was better than her, she really wanted to see that for herself.

The beeping of the phone indicated a message had come through. Ola was excited as Jennifer seemed to have swallowed the bait and replied the text. OK, dat's gr8. What hapnd did u c my missed calls? Called u 2X in d morn. How r u anyway, sorry I was in a meeting, still in a meeting, C U L8r. Ola replied as Deji.

The woman's reply incensed Ola even more.

"The slapper!" Ola raged,

"She will get what is due her. She wants to reap where she has not sown. Where was she when I suffered to bring my husband to Dublin? All the money I borrowed to pay his first school fees so that they could give him a student visa. This is how he chooses to pay me? I thought all these years Deji was working for the family not knowing that he has his own agenda! I will frustrate Deji in this town. He did the same thing last year and now he has started again."

Ola playing Sherlock Holmes to uncover Deji's cheating had a few logistical problems. She was not sure how she would recognise Jennifer when she arrived but she hoped few women would be driving into the pub at about three pm—that's why she had chosen a place like that, hopeful she'd be easily identified. She didn't want to be seen as a pushover seeing that she was going to meet her competition or one of the competitions! Ola dressed up nicely with her hair properly styled. At 2:30pm, Ola made a detour first to pick the kids from school. She was so distracted she didn't hear any of the chatter from Alicia who went on and on about who said what in school and what they did during PE. Ola heard something about someone being on green throughout the day in school.

"Good girl" Ola seemed to have said the right thing as Alicia brimmed with joy. Ola hoped no one noticed how preoccupied she was.

As she drove into the parking lot of the pub, she wanted to say game on! She parked close to the entrance of the pub and with each car that drove in her heart gave a loud thud. Ola sat waiting, watching the entrance like a hunter poised waiting for prey.

"Husband snatcher . . . !" Ola huffed cursing her prey even as she began to have second thoughts. She realised she had not thought it through and she was plagued with thoughts of what to say to this Jennifer woman when she met her. Ola pondered as to what the woman's part was in her marriage's mess up. If Deji kept it zipped up, if he kept it within his pants, they wouldn't be in this position—she wouldn't be in this position now.

CHAPTER TEN

SHOW TIME THOUGHT OLA AS her attention was aroused by the arrival of a grey 2005 Mitsubishi carrying a dark skinned African woman. Ola was quick to notice they were about the same size, though the woman had slightly broader shoulders. Ola frowned disapprovingly as she noticed the amount of makeup on her face. She wondered if she was Jennifer crouching lower into the sit as the car drove towards her.

"Hey mum, are you hiding from someone?" asked Michael

Ola was startled by Michael's question which seemed to come from a long way off. She had forgotten the kids were with her, not a good plan she realised too late. Ola mumbled an undecipherable reply which seemed to satisfy Michael who happily returned to fiddling with his phone. She took another peek at the lady who seemed to be driving around looking for someone or maybe a car she guessed. She watched her until she drove into a marked parking space. Her unhurried movements were beginning to irritate Ola who was still contemplating how to avoid embarrassing herself by approaching the wrong person! From her vantage position in the car park, Ola noticed the woman's head bent over something in her lap—she was searching through a bag resting on her laps. Her smile of victory was accompanied by a phone which she waved around like a trophy making Ola's blood boil as she noticed the woman's brightly coloured well-manicured nails. Ola had stopped fixing nail extensions when she couldn't afford them anymore. In fact after buying groceries and food stuff from the shops, what little she had left went towards school trips and little bits for the kids . . .

"Hum mm . . . hum mm," the vibrating hum of the mystery phone she found earlier in the day broke into Ola's thoughts. A call was coming through with the name Jennifer flashing on the screen. It had to be her Ola concluded as she looked up and saw the husband snatcher with a phone to her ears apparently making a call to her lover - my husband! Ola thought with as much venom as she could muster blinded with rage.

Ola drew in deep bursts of breath to ease the constriction in her chest which suddenly felt too tight. She was now sure this was the Jennifer woman and seeing her blinded Ola with renewed rage. The woman looked vaguely familiar, but she couldn't be too sure . . . maybe from the children's school . . . community or maybe from a party or something. Ola was definitely sure she had seen that face before. Before she lost her resolve, Ola climbed out of the car and headed straight for the grey Mitsubishi.

"Hello" said Ola tapping her knuckles on the window of the driver's side of the car to get the evil woman's attention. . . .

"Look at the Jezebel . . ." thought Ola in a temper, "She even looks like a modern day witch with the talons she calls nails!"

"Hello?" she replied curiously as she stepped out of her car.

"Are you here to meet Deji?"

"Sorry . . ." she said very slowly with a frown on her face as she drew out the answer. The woman's hand went to the door of her car as she sensed everything was not as it should be.

"Well Deji sent me to you. He said he can't get here to meet you but since you are a hooker . . . I can give you another person's number whom you can start to bother."

"I beg your pardon . . . , what did you just say?"

"He said you are a hooker and that I should give you another number so you don't have a wasted afternoon, or don't you understand what I am saying?"

"Who are you?"

"You should have asked when you started sleeping with a married man," Ola screamed at her. Ola was so upset she just wanted to wipe the smug smile off her face. She wanted to push her . . . she wanted to punch her. Ola wanted to make her pay for what she had done to her family.

The pain of Deji's betrayal with this home wrecker pushed Ola beyond personal consideration she just wanted to embarrass and disgrace her in public.

"So you cannot find your own man, you decided that stealing someone else's is what you should do?"

"I don't have time for this nonsense," the woman replied sarcastically as she made to move back into her car, but Ola was not having any of that. She grabbed the woman by the hand pulling her towards her own car.

"Come and see the children you will have to take care of . . . you husband snatcher!" Two women pulling at each with raised, angry voices is a guaranteed crowd puller any day at a Dublin pub. To now have two black African women shoving and shouting obscenities at each other was like providing free VIP seats for a movie on exclusive viewing . . . , the crowd for the showing was building quickly.

"You are embarrassing yourself . . . please go home!"

"Go home you say? The home you want to destroy . . . ? The home you are so desperate to enter . . . *ashawoooooo*, prostitute . . . , *whoo . . . , whoo . . . , whoo . . .* !" Ola screeched bouncing the palm of her hand against her mouth back and forth to make a childish jeering sound. Ola was losing it but she was past caring. It was her moment of madness which she could not awaken from.

"*Ashawo*" Ola continued to make jeering sounds emphasising the name calling.

"Can you keep your voice down you demented woman. No wonder Deji is finding solace in other women's arms."

Jennifer's goading was the final straw as Ola lunged for her with only one goal on her mind—to inflict as much pain as she was feeling in her heart. She wasn't bothered about the small details as she was prepared to employ any means possible to humiliate this thieving Jennifer as much as she and Deji had humiliated her. Ola wanted to scratch her face and put a few permanent marks on her skin that Deji would see. Marks she would never forget . . . , marks that would deter her from trying to steal other people's husbands next time. Ola plotted how to use her chapped nails to draw some of those tribal marks the Yoruba's used to put on their children's faces to ward off evil spirits especially children who suffered from spells of fainting and epileptic fits.

The woman's attempts to get away from Ola who was determined to pull her hair out of its neat plait intensified the scuffle.

"*Aji oko olo ko*" Ola cried out in Yoruba, meaning husband snatcher. "Go and find your own, you stupid husband snatcher."

Some of the men around the pub who had been watching the exchange suddenly stepped into action separating them. Ola violently resisted being pulled away from Jennifer, she hadn't exorcised her anger yet . . . until she looked up and her heart sank as she saw her children standing beside them with Michael screaming.

"Mum? Mum! What are you doing?"

Jennifer apparently seeing that as an opportunity quickly got into her car screaming.

"You have not heard the last of this. You want humiliation? I will give it to you big time. This is war now! This is war you demented woman. He looks for me, he begs me to be with him. He tells me how lousy you are in and out of bed. I have been told by D that you are a dirty pig who cannot keep the house clean. You refuse to work . . . , you refuse to go to school even when he has paid the fees you dropped out of college and wasted his money. I know your story you dirty pig! Now this is out in the open I will take that man from you because you don't deserve him. He stayed with you because of his kids and out of pity but you have crossed the line. You have crossed the line . . . ," she screamed as she reversed her car and zoomed off leaving Ola with the watching crowd.

Ola's heart sank as she became conscious of the sea of white faces and even a few black Africans she recognised.

"Oh no . . . my story will be all over town in no time," lamented Ola mortified by the scene she had just created. Her biggest regret was that the children had seen it all, they even heard the vile words from that evil woman! Ola regretted exposing the children to more harm.

"Ola . . . , are you okay?" Bimbo a woman Ola recognised from her neighbourhood ran towards her in concern.

"Thanks I am fine."

"What was all that about?"

"Nothing . . ."

"It didn't look like nothing."

"It was nothing."

"I am sorry Ola, look there is no need pretending. I heard everything and I . . . , we have all known all this while about Deji . . . your husband and that woman, we thought you knew and that you were okay with it, after all some men have two wives—you know that. They are usually everywhere together. Parties, shopping . . . she's always with him. I was so sure you knew. People just thought you had that kind of arrangement because he wasn't hiding it."

"Thank you, I didn't know." Ola said moving away to put an end to the conversation as the small crowd thankfully dispersed.

Ola grabbed Alicia and Michael and quickly made her way to the car. Michael wasn't to be easily silenced and who could blame him thought Ola as she wiped a tear from her eyes. Ola berated herself for involving the kids. One look at Alicia was enough confirmation that this had been a wrong move. The poor thing . . . , Alicia was in a flood of tears.

"Mummy you were fighting with a woman, I was scared."

"It was nothing darling, mummy made a mistake, she was just angry and didn't think."

"Is Daddy in trouble, is he a bad man now?"

"No honey daddy is not in trouble"

"But I heard mummy, are you going to fight tonight, will I have to hide if you are fighting?"

"I am sorry darling we are not going to fight. It was a stupid mistake. Let's go home and have lunch."

The last set of bystanders finally left giving Ola and her kids' funny looks. Ola started the car and drove home. In spite of what she'd told Alicia, Ola knew she was in for a fight with Deji. There was no way he was going to let this lie, obviously the stupid woman would go crying to him . . .

Chapter Eleven

"How long are you going to ignore me?"

Deji continued to give Ola the silent treatment since her fiasco with that Jennifer woman.

"Your dinner is on the table, please come and eat your food."

More silence . . .

"Deji . . . you can't just keep silent in this house. If you have something to say, then say it. Two weeks now you have refused to eat . . . , you come and go without caring for those at home. Talk to me please . . ."

Ola was exasperated by Deji's behaviour. If he'd shouted or even insulted her as he usually did it would have been painful but better. Ola realised she might as well be talking to herself with the deafening silence in the house anytime Deji came home.

Ola decided to appeal to him again. Calling his name softly, she moved toward him smiling enticingly as she grabbed his arms. Deji turned sharply with a murderous look in his eyes which was enough to put a stop to her attempts.

"Move out of my way now before I do something I will regret."

Opening her eyes wide in exaggerated apology, Ola cautiously moved away from blocking the door to let him through. Since her public debacle with Jennifer or Jen or whatever her name was, it had been silent war in the house.

"Okay, you go. Two can play this game you know . . . , two can play the game!" Ola shouted.

The bang of the door as Deji stormed out was enough to calm her down.

Storming angrily to the dining room, Ola grabbed the bowls of food and emptied them into the bin with as much loud banging as she could muster without breaking the bowls!

"I don't care," Ola repeated over and over as she tried to convince herself she didn't care . . .

"Are you okay mum?" a bewildered Michael asked as he came running into the kitchen. His voice made her snap out of her musing.

"Yes I am fine love . . . , the wind made the door slam louder than was intended, go and finish your homework," Ola soothed Michael but she was at breaking point herself. She needed to talk to someone as she was finding the silence in the house frustrating. Ola knew it was a game meant to frustrate her and teach her a lesson. The truth was that it was working. Deji knew her weakness and he played it any time he needed to. She didn't know why some men did the silly *'I am not eating your food thing!'* wondering who suffered. She wouldn't have minded if he was refusing to eat her food but was providing for the house, but this *'we are not talking phase'* meant she couldn't ask him for money for gas for the car and she didn't get money to buy groceries. It was a total black out or block out thought Ola, uncertain which one suited. Ola decided to seek advice from a more mature Nigerian woman. She had been married for over eighteen years and they seemed like a happy couple.

"Aunty Favour? I hope I didn't disturb you."

"No you're alright my dear, how are you doing . . . ?"

Ola told Mrs Bamidele whom most people called Aunty Favour all that happened with the Jennifer woman including the outcome.

"Aunty, I don't know what to do, honestly. Deji is not eating at home, he's not talking to me . . . I mean we've not spoken more than a handful of words to each other."

"Have you guys talked about your allegations against him or the altercation you had with that woman you had a fight with?"

"We haven't and honestly I don't know where to start from. I thought he would bring it up but nothing, not a word and I don't even know if I want him to anymore. I am really afraid of what he will say."

"You know we are African women . . . you have to remember one thing that the man is the head of the home and you must respect him. If there is a problem and he is angry with you, then you must make the first move and apologise."

". . . but he did wrong. He was cheating on me . . ."

". . . I know my darling, I know what you said. At the end of the day do you want to drive him completely into another woman's hands . . . is that what you want? To be alone after all you have been through together?"

"No Aunty."

"Then apologise and try and draw your husband back home."

"It just feels so unfair . . ."

"I understand what you are saying, but do you understand what I am saying to you? Because what seems unfair to me is for you to allow one floozy out there to take your husband, the father of your children . . . that is what is unfair. You must fight for what you want . . . , you must fight for your home."

"I don't know aunty, I am so confused . . ."

"There is nothing to be confused about, remember my dear a wise woman builds her home but a foolish woman pulls it down with her own hands. Feeling a sense of injustice will not satisfy you on cold nights neither will it provide for you."

"Aunty . . . there is so much you don't know . . . so much I can't begin to tell you."

"My dear, I might not know your specifics, but I assure you I know many women's stories. It cannot be worse than a man bringing another woman home to your marriage bed and I tell you I have heard so many of it happening and the relationship still survives it. There is nothing that commitment and patience cannot overcome . . . you are the woman so you have to take the first step."

"He's not talking to me so I really don't know what to do."

"You are an African woman, you know what to do. Remember 'the head does not go to the hand; the hand goes to the head.'"

". . . hmm, that is a deep saying."

"Look when Deji comes home, honour him as your head, as your husband. Swallow your pride if you have to. After all you know what you want."

"I do . . . ?"

"Do you want Deji or do you want to drive him back into her arms."

"I want my husband . . ."

"Then look, when he comes home tonight, prepare his favourite meal. Serve it well with your good dishes and then go and kneel before him and plead with him to come and eat your cooking. That is the first step. You need to swallow your pride and apologise because those who say pride goes before a fall are not mad. The sad thing is that the fall will be yours."

". . . Mm mm . . ."

"A word they say is enough for the wise," Aunty Favour added with an ominous sigh.

"Okay Aunty, thanks for your advice."

"You are welcome my dear, just try your best to make it work. Don't lose your husband because of pride . . . it is all in your hands."

Ola was used to Aunty Favour's advice, what else had she expected her to say anyway. It was the typical advice—a list of things she is supposed to change about herself to make Deji feel loved and respected. Ola was bothered by the responsibility placed on her to make the first move. She wished someone would just be bold for once and say it as it really was. Someone who could really tell Deji the truth and make him own up to his responsibility not pussy footing around or mollycoddling him Ola sighed angrily. Why couldn't they ask him to do things to make her feel loved? Or did they think women were immune to being loved . . . or maybe they thought women didn't deserve respect or consideration?

Ola was consumed by a sense of injustice but she was also caught between two very difficult options, either humiliating or humbling herself as some called it to keep Deji, her man or refuse to give in and drive him further into the arms of that desperate prostitute! Ola felt a bit guilty insulting the woman, Jennifer or whatever her name was. She knew Deji had to be a willing participant in the liaison for it to develop. She was sure he probably initiated it and pursed the woman! But Ola was not really listening to reason. She was too mad and at least cursing the woman made her feel a little bit vindicated.

Ola was hurt and still hurting but she could not deny what she had to do if she wanted Deji and she did.

"Silly, people will think, but he is mine. I can't just give him away to any woman out there like a stray dog!"

Her frustration was in not knowing how to get her husband back. Ola would have preferred him to apologise to her. She wished he would bring her flowers and say he was sorry and that it wouldn't happen again. She would have loved him to plead with her to the point of grovelling . . . but he had the upper hand this time because anything at all would have been better than this silence.

Ola was frustrated with her life to the point of hating it. She was so full of hate these days—she hated that she had to apologise even when she knew she was right. . . . she hated that she didn't have the luxury to be angry. Her life as a woman felt like a living hell, a life sentence from which there was no escape. Ola thought of some of the women she knew who seemed genuinely happy. She couldn't help wondering if it was real or if all women lived like her or if some women had different lives from others. She knew it wasn't education because she had seen very educated women who were treated badly by their spouses. It definitely wasn't beauty as many beautiful women had been divorced. Ola wished someone would come and give her answers but she wasn't willing to take the one that said behave like a fool so he can love you!

This spectacle of a marriage that hers had turned into was not working for Ola and it wasn't making her happy.

". . . But it gave you the children who make you happy," a small voice reminded her in a tiny whisper. Oh heck, thought Ola wondering what she was going to do . . .

. . . No, Ola knew what to do—apologise and be the good and dutiful wife! Maybe tomorrow . . . , yeah, she chickened out. I'll leave it till tomorrow . . .

The next evening, Ola forcefully swallowed her pride, she dressed as nicely as possible with a lovely sheer nightdress and matching dressing

Page
86

gown. The kids were safely in bed and she could hear Deji pottering around downstairs.

"Well, this is it. " Ola knew they had to sort things out one way or the other.

"He is my husband and I don't want to lose him," Ola concluded.

"Welcome," Ola greeted Deji as he came into their bedroom, again getting no answer. Ola knew how easily their squabbles could have degenerated into becoming two strangers sharing a house if not for the advice from her mother during their traditional wedding. She'd advised them that no matter what happened, they must always share the same room. That way she said it was easier to keep seeing each other and then to apologise if one needed to. Her mum said it made the heart softer. Though on reflection on the statistics of women killed in their own homes in the western world, Ola wondered if she was not tempting fate by sleeping in the same room, on the same bed with someone who abhorred animosity and anger against her. She could not decide really which was worse to actually be deep in sleep beside someone who was mad at her, who if the look on his face was anything to go by actually hated her or to take the risk and remove herself and her children from insulting treatment and harm!

Ola concluded it was her fault and so she was going to do whatever it took to fix it . . .

Ola continued watching Deji move around the room as he went through his bedtime routine. It was the same on the nights he stayed at home, the only difference now was the scowl on his face and the moody silence which was becoming really nerve racking for her. Ola listened for his next step as Deji went into the bathroom where she heard him gurgling after brushing his teeth.

This is it Ola decided—her plan was to tempt Deji into submission if she had to! She lit the scented candles in the room and made the light a bit dim. She desperately hoped a bit of seduction would work on that stubborn husband of hers. As the door creaked, Ola quickly scuttled to her side of the bed poised and waiting for him to come back in.

Deji gave one sweeping look at the candles, lifting his eyebrows questioningly eyeing Ola and the room. The slight movement of his head and the curl of his lips at the sides made Ola's heart drop with dread. She had a bad feeling about it but she was determined to see it through. She had made up her mind to fight for what she wanted—her man and her family together . . . or was it? Ola's heart twigged a little as she thought about her reason. . . . which is what exactly? She paused to ponder over the question. From the corner of her eyes, she noticed Deji move with deliberate precision to prevent his body from touching her as he tucked himself neatly under the covers.

Ten, nine, eight . . . Ola closed her eyes and counted down from ten to zero to calm her nerves and motivate herself to make the move. She gently climbed out from the bed moving round towards the side closer to the door where Deji lay. With her heart in her mouth, Ola gingerly knelt down before Deji with a remorseful look on her face as she proceeded to pour her heart out to him.

"I am sorry. . . . I am really, really sorry for my behaviour. Please forgive me." Ola carried on at Deji's silence taking it as a good sign.

"I don't want our relationship to be like this. . . . I love you and I want our home . . . , our marriage to work. I will do whatever it takes to make this work for us. Please forgive me and let us put this all behind us." His silence was once again becoming unnerving for Ola. She was afraid that she would have to drag herself all over the floor to show her remorse!

". . . you are my husband and I accept you as the head of this home. I can't stand it that we are not talking to each other. I can't stand it that you are not eating my cooking. . . . even the children are affected by it. You can see the way they scuttle away once you come home and they keep to themselves almost walking on egg shells. It can't be good for them, they are only kids and the atmosphere at home is too fraught with tension for them . . ."

"Don't you think you should have thought about that before you went to behave like a lunatic on the streets of Dublin? Now you make out it's because of me the children can't feel free at home?" He snapped almost biting her head off as he jack-knifed into a sitting position on the bed.

That's something, Ola thought, happy that she was getting some form of reaction out of him. Now all that was left was to calm him down, after all what's that saying, it gets worse before it gets better.

"Please Deji, I am sorry . . . , that's not what I meant at all. I am not even laying any blame. I am just saying that it is not good for the children and it is not good for us."

"Speak for yourself! . . . at least this way I don't have to give account to you. Just look at you . . . everything hanging lose, look at all the flab on your fat belly. What kind of woman are you anyway, you dare to go out there and embarrass me, no actually, not me but yourself all for what eh . . . , your stupid insecurity?"

"Deji! Please I am on my knees here trying to apologise for something tha . . . that . . . , hmm mm . . . , look what more do you want from me. You need to slow down on the insults please, I am apologising . . . , for peace sake in our home and in this relationship . . . please!"

The silence stretched between then for a long time as Deji appeared to be contemplating what to do and how to respond to her change of plan from aggression to plea.

"Come here" Deji said after what seemed like an eternity. Deji stretched out his hand towards Ola and stared at her, into her eyes with that look that made her forget all the things she was angry about. She loved being with this man, she thought if they just both tried harder it could be a good relationship. Looking into Deji's eyes always did it for Ola. It made her go mushy inside. For an extended moment, Ola forgot all about the strife, the pain and the cheating. She remembered how it had been between them when they first meet . . . when they were dating . . . When the sun seemed to shine out of everything Deji said . . . Ola notice Deji was still waiting for her and she gingerly placed her right hand into his outstretched hand. Deji's look darkened and he slowly pulled her up off the floor where she had been kneeling onto the bed beside him. As if transfixed, Ola watched as Deji lowered his head towards her blocking out the light and they slowly locked their lips together in a passionate kiss. Ola spread her fingers over his shoulders pulling him in closer to her breasts which had been flattened between them. Deepening the kiss, Deji moved over Ola and joined his body to hers.

As Ola drifted off to sleep still wrapped in Deji's arms where she was relishing the aftermath of the passionate exchange between them, she sent a silent prayer to the man up there as some of her worries came flooding back. She wished they had addressed the issue about the Jennifer woman but they didn't. She didn't understand how it suddenly became about her wrong doing and not what he did. Ola was apprehensive about being able to live with the choice she'd just made—to stand for her marriage and let it all go.

". . . this is my life . . . this is my choice . . . , the choice that society expects from me . . . ," she convinced herself as she drifted off to sleep.

CHAPTER TWELVE

"HI HONEY, HOW WAS WORK?" asked Ola reaching up to give Deji a kiss as he returned from work.

"Just hectic, I am so exhausted . . . , I can't wait for my holidays."

"Well, you can have a few hours of quiet tonight as the kids have gone for a sleepover at Rita's place."

"What do you mean?" Deji asked in that ominous sounding voice that usually spelled trouble.

"Oh . . . , you know my friend Rita, the kids are spending the night at hers with her kids and they are having a movie and popcorn night. She kindly offered to take them to give me a little break as I mentioned I was not feeling too well. She thought we might enjoy having some time to ourselves."

"I don't want my kids going anywhere without my say so."

Ola's jaw dropped open in surprise as she stared open mouthed at Deji

"Do you understand?"

"Oo . . . oo . . . okay."

"You need to go and get them back right now."

"That will be kind of awkward for me to go and pick them up and the kids will be really disappointed as they are there already. What will I say, how will I explain it?"

"I don't really care, you just need to go and bring them back now."

"Deji . . ."

"No Ola, get the kids back home now!" he shouted and stormed upstairs

So much for peace at home Ola thought regretfully.

Driving down to Rita's house a fuming Ola took out her anger on the gears as she scrunched and pushed the car 20 km above the recommended speed limit. She kept looking over her shoulders hoping there were no speeding cameras around her or worse still, one of those mobile camera things they'd been talking about on the news. The last thing she needed was getting a speeding ticket or a fine. She knew her inability to pay a fine would definitely make Deji's day and Ola wasn't in the mood to add to his pleasure. She was confused by her love/hate relationship with Deji as on some days she was so hooked on being with him that it felt like a drug addiction and on other days she hated the man so much she could taste it in her mouth. Those were the bad days when she had those really terrible thoughts that she dared not tell anyone about . . . maybe hate was too strong a word to use but she was glad no one could see into her thoughts.

Ola was infuriated by Deji's behaviour and it got even worse particularly when he adamantly insisted that she obey his decisions leaving no room for negotiation or discussion.

"Hmm" huffed Ola feeling helpless . . .

"Hey, what's up?" asked Rita in surprise as she opened the door to Ola's persistent ringing of the doorbell.

"Don't tell me you are missing the kids already," she teased without giving Ola a chance to answer.

"Where are the kids?"

"They are upstairs playing. Is everything alright, can I get you a drink?"

"Thanks, tea, no sugar."

"Maybe the heat of the tea will warm my insides," thought Ola whose heart felt cold from the force of keeping her emotions bottled-up.

"Are you okay?" Rita asked as she suddenly seemed to take in Ola's strained look.

"I have to take the kids back home, Deji doesn't want them to stay for a sleepover and his reason is that I should have asked him first."

"Okay . . ."

"I mean, he was at work when we decided after school and it's no big deal anyway. I am their mother for Christ's sake but he acts as if suddenly I am one of the kids and I have to ask his permission before I do anything. . . . That is the problem, you know . . . not about them coming out to yours, but his need to prove his power over me, just to degrade me and make me feel small. I am really tired Rita. I am close to the edge, I swear I am."

"I am sorry Ola, I don't even know what to say, because if that is your system in your home I can't advice you otherwise. You need to find what works for you guys and use it. What makes you both happy . . . you know what I mean . . ."

"I know I have to do something about all this but I don't know where or how to start."

"Hmmm"

"Let me go and break the bad news to the kids that I am going to spoil their fun tonight" grumbled Ola walking dejectedly from the room feeling hurt like a helpless child.

As Ola bounced up the stairs she was impressed by the stylish decorations and the unique pieces in Rita's house. The place always looked so serene it was hard to believe there were six people living there.

The kids all looked really happy in their night clothes pretending they were at a movie theatre with the lights off hugging their popcorn bowls and drinks. Ola at once knew she didn't have the heart to be the bad guy that night. She wasn't about to spoil their fun just to please Deji . . .

"Mummy!" shouted Alicia as she noticed her watching them from the door. There was a chorus of greetings from the other three in the room as the older kids were doing their own stuff in their rooms.

"Come and see mummy" Alicia said as she pulled Ola by the hand into the room.

"Jade has a big TV in her room. It's just like in the cinema and we are watching Puss in Boots. It is really cool! Come mom, do you want to

watch mummy . . . ? Come and have some popcorn. This is really
coooool . . ."

"Thanks honey, I just came to kiss you goodnight." Ola fibbed "I
don't need to ask if you are having fun as I can see that myself." Ola
jested about with the kids pretending to eat imaginary popcorn from all
their bowls. Finally exhausted, she said her goodnights and headed for
the door.

"Where are the kids?" asked Rita.

"I just couldn't spoil their fun. They seemed so settled and happy I
decided to just leave them. I will go and face Deji myself." One thing
Ola was sure of was that Deji liked to keep his good boy image and that
reassured her that he would not make the journey to harass Rita himself.
He would rather Ola did such dirty work for him . . .

"Do you think . . . ?"

"I am not . . . really thinking. I am tired of thinking!" Ola interrupted
her bosom friend Rita who was ever so wise and helpful.

". . . Its okay, I am going home. I can allow him play his power
games with me but I absolutely refuse to allow him involve the kids."

The minute Ola drew up in front of the house her bravado left her
as her mind became swamped with thoughts of Deji's irrationality. Ola
prepared herself as she approached him.

"Deji, please I don't want us to fight but I have obeyed you and I
went to try and get the kids but they are settled for the night and I felt it
would be cruel of me to spoil their fun. I am sorry."

"So in other words, you decided to disobey me again."

"No Deji, I just thought to appeal to you that we should place the
children first instead of our desires and wants."

"So you want to take my place now is that it? You want to show me
that you can think? You have now become the head of the house."

"Deji that is not the case please and I'm sorry."

"No worries Ola, you head the home and also remember with being
the head you also have the responsibility of taking care of the house as
well. Since you do not consult with me and ask for my permission to do
things, that's okay! You can feed the house and pay all the bills as well."

"Deji it's not fair to keep threatening me all the time like that, it's not fair."

"So now I am a monster because I ask you to run things by me before you do them eh . . . ?"

"No, it's just that you make it sound as if I am one of the kids rather than your wife and your mate."

"I have told you that you can be my mate. In fact you can be my equal and my head but you also have to foot your share of the responsibility that's all I am saying." Deji replied with each word dripping with sarcasm.

Ola knew it was time to just keep quiet because the back and forth was not taking them anywhere.

"I am going out, don't wait up," the door slammed and he was gone. . . . So much for my romantic time at home without the kids Ola grumbled in resignation.

At a loose end, Ola wondered listlessly from room to room picking up things and putting them back in place. She spent the next half hour cleaning out the kids' bathroom and toilet as her mum's favourite quote flashed in her mind—'*an idle mind is the devils workshop*'. With three hours pottering around the house on her own, Ola had cooked up different conspiracies driven by Deji deliberately picking a fight with her. She was mad that she'd played into his hands, that she gave him the perfect reason to pretend to be angry and storm out of the house without needing to say where he was going. Ola decided to have an early night. She knew there was no need to continue on that path of thinking as it only left her depressed.

As usual, Deji's trousers and shirt were hanging over the chair, and Ola picked them up placing them on the wooden hanger. She noticed something fall out of a trouser pocket. Ola's heart jumped as the threads of suspicion snaked into her mind. She quickly let the clothes drop back down to the floor in exchange for the fallen piece. It turned out to be nothing, at least not what she suspected! It was a slip of paper Deji had scribbled something unimportant on but it was enough to awaken the Sherlock Holmes in her and set her thoughts rolling. Ola searched through both pockets without much result. She progressed to his other jackets in the wardrobe and uncovered a few suspicious looking receipts for restaurants that showed a bill for two from two weeks before. She went back downstairs and checked the pocket of Deji's outdoor jacket, nothing much in them, at least not the evidence she was afraid of finding. Ola berated herself for her stupidity, she couldn't understand why she was looking for what she didn't want to find! She knew she was torturing herself by searching through Deji's stuff but she felt driven to stay at least one step ahead of her cheating husband. She had been there before where his actions took her by surprise and she didn't want that to happen again. She loathed the idea of being the last to hear about Deji's philandering and she could see the signs again.

Once Ola's suspicion was aroused there was no stopping the investigator in her! She riffled through Deji's mail and found a few bank statements from his credit card and bank account. Ola was very shocked by his salary for the previous month when he'd almost killed her for asking for money. She was pissed off at how much he earned the same month he refused to give her money to buy a good present for Michael's birthday.

"This is wrong" Ola cried in dismay ". . . so . . . so wrong."

She noticed a few cheque stubs for various amounts. . . . Ola wondered who they were made out to and why! She decided to search through his work briefcase for the cheque book in her quest for answers. Though she wasn't expecting Deji back any moment soon, it didn't stop the adrenaline from pumping through her system as her head swelled with the fear of being caught. Ola quickly riffled through Deji's case which didn't turn up anything. She wasn't really surprised, in fact she would have been more surprised if she found any incriminating evidence as Deji had been burnt by her investigative searches through his pockets too many times before. Ola was sure he knew better than to leave stuff lying around for her to find.

"Damn" Ola swore loudly in frustration as she decided to give up on this foolishness and go to bed.

". . . Maybe . . . , no, no. no . . ." Ola squashed the thought that snaked into her mind as she spied Deji's laptop on the table. Anyhow, she was certain he would have changed his password by now or . . . maybe not . . . giving in to temptation she turned on the laptop.

"Yeeyiiii!" Ola yelped delighted that the password she had for his laptop still worked! "Surprise . . . surprise." She laughed with her eyes opening wide like round saucers.

Ola was plagued by a pang of guilt. She felt like a crook sneaking into Deji's private things.

"Heck," said Ola excusing her actions, ". . . this is what I have been reduced to."

She didn't trust this husband of hers and to get any information she had to dig for it or wait till it became public knowledge which meant shame and public disgrace for her. Sadly Ola realised that when she had funny feelings about Deji like this, her instincts were usually right.

"Oh! This is gold" she mouthed as Deji's laptop opened onto his email page, from hibernation ". . . yeah!" Ola's laughter bubbled over.

"Okay," she gave herself a congratulatory nod. Ola was excited at the prospect of finding out what Deji had been up to . . . She hesitated momentarily as she realised that going further could either satisfy her curiosity or break her heart. Even as she knew she might not be able to do anything if she knew Deji was having an affair, the curiosity to know still won over.

The choice made, Ola settled comfortably on a chair as she started scrolling through his emails. There were so many emails from different people. It seemed her husband had hooked on to a dating network, as many of the emails referred to. Phone numbers were exchanged in some of the emails and suggestive pictures which made Ola exclaim in shock. It was more than she thought was going on. Some of the women had made different requests from Deji . . . one particular email thanking him for the things he sent to her! Women from different countries!

As she read on, she was able to piece together his profile as most of the emails were coming from a dating site. Apparently Deji's profile stated he was single. Ola looked at the time and in a blind rage she started typing up replies to the emails.

"Hell! This can't be happening to me again," Ola raged. "When will it stop?"

She started with the new emails and progressed to the older ones informing all of them of Deji's marital status and the small detail of his two children. She hoped that would put a stop to the whore mongering women . . . but would that stop Deji? She wondered why all this was happening to her as if she didn't have enough stress in her life!

"It's not even that he's such a stud," raged Ola criticising him. "What were they looking for with him ehn . . . ? Why couldn't they just leave him alone . . . why oh God couldn't he leave them alone? Ola lamented as she wondered who she was going to share her latest predicament with. Ola balked at the thought of telling anyone. She knew they would just laugh at her the minute her back was turned.

Ola realised the email address was different from Deji's regular one. She was worried that her husband, the father of her children, Deji her love, seemed to have this other life and identity that he was living simultaneously with the one with her. Ola became afraid that she didn't know where exactly she fitted into Deji's life. She didn't want to wake up one day to find out her whole life had been one big lie after all she has endured at the hands of Deji for the sake of staying married.

Ola's computer skills were not excellent but she could get by. She noticed a window opened that had been minimised and curiosity got the better of her and she clicked on it.

"Hah! Jackpot," she exclaimed as it turned out to be the dating site and Deji's page was still open!

"Nice one . . . nice one." Ola was excited by her discovery even when she was uncertain what to do with it. She knew Deji wasn't expecting her to check his laptop because he left home suddenly in a hissy fit. She was sure he would hate himself for this mistake and she planned to make sure he did. Ola laughed as a sinister plan began forming in her mind. She was going to make sure of it even if it was the last thing she did in this relationship with Deji. She was at her wits' end with Deji and she promised not to allow him keep making a fool of her

". . . or maybe she was the one making a fool of herself by always taking him back and fighting the wrong people," a small voice cautioned her in her thoughts.

"Ha . . . ha . . . ha . . . ," laughed Ola as she read Deji's profile name, "Jerry indeed!" then she became embarrassed as she remembered the part of his anatomy he called MR. Jerry. It had to be his alter ego—double or whatever name Freud called it in psychology! . . . Single, 36 she read from Deji's fake profile.

"Hah! The lying, cheating rat!" Ola discovered that Deji had reduced his age by twelve years or maybe they were the lie - her children and her . . . she wondered. She was upset and didn't seem to know the truth anymore with Deji's constant stream of atrocities. Her husband's profile read . . . *looking for a serious relationship.* So what were they thought Ola . . . , her children and her were what . . . , ehn . . . ? Well, they would see how serious they would be after she was done with that profile. Ola decided to help her husband fill in the blank spaces in case he had suffered from a temporary memory loss when he was creating the profile.

Ola realised this could turn out to be a lot of fun even as she worried about the consequences of upsetting Deji. It didn't stop her from executing her plan.

She titled his picture *'The face of a liar'* and increased his age by twelve years to a very nice *'60'.*

"Ha . . . ha . . . ha . . . ! Let's see who is laughing now," laughed Ola at the mayhem she was creating for Deji as she updated the changes. For status she change it to *'married polygamist'* and for interests, "Hmm mm . . . , let's see" thought Ola as she tried to be creative. *Loose Slappers*, then she deleted it on second thoughts as she wasn't sure if Deji's fan club would understand the word. Okay *'cheap, loose hookers willing to give it for free'.* Ola was breaking her heart laughing and thanking God she could get a bit of pleasure from such a disheartening thing. Her husband on a dating site!

For his qualities Ola went to work on the profile and changed it to *'cheat, liar, selfish pig, low self-esteem, violent abuser and domineering.'* Ola wanted to write more but thought better of it.

"OMG, ha . . . ha . . . ha . . . ," Ola burst out laughing, she had not had this much fun in a very long time.

"Okay, enough," she stopped herself as she saved the final changes and put the laptop on hibernate again.

"Well, it's his fault for his lack of internet security . . . ," Ola appeased her conscience as remorse and fear crept in to drive away her bravado.

As the wise people say, *as you make your bed so you lie in it . . .* or is it *if you can't do the time don't do the crime.* Whichever one he preferred, Ola was good with it.

"Bloody bastard . . . !" She swore violently as she slammed the laptop shut, finally giving vent and insight into her feelings . . .

CHAPTER THIRTEEN

FOR THREE DAYS OLA WAITED dreading the explosion to come from Deji but as each day went by she began to think maybe the prank she'd pulled hadn't worked. Maybe the changes to his dating site profile hadn't saved . . . She'd had a change of heart about the drastic nature of her reactions since then and was regretting it but it was too late to undo anything. She hoped that Deji's lack of reaction meant the changes had not have been saved either by an act of God or her computer inaptitude! Whichever one, Ola had her fingers crossed in hope . . .

Ola was worried and wracked with guilt and needed to off load on someone. She decided to try Rita her good friend who had become like her guardian angel these last few years. Grabbing the phone, Ola placed a call to her.

"Hi Rita, it's me Ola, can you talk for a minute?

"Yeah sure . . . , how are you? Do you want to drop down? I am actually on a few days leave from work, I could do with some girly company right now," Rita answered cheerfully.

"You don't mind do you?"

"Of course not I asked you to come didn't I?"

"I don't know . . . it's just that I think I need to see a doctor or someone. I am either getting paranoid or maybe something is seriously wrong with me."

"Look, come over and we can talk better."

"Okay, see you in a few."

Driving down to Rita's gave Ola some time to gather her thoughts and growing panic.

"So how are things going on at home now?" Rita got right down to it without much preamble. That's what Ola loved so much about their friendship. They didn't stand on formalities neither did they sugar coat things unless absolutely necessary.

"All good I can say. Family life has settled into routine again and things on the surface seem to be going on okay and I am grateful to God that Deji has been coming home every night and we seem to make an effort to talk to each other."

". . . but? Why do I feel there is a . . . *But* coming?" asked Rita.

"Oh I don't know. It's just that I always have at the back of my mind Jennifer, you know the lady I had the fight with? I am so afraid to ask Deji about her. I don't want to rock the boat . . . yet she stays with me, always in my head . . . in my thoughts if you know what I mean."

"What's troubling you about it?"

"I guess I don't know if he broke things off with her or not, though the last time I looked through his phone there were no text messages or names that raised my antenna or looked suspicious."

"So if I get you right Ola, you are using your time being a detective at home . . . ? That must be hard for you."

"Rita you don't know the half of it. I am checking his emails, pockets, phone book, address book, bank statements, credit card statements, anything I can get my hands on to give me some information about what Deji is up to."

"That must be really, really hard for you. I can't even begin to imagine living like that. Look, why can't you just talk to Deji . . . ask him if you have questions or doubts?"

"It's not that simple and the truth is I don't know if I can stand the answer or if I am ready for him to own up to me. Anyway, talking to Deji always results in a fight . . . then what? Do I leave him? . . . by now we . . . we both know I can't! Think about it, what will happen to the kids and . . . me as well? Where will I go, how will I live . . . what kind of life will I have? Look, I have had this conversation with myself many times and I am still not any closer to an answer than I was before.

"What next for you Sherlock Holms?" asked Rita in an attempt to lighten the mood as she noticed the despondency in Ola's voice.

"No I won't go that far . . . but I did some pretty bad things. I found Deji had this whole online dating life and you can say I edited his profile." Ola told Rira with a sheepish smile.

"Noooo . . . !" Rita said as she doubled up in laughter.

"Yes! And you don't want to know what I changed it to but I tell you it was sweet revenge but I think I must have done it wrong because it's been three days and he's not said a word . . . no strange looks or attitude from him. So maybe I am in the clear."

"I knew you were mad but I didn't know you were this mad ha . . . ha . . . ha . . ."

"I know but it was such a wonderful feeling I couldn't help myself."

"God help you because it's as if you have a death wish."

"If I can't beat him physically this is my way of hitting him in a way that hurts.

"Well, be careful because revenge sometimes always ends in tears."

"My life is already in tears as I am anyway."

"If you say so . . . what's next for you? Many times we talk about what Deji wants and how you can give him what he wants or be a better person for him but what do you want for yourself? Where would you like to see your life going?"

"From now I am going to concentrate on myself. I am hoping to go back to school . . . maybe get a job or something. At least the kids are in school now. You know Deji is the only one working now and that is the major problem we have or that I have. I have to be 'good' to get anything for the kids and myself. Once he is angry with me . . . that's it! No money for gas, no money for groceries. Anyway enough of my moaning, I am getting my life in shape!" Ola waved her hand dismissively to try and disguise how troubled she was by her situation and her complete dependency on Deji's goodwill.

"Good on you girl, it's really good for you to get a life and do something for yourself. It might make a difference for your home if your existence did not revolve around Deji. But please keep safe, remember the saying, a living dog is better than a dead lion. Don't play with your life or your children's lives."

"Easier said than done though."

"I know but remember hard is not the same as impossible. Well, if there is any way I can help, you only have to ask."

"Thanks Rita, you are a good friend."

". . . hmm mm, I don't know about that."

"Trust me you are."

"I hear you. Anyway, you know where I am."

By Thursday Ola had grown tired of waiting for a reaction from Deji. It was obvious her attempt at revenge hadn't worked. From her experience with Deji, she knew there was no way he would have taken that stunt lightly. To be honest she was kind of disappointed the changes didn't go through. She looked around the room where the kids were quietly completing their home work from school. Taking care of the kids was one thing that took her mind off her own problems. She enjoyed losing herself in their lives . . .

"Mum I need some help with these sums, can you come?" Michael's voice broke into her thoughts. Ola cringed at the daunting task of wracking her brain with elementary maths. She tried to remember if they had to deal with this level of multiplications and divisions when she was Michael's age.

"Sure love, let me see . . ."

"Daddy . . . ! Dad's home" Alicia's screamed just as Ola heard the door handle rattle. Alicia used this as her perfect getaway from the homework table . . . pushing back her chair noisily she ran to open the door for her dad. It never ceased to amaze Ola how well Alicia got on with her dad. Sometimes Ola even used Alicia as an excuse to get things from Deji. Ola groaned as she thought of how long it would take her to get Alicia to concentrate again on her homework.

"Welcome Dad," she ran straight into her dad's arms and he bent down to pick her up swinging her up in the air.

"How is my princess today?"

"I am fine daddy. I got a yellow star in school today and my teacher was not in so we had to go into another class . . ." Ola tuned out a bit as

Alicia went cha, cha, cha to her dad. Alicia could be a talker sometimes, in fact Ola always teased that she could talk for Ireland. The good thing though was her dad always has the patience for her.

"Welcome Dad." That was Michael . . . he was still at the table focusing on his homework. He was always cool with his emotions especially with his dad. Ola did not know when their relationship changed or even how it changed. They used to be so close but now they didn't seem to say more than monosyllabic words to each other.

"Michael, can you take your sister up to her room for a minute, I need to talk to your mum." Deji's voice sent uncomfortable shivers down Ola's spine. . . . It didn't sound good

"Come on Alicia, bring your homework upstairs." Michael picked up his books and waited by the door for his sister and they both marched up the stairs. Turning to Deji as the kids closed the door, Ola moved forward with her hands stretched towards him.

"Hi honey, is everything okay ehhhh . . . !" the whack of the back of Deji's hands across the right side of Ola's face forced the words back into her mouth and filled her eyes with stars for a few minutes.

"Hey y y . . . ," Ola stammered in protest as she put her hand up to her face to ease the sting of the blow.

"What kind of a monster are you?" She heard Deji as if from a faraway place as he grabbed Ola by the collar of her jumper and began to shake her. Ola clenched her teeth to prevent herself from crying out as the kids were just upstairs.

". . . Deji! What is the matter, what is wrong, what have I done?"

Slap after slap after slap landed around Ola's head as Deji continued to pound at her with his right hand while using his left hand to hold her up against the wall

"Deji, Deji, please stop you are hurting me, please, what did I do, let's talk about it the kids are upstairs they can hear . . ." Gripped by fear and confusion Ola tried to protect her head as the thuds of his clenched fist kept pounding on her head. It would have been funny if it wasn't so painful as the thuds reminded her of the traditional method of making pounded yam, one of Nigeria's delicacies. Boiled Yam which Ola sometimes described as big potatoes were placed in small potions in a wooden mortar and a long wooden stick bearing a big fat head like a man's fist was then used to pound the yam beating it as fast as the person pounding could till it formed a sticky smooth mash. Ola went from protecting her head from being mashed like stubborn yam to prying Deji's left hand from his grip on her neck. Ola's panic increased as she began to feel faint as she struggled for air. She could not understand why he always seemed to go for her neck as if he had a wish to cut off her air supply which she suspected right now. Ola reached up for his face to try and scratch him hoping he would release his grip on her neck. That only seemed to aggravate the situation as suddenly her feet left the ground where Deji lifted her up and slammed her against the wall really hard that Ola thought her bones were going to break.

". . . aahhhhhh!" Ola let out a shrill scream and grabbed the nearest part of his body that she could grab with her teeth which happened to be his shoulders.

"Ahhhh! You stupid bitch you bit me, I will knock those teeth out of your mouth."

"Deji, please," Ola struggled some more "you are hurting me!"

"You have not known what pain is. By the time I am done, you will be living in permanent pain. Did I force you to stay with me you foolish woman. Who gave you the right to go to my laptop?" As realisation dawned on her, Ola burst into her own defence and counterattack.

". . . but Deji you are a married man, you are supposed to be my husband, what part of what you did is good? What part of what you did is a married man supposed to do that you feel you have the right to beat me tonight, eh Deji?" She was in so much pain and could not control the tears as they ran down her face.

". . . You lying thief, so you are now a computer hacker, yet you cannot go and be a computer expert and go and get a job? You are going to jail I tell you, hacking into someone's email is a crime. I will report you to the police that you are a criminal. I tell you by the time I am through with you eh, you will be deported from this country and you will never see the children again."

". . . you will have to kill me first Deji, you will have to kill me first. You are beating me because I caught you as a cheat, because I told the people you are posing for exactly what you are, you better finish the job now because after this, if I get up from here I am going to your work place. I am going to tell them you are a wife beater. I will tell them how you lied on a dating website. I will send that link to all your bosses at work. I will ruin you. I promise you . . . I will . . . ah . . . ahh . . . ahhhhh! Deji stop, help! Help meeee!" Ola began to scream at the top of her voice as she fell down and Deji began kicking her all over with his shoed feet where she lay curled on the floor.

"You bitch! . . . stupid idiot! You dare me to kill you . . . I promise you I will enjoy killing you. You are a burden in my life, a weight dragging me down . . ."

With each word Deji kicked harder and faster into any part of her body his foot found. As Ola slowly stopped struggling she heard the door opening. Oh God no please she prayed silently, the kids were coming in and she didn't want them to see her like that. She licked the blood off her bloodied lips as she tried to open her eyes to talk to them.

"Dad, what are you doing? Daddy, stop!" A screaming Michael jumped his dad from behind as if to try and stop his flaying fist. Ola could hear Alicia's soft voice crying. She knew she needed an adult's help right then, she was of no help to herself or the kids. Ola realised that's what Rita was talking about when she warned her about not getting the kids in the middle of their row!

"Go back upstairs now Michael!" Deji screamed at him shaking him violently off his back.

"Michael, go and call Aunty Rita." Ola croaked slowly as she tried to muster all her strength together to issue instructions to the kids. Ola knew that no matter what happened to her, she would never forgive herself if they got hurt. She was usually able to take the beating without screaming and alerting the kids. Though Ola was scared with the force of the punches she was angry with herself for screaming as she blamed herself for the kids coming downstairs.

"Alicia, go upstairs and play hide and seek till I come and find you. Go on play a game with me." She just stayed by the door crying.

"Go now!" Ola shouted. The force of her voice must have gotten through to her and galvanised her into action and she ran after her brother.

"Help me . . . Deji pleasseee . . . , I can't breathe . . . ," Ola cried out in a hoarse voice and she renewed her attempts to break free as Deji's knee pressing against her chest inched higher towards her neckline cutting off her air supply. Ola was afraid the kids were going to watch her being killed. She was afraid of the kind of scars it would leave on their young minds. "Oh God, help me please . . ."

"Shut up! You see what can happen when you cross me! You see!"

"Please . . . ssee, I am sorry."

"You are not sorry enough! I will mark you so you will never forget," Deji promised her in an ominous voice under his breath.

Ola prayed help would come soon as she strained to hear Michael's faintly speaking behind the closed door.

". . . Yes you need to send the police. He's going to kill her. My dad is going to kill my mum. . . . Yes we are at home . . . no I am the oldest person at home."

"Who are you talking to? Michael! Michael! I say who is that you are talking to?" Deji roared at the little boy with that voice of his that ordinarily was quite intimidating and threatening not to mention when he roared in anger.

"I am calling the police . . . stop daddy please . . . ," Michael cried out at his dad as he stood poised beside the door.

"Turn off that phone now!" Ola heard him shout at Michael as her vision began to blur and her head throbbed with pain. As if as an afterthought, Deji softened his voice as he did an about turn to convince Michael to hand over the phone.

"No . . . no . . . no Michael, Michael . . . ? Hey, you got it wrong, what do you think happened buddy? Mummy just fell and hurt herself, come and see, she's okay. I am just helping her with her injuries. Give me the phone," stretching out his hands towards a reluctant Michael. He took the phone off him and cut off the telephone connection.

The doorbell and phone as if in unison began to ring at the same time very loudly sounding like an African conga drum rolling right inside Ola's head. Thank God for small mercies was all she could think as Deji had to release her from the knee drop he'd pinned her down with for minutes. Deji's body had been shielding Ola's view from Michael but as he moved away, Ola was afraid of what the sight of her bloodied face would do to Michael so she curled up and turned her body away from him. Even that simple movement felt like pure hell as her whole body was wracked with pain.

"God . . . ! What did I do to deserve this, what did I do to deserve this life . . . ?" Ola sobbed silently as she tried to muffle the sound and hide her pain from the kids.

"Are you okay mum?" Michael thought he was helping but his gentle hands rocking her shoulders sent even more pain down her spine as she remained on the cold kitchen floor.

"I am okay . . . go upstairs to your sister. Go and make sure she is okay and not scared where she is hiding . . ."

"No we are okay . . . ," Ola heard Deji saying to someone at the door

"We heard a woman's voice screaming . . . is everything okay . . . , is Ola okay . . . ?" interjected a female voice which Ola was sure had to be Vera and John, bless their soul . . . her Irish neighbours. Ola had become friends with them in the past six years they'd been living in the street.

Ola decided to take the opportunity and move before Deji came and finished the job. She expected him to be mad when he found out about her fumbling with his profile but to say she was shocked by the level of his reaction was an understatement. Ola truly assumed that because what he had been doing was so embarrassingly wrong on his part he wouldn't have the boldness to be massively angry but little did she know . . . little did she know she thought as she shook her head in regret. Ola knew she would have been all black and blue by the morning if not for her dark skin which seemed to have its advantages. At least it covers a lot of bruising. Ola shuddered as she imagined what she would look like if she had been a light skinned person taking this amount of beating. She tried to laugh as the picture of a black and blue collage with a hint of pale pink flashed through her mind. "Uhh" Ola grunted as pain shot across her broken lips as she attempted to laugh at her predicament.

"Thanks for your concern, everything is fine . . . we appreciate . . ." She heard Deji dismissing their neighbours. Ola grunted again as she tried more determinedly to drag herself off the floor as she heard the bang of the front door.

"Stay put!" Deji's barked command stopped her feeble attempts to lift myself off the floor as he came back in the room.

"You see what you make me do when you make me mad, you see?" Stretching his hands as if exasperated he walked towards the kitchen sink and ran a bowl of warm water and then grabbed a cloth and began cleaning the blood off Ola's face. She winced as the first splash of warm water touched her face. Ola wasn't sure if her movement away from Deji's hand was more from not wanting his touch or from the stinging of the water in some painful parts. As the truth stared her in the face, big drops of tears welled up in her eyes. Ola didn't want his touch anymore, not now . . . , she cried as she turned her face away from him in rejection of his touch and help.

"Stop and let me look at you," he insisted.

They both froze as they heard siren sounds outside their house at the same time. If she was in doubt that the siren bearers were at her house they disappeared as she saw through the window the flashing lights stationed outside their door followed by the loud insistent ringing of the doorbell. Ola remained sitting on the floor with her back against the cupboard as Deji went to answer the door for the second time in less than five minutes. She thought how popular they must be that night as it seemed more people wanted to come and witness her humiliation.

Ola clutched at anywhere she could lay some of the hurt and shame she was feeling. She was embarrassed that her neighbours and even her children heard her, a 35 years old woman being thrashed like an unwanted animal. No . . . , Ola didn't want anyone at her door sharing that humiliation with her because she was so sure they'd all heard.

"Oh God . . . just kill me now won't you, just kill me now pleaseee . . . ," Ola cried a silent prayer.

"We had an emergency call from this address," a male voice said very authoritatively.

"I am sorry we didn't make any call officer." Ola heard Deji saying.

"A young lad placed an emergency call to say his mother was being attacked and we had two other calls saying there were shouts for help from this address in a woman's voice."

"Oh, I am sorry officer for wasting your time with those calls. My son made a mistake you see because my wife had a fall and he probably panicked as she screamed when she was tumbling down the stairs, but she's okay." As those words left his mouth Ola wanted to scream 'liar . . . ! Liar . . . ! Pants on fire". She felt like one of the kids with such silliness coming into her mind.

"Can we see your partner? The caller said his mother was being hurt."

"No officer, he made a mistake."

"Can we see her now?" The officer asked sternly refusing to be swayed by Deji's answer.

"Ola! The Garda Officers are here to see if you are okay" Deji called out loudly from behind the door in the other room probably to alert her of the presence of the Garda. Ola fumed as she decoded Deji's message. He wanted her to pretend all was okay . . . but it was not okay! Wife beater Ola ranted calling Deji names she dared not speak out openly. Ola felt ashamed as she considered the kind of punishment Deji had given her. It reminded her of common criminals caught stealing in a public Nigeria market who had been left to mob action punishment by the locals in what they called jungle justice. As the Garda Officers walked towards the kitchen Ola toyed with the idea of speaking the truth, or just saying to them that she had been beaten within an inch of her life by her husband. What kind of woman would that make her then . . . , what kind of woman she asked herself?

"Are you okay lady . . . what is your name?" the female Officer asked on seeing the state Ola was in. Ola knew that if the Garda went through their records their address would be known to them because this was not the first time people had called the police because of the fights in their house. Ola had always thought if her family was known to the authorities in Ireland it would be for their outstanding contribution in the state. Little did she know that she would end up like this many years ago when she'd waited anxiously for Deji to join her.

"I am sorry Mam. I was upset coming down the stairs and I tripped and I had like a free-fall down the stairs. I seem to have knocked every joint in my body." Ola spewed out the well-rehearsed story as she tried to deflect their suspicion by injecting a bit of humour into the situation.

"Don't try and talk, the ambulance is just arriving and they will come and check you out." As the paramedics came into the kitchen, Ola recognized the ambulance man as she liked to call him. Her heart dropped because it was the same African ambulance attendant who transported her the first time she had a fall and lost her baby. He had actually been on call out to her house a number of times over the years.

"Only I would be unlucky enough to keep getting possibly the only African attendant on call out to my house," she huffed in self-disgust at her ill luck. Ola's religious beliefs didn't believe in luck which was good enough for her considering that her recent fortune or misfortune would have proved beyond any doubt that lucky was one thing she was not!

"Good evening Mam, can you tell me your name?" asked the paramedic

"Ola" she answered wondering why he was going through the formalities, he must know her name by now! After all he had answered at least three call outs to her house she fumed!

"Okay Ola, can you tell me what happened and are you hurt?" Ola repeated her ready prepared story to the paramedic even as she could hear Garda officers quizzing Deji. Ola knew what she really wanted to say but she was very conscious of the consequences. What could she say really . . . ? What? Could she say that her husband beat her and hurt her? What then, when she knew she would simple let it go, again. It wasn't that Ola didn't want to report him, it was the price . . . the price for her and her kids.

. . . No. Ola decided Deji's version of the story was okay.

"I am sorry, I was upset coming down the stairs and I tripped and I had like a free-fall down the flight of stairs and I seem to have knocked every joint in my body."

"Can you tell me where it hurts?"

All over, Ola indicated with her hand too embarrassed to speak to the paramedics.

"We have to take you in for observation to make sure you are not suffering from a concussion."

Great! Just great Mr here to help! Ola seethed silently. So who was going to take care of the kids? She fumed at the disruption to her life and routine. Ola desperately needed someone to pay for her humiliation, she needed someone to take this pain and stress out on. She knew the paramedic was just doing his job, him and all the usual cohorts of social workers she knew would be waiting at the hospital.

The Garda returned from quizzing Deji in the sitting room.

"We are sorry to disturb you, but can you confirm the calls we had that you were being hurt by someone?"

Ola was seriously tempted to drop Deji in it and see his sorry arse banged up. Maybe he could be on the next 'banged up abroad' episode she thought, but she could not. She had to think about the kids, she had to think of them.

"I am sorry officer, it was as my husband said earlier, I fell down the stairs, I wasn't looking where I was going and I tripped on the washing I was bringing down the stairs." The frustrated look on the Garda Officer's face said it all 'you stupid woman!' . . . but they didn't understand how hard it was or the choices she was faced with.

"Okay." The officer said in defeat as she watched the ambulance attendants assist Ola to the ambulance. Going out the door she put her face down as she saw her neighbours looking from their front gardens in interest. Ola jumped as she accidentally bumped into someone, causing her to look up.

"Ola . . . oh my God, Ola . . . ! Are you okay?" Rita exclaimed as she saw her battered face.

"How did you know . . . what are you doing here?"

"Michael called me. Sorry I left home as soon as I got the call there was a lot of traffic."

"It's good that you are here now. Can you take the kids for me till I come back?"

"Off course! I will."

"Sorry, can you help me alert the officers?" Ola asked the ambulance attendant who was assisting her into the vehicle.

"Okay."

It was as if the presence of her friend Rita suddenly reminded her she was not alone, not locked in with Deji. Ola knew it was going to be difficult but she was going to do the right thing for the first time. Even if not for herself, then she would do it for her children.

"Sir, I would like to change my statement. My husband physically abused me, endangered my children's lives and I am afraid for my life and my children's lives. I was afraid but I would like to press charges."

"Okay, we will take him in for questioning and take his statement. The best we can do right now is to ask him to find a place to stay tonight but here is the address and number you need to make a formal complaint to get a barring order.

"Thank you officer," Ola replied respectfully in appreciation for their patience. As the ambulance pulled away from the house, Ola saw Deji being led into the marked police car with the flashing light. She wished she had a camera to photograph him and maybe use it as his profile picture for his dating site with his whores she raged. Ola really didn't know what to do or even if this was the answer because this was guaranteed to get her into even more trouble with Deji. All she knew was that she needed to do something before she truly got killed. Ola turned away from the ambulance attendant in embarrassment as he tried to ask her more questions. She pretended to be in too much pain to talk.

Just before Ola was discharged from the hospital, a social worker came to see her to give her the spiel about domestic violence. Ola tried to listen but her mind was plagued by Deji and what to do about her situation with him. She offered to arrange contact for Ola with people who could support her since she was pressing charges. Ola panicked when she gave her information about some emergency accommodation and refuge for women and children. She could not help remembering what Deji had said about such places. She knew he must have been lying just to scare her about using such services but it had taken root and was now influencing her decisions

"Thank you. I am okay now," said Ola as she tried to shut the social worker up and dismiss her but she was probably experienced and she seemed bent on finishing her talk.

"Facing abusive partners can be quite intimidating and sometimes even dangerous for the person facing the situation especially when they are reporting. There is support so you don't need to go through it alone."

"What dangers would you know of?" Ola quizzed the woman letting out her fear as irritation.

"I am aware you are pressing charges against your partner and we are just offering advice and we would like to help you see all the options. It can be a dangerous time because sometimes the abusive partner doesn't want their victims to leave neither do they want to leave themselves and so they can become even more violent once their partners presses charges. What I am saying is that you don't need to do this on your own there are supports in place that you might not know of."

"Okay, thank you and I will bear that in mind and thanks for all the information and contact details. I will use them if and when I need to," replied Ola sounding self-assured all the while quaking inside . . . she was really scared of the consequences because she knew Deji wouldn't take this lightly, but she decided to take things one step at a time and cross that bridge when she got there. So bandaged up and filled will pain killers Ola was discharged to go home . . . wherever that was . . .

"God help me," cried Ola. That has become her silent prayer. God help her indeed . . .

CHAPTER FOURTEEN

ARRIVING BACK ON THE STREET was quite an embarrassment for Ola after the public farce she and Deji had made of themselves the previous night.

Ola was frustrated in no small way as she wanted to swear at the way her life was turning out. She could see some curtains pulling back as the taxi dropped her off in front of the house she had lived with Deji for six years. She was certain she had been many of her neighbours' tea time conversation the day before or the subject of their office gossip. Ola put her head down in shame but she was determined to survive this. She knew she had to for the kids' sake . . . she said to herself vehemently.

Stepping into the house cautiously, everything looked a bit strange with the kitchen upside down. Ola had this habit of never leaving the house in a mess no matter how much of a hurry she was in but these were not normal circumstances. The phone light was flashing with messages . . . chairs strewn all over the place around the kitchen table and unwashed dishes piled up high in the kitchen sink. She unconsciously began to pick up stuff and put them back in place as she walked restlessly around the house.

Ola turned the answering machine on speaker as she went about tidying the house, a move she immediately regretted after the automated voice droned out "you have six new messages." The blast of anger and accusations stopped Ola in her tracks and sent the little calm she had been feeling out the window.

"What are you thinking off . . . you have sent my brother to prison, if you don't want to stay married do you have to kill my brother, ehn? Ola, what kind of trouble is this? Call me! You hear call me!" That was Josephine, Deji's sister living in France. Ola didn't have much contact with her anymore these days, come to think of it, neither did Deji.

The next few message sounded the same . . . more or less.

"Madam, what is this I hear, my friend has been arrested, why didn't you call me? Why such a drastic action? I can't get you on your mobile. Can you answer your phone, we need to talk." "This is not our home, you want Deji to go and rut in Oyinbo jail, can you carry his death on your conscience.' '. . . Sister, we are African's oh, don't let this Oyinbo land confuse you.' . . . on and on the messages went.

"Did he tell you what he did? Did he tell you how he kicked me on my tummy? Did he tell you of the time he beat me so much I lost my baby?"

Coming to herself Ola realised she was alone at home and she was screaming around the house but there was no one to hear her . . . She was appalled that Deji was telling false stories about her everywhere. He must have been telling people his version of the story. Ola expected this but she was still shocked by the recriminations in the messages. She could not understand why they were acting as if this was new.

She wanted to ask them why they didn't stop Deji all these years when he was sleeping around and hurting her and her children—his own family!

"Why?" She cried. Giving in to her feelings, Ola broke down in a renewed bout of tears.

Ola wondered if they would be that lenient with Deji if she were their sister. Her answer came much faster than she would have liked as the next message was from her mum. Her mum . . . , can you imagine raged Ola.

". . . please Ola my daughter, a woman does not use the police to solve a problem between herself and her husband. Please my dear, don't let them call us a bad name oh. You know Deji's mother and I are in the same meeting group and she was crying to the club president. . . . please my dear, suru- gently. That is Oyinbo style, let us use our style to solve this."

". . . Our style! Can you imagine . . . our style she says? What is our style?" raged Ola.

She wondered how people came from Africa to Europe and are happy to spend Euros as the means of exchange. None insisted on spending Naira or other such foreign currency to see how far that got them and even the ridiculous nature of it. But a man beats his wife, nearly kills her and suddenly she had to be an African woman! Where did they see it in African culture that a man was supposed to beat his wife, where? She asked rhetorically. Even the tradition concerning the wall Gecko disallowed people from attacking it. If it was irritating, you were supposed to lift it up cautiously and put it outside but never to hit or kill it because they claimed doing so would bring bad luck. Though it was based on superstition, it was packed with wisdom. Ola could not imagine why a culture that believed that would want to blame her for trying to protect herself and her kids. After all there were legalised places where people could beat each other—in the boxing ring!

"They can all get lost!" Ola screamed as she pushed the phone off the table with one mighty crash onto the kitchen floor. Just then the doorbell started ringing drawing her attention again to the decisions before her.

Ola wasn't really in the mood for visitors but she had to check as she wasn't sure if it was the Garda back with more questions . . . it turned out to be Chike, Deji's friend.

"Good afternoon Sir, you are welcome." Ola greeted him in the way that was demanded of her as a good respectful Nigerian woman. He was only 41 years old but Ola referred to him as sir. He was not really like a religious Sir or a Knight but she had to show him respect and he too showed her respect by calling her madam, not like the madam that owns a brothel! Many Nigerians feel that you cannot call another woman's husband by their first name or call another man's wife by her first name so they do the madam/sir thing or sometimes they address each other as the parent of so and so, Ola would have been Mama Michael, but she hated that form of greeting because it was not her whole identity!

Ugh . . . groaned Ola as she rolled her eyes.

"Madam, what is this thing that I am hearing, why didn't you call me before you took any action?"

"I am sorry sir, it's just that it was sudden and things have been getting out of hand."

"Okay madam, you have proved your point and you have shaken him a bit, we need to go and make a new statement and tell the police that nothing happened."

"Oga Chike, you have not even asked me what happened you just want me to go and lie to the police that nothing happened, what will happen when he hurts me again?"

"My dear, the important thing now is to get Deji away from the clutches of the police. You know the way they are and even seeing that he is an immigrant. Do you want them to hurt him, is that what you want for your husband? You want to bury him here is that what you want madam?"

"No . . . off course not!"

"Then you will go and do the right thing and get him away from there. Look my dear, I know you are angry, but you know the way we men are. If my wife reports me every time I just push her a little I will be in jail every day. You have to take this in your stride madam. You know, it's not as if this is new to you, we men are like that. How many times did you see your parents fight, did your mother ever take him to jail?

"uhum . . ." Ola muttered under her breath. She knew Chike wasn't actually there to listen to her side, he'd probably been told to go and talk *'sense'* into her. True to what Ola thought, he carried on with his own plans.

"So why are we allowing Oyinbo system distort our African values and culture? We are African's oh, that is what we are . . . ehnn . . . please let us go and change the statement before they charge him. I know that you Ola you are a very good woman and you don't want anything to happen to your lovely family. Even the children will not forgive you if something happens to their dad because of you. Come on, let's go to the station."

He wasn't there for her . . . he was just there to get Deji off the hook that was all! Ola fumed. What had she expected anyway? He was probably the same in his home. After all by his own admission he 'pushes' his wife. Ola sniggered as she pasted a thankful smile on her face.

"Thank you for coming sir, I appreciate your intervention."

"It is okay madam, we cannot always react the way we feel things. One must always look at the consequences and what we have to gain from our actions. Don't worry things will get better ehn . . . , please don't look back."

"Thank you sir, it is okay, I will go to the Garda and change what I said because it's not as if I want my husband in trouble. I can't bear it."

Ola knew there was no going back in the relationship but she had no plan. She wanted out that was the only thing she was sure of—oh yes . . . and tired of being treated like an inanimate object, like a property. Ola didn't see herself as a very desirable woman, but she was convinced she deserved a little better than what she had with Deji. . . . at least she hoped she could get better from life.

Ola's mind drifted to the time before she got married, when she was greatly admired. She was frequently described as beautiful and confident and many envied her for her brains. Her final results from college surprised many when she graduated with first class honours. Ola was saddened as she reflected on what she had done . . . or rather not done with all her dreams and ambitions. . . . no job . . . no prospects apart from being a stay at home mum. Deji was right, who would want to employ her? Ola wondered what she would say on her curriculum vitae. Maybe cook, cleaner, driver, child minder and the crowning quality . . . punching bag.

Ola was worried that she might be seen to have behaved like every other silly woman being abused by their partner. She knew it was hard to understand but Ola was swayed by Deji's position as her husband and the father of her children. So allowing Deji to be arrested or even persecuted was like sending herself to jail. It didn't make sense but Ola was convinced and there was no stopping her. She was going to have to drop the charges against Deji.

The Garda tried to investigate if Ola was being intimidated into changing her story but she refused to be swayed. Ola apologised for wasting police time and fibbed that she was angry that's why she'd made those allegations against Deji. Despite telling her that Deji would be free to return to the house unless she proceeded with obtaining a barring order, Ola was still reluctant to proceed with her case. She was however surprised that contrary to her belief that Deji was arrested, it seemed the law could not arrest him unless he violated a barring order. It made her wonder where Deji was or even where he spent the night when the Garda officer informed her that he had been released the same day after questioning but they had advised him to stay at a friend's for the night.

If she expected gratitude from Deji for dropping the charges against him, she had another think coming! Deji arrived back home on a war part with his face set like flint—hard and unyielding. It had the makings of their usual silent war but Ola wasn't playing it his way this time . . . she was going to turn the game on him. His usual strategy was to keep malice with her refusing to talk to her for days on end. Ola usually would become weary and she always gave in first because she couldn't stand the tension at home. This time Ola had a game of her own. She bypassed the days of malice and went for broke. Immediately Deji stepped into the house, she knelt before him and apologised for her actions looking very remorseful with tears in her eyes.

Ola had a plan . . . but it needed time . . . she needed time . . .

Ola's plan began with her first appointment to suss out the supports the social workers said were available to help women experiencing difficulty. She felt really odd attending a welfare clinic as Deji had been working for the past ten years so they were not on a state payment. As Ola arrived at the Welfare office, she took a ticket and found a sit on the cold hard chairs in the starkly furnished room. She was disappointed that she could not just walk away from Deji but she had to go cap in hand looking for support. Ola saw this as part of the problem. She was displeased that she was either begging Deji or the welfare office. Either way, she saw her self-esteem on the floor, but at least this was definitely better. This at least guaranteed that she wouldn't be killed or infected by a sexually transmitted disease from a husband who couldn't keep it zipped up!

Ola was confused by what her friends wanted her to do. First they thought she was stupid for not kicking Deji out of her life, then the same people called her a bad woman for taking steps to prevent him from destroying her completely. Ola knew the implications of Deji having affairs and sleeping around. She just didn't know what the general consensus was or the best way to deal with them. She wished someone would just come and tell her what to do . . .

Ola had to snap out of her musings as her number came up on the counter.

"I am sorry Ms Ola, for us to put you on a payment you have to make a written application and because you are married you have to bring your husband's payslips for us to know that he cannot afford to take care of the family." The lady at the welfare office informed Ola kindly.

"You don't understand, we are having real difficulties and he is very abusive and I am afraid for my life. I need to leave him and move out to protect myself and the kids. My being here is all done secretly so he doesn't know that I am planning to leave. The lady at the hospital said it is usually dangerous if the abusive partner knows you want to leave that is why I am planning secretly."

"I understand but there is not much I can do unless you have formal separation documents in place because my records show you as married. Look depending on how desperate it is you might want to try emergency accommodation in one of the women's refuge centres or see if the council can give you a flat. I am sorry I can't be of more help."

Disappointed and deflated Ola thanked the officer and left. She knew she had to come up with an alternative for her plan to work.

Ola was not prepared to go to one of those refuge places. She was scared because Deji had told her things that could happen to the kids or the possibility of drunks around the place. She knew it was a farfetched story by Deji to deter her from ever thinking of leaving him but the story was stuck in her head and she knew she would never forgive herself if something happened to the kids.

Ola decided to go and try the council Officers for a flat . . . she'd heard rumours that it literally took forever to get one but she would at least try and put her name on the list.

"You have to fill all the forms but there is a long waiting list before it gets to your turn."

"What is the waiting time for an average family?" Ola asked the lady at the council offices.

"It is not so straight forward you know, depending on your circumstances, if there are people with worse conditions they will be moved ahead of you. But on the average we are looking at say three years."

". . . Oh no!" Ola groaned in defeat as she couldn't help letting her disappointment show feeling this was the end. Deflated by the massive holes punched in her bubble as it became obvious that her plans were not going to be easy to achieve, Ola thanked the officer politely even as her insides were crumbling.

"It's not over yet!" Ola encouraged herself. She didn't know how but she was determined to make her plans work. Her next option was finding a job. Ordinarily that would have been Ola's first option but her main challenge with it was her lack of relevant experience!

Refusing to be deterred, Ola braced herself and marched determinedly towards the recruitment agency at the City centre along the quays. She was buoyed with her previous customer service experience and a barrel of hope. But immediately Ola got to the centre, she knew it was a mistake as her naivety became obvious. She actually assumed that the agency would consider her ten year old sales assistant experience for a job today!

The information officer at the front desk of the agency put the final hole in Ola's bubble. She pushed a clipboard to Ola with a questionnaire and a pen to fill in her details . . . education, work experience . . . references. Ola didn't know where to start, she didn't know if the company where she'd been employed briefly over ten years ago would remember her or if they would even be willing to give her a reference. She still took the chance and filled the form with her stale details, all of which fitted on half a page. Discouraged, Ola handed the form back.

"Well Ola, considering your experience, we don't really have much now but I will keep your form on file and we will let you know if we have any opportunities that will match your skills," . . . blah, blah . . . blah was all Ola heard because she knew she was being given the polite brush off . . . another brush off. Ola thanked her again and walked blindly onto the street.

It was proving too much for Ola and she began to cry . . . just too much she cried wondering why her life was so messed up.

Ola felt heaviness in her chest giving her painful constrictions as she walked onto the cobbles. Ola's knees began to shake. . . .

"Oh God," she panicked "I am going to have a heart attack." She held out one hand over her chest and with the other she wiped the tears streaming down her face and walked smack into a hard wall. Ola raged at her silliness when she realised she had walked into someone.

"Steady," a deep baritone male voice said as warm hands reached out for her shoulders steadying her.

"So . . . sorr . . . sorrr," was the last thing Ola remembered as she felt herself falling headlong into a dark pool.

"I can't breathe," she croaked hoarsely. Ola was shocked to see that she was half resting on the knee of a man with a dark coloured suit with her butt on the cold paving stone.

"I can't breathe!" She cried louder as she felt panic rising in her. Ola was amazed at how quickly a small crowd was forming.

"Can I have some space please, I am a paramedic . . . can you step back please?" The owner of the baritone voice asked with assured authority in his voice as he proceeded to lay her gently flat on the ground. He seemed to know what he was doing reasoned Ola as the owner of the voice took her hand by the wrist for a short period. Ola realised he was taking her pulse. He seemed satisfied with the result as he turned and directed his gaze fully to her. Ola's eyes widened in recognition—in fact both their eyes widened in recognition as they both seemed to see each other fully almost at the same minute. It would have been comical if it wasn't so damn embarrassing thought Ola.

Ola took this as another proof of her lack of luck. These things according to superstition were supposed to happen in threes she grumbled as she calculated that she'd four unlucky things in one day. For her it was one too many. To bump into no other than the Mr Know it all Ambulance Man of all people!

"Ola?" he called her name hesitantly trying to ascertain it was her.
"Yes."

"Are you still in pain?"

"I feel tightness in my chest," Ola muttered in a low tone.

"You need to breathe . . . slowly, you are having a panic attack, just relax and breathe . . . breathe, keep breathing." His gentle voice seemed to have a calming effect on Ola. Mr Ambulance man picked up her hand again and placed his other hand against her shoulder. As she fixed her gaze on him she felt a release of the tension from her body and her breathing calmed.

"Are you still in pain?"

"No thank you, I feel better." Stretching out his hands he helped her to her feet. Ola was mortified by the encounter but manners demanded she show appreciation again!

"Thank you, lucky me that you were here."

"I don't know about that . . . , I think bumping into me must have sacred you into having a panic attack. Look it might be good for you to sit down for a few minutes just to get your blood circulation flowing better again and to calm down."

"Thanks I will find a place to sit."

"Let me buy you a coffee across the road to apologise for tripping you over."

"It's okay, I have to go anyway."

"Look, indulge me . . . for medical reasons that is, I would like you to sit down for a few minutes just to make sure you are okay before you start moving again."

"Oh all right" Ola finally gave in and went across the road to the coffee shop. Ola wasn't in the humour for anything, she was embarrassed enough as it was.

"At least this time I did fall." Ola joked nervously in an attempt to cover the awkwardness.

Ambulance guy either didn't like her joke or he was just a moody person thought Ola as he didn't laugh. He didn't even make any attempt to crack a smile. Ola noticed a slight twitch along his jaw line as he pursed his lips as if thinking of how to say what he wanted to say.

"I hope you know I am not judging you so you don't have to do that or feel embarrassed. I just want you to take a few minutes to relax and we can both be sure you are okay."

"If you say so ambulance guy."

"I say so and it's Raymond . . . my name that is. You can call me Ray."

"Where are you originally from?"

"Nigeria . . . and you?"

"Same place. How did you get to be a paramedic, it's such a strange profession for many of our people. You are the first Nigerian . . . in fact African paramedic I have ever known in Ireland. Well it's not as if I know many . . . ," Ola's voice trailed away as she realised she was blabbering.

"Yeah, well it was the closest I could get to being a doctor without having to spend so many years in college," Ray replied ignoring her self-conscious chatter.

"Did you want to be a doctor?" Ola asked allowing her curiosity get the better part of her and drew her into further conversation with Ray.

"Yes, on a good day. But I am happy here, this is a good job and I like it."

". . . Yeah, I wish I had a job. I am looking for one now but I have no experience . . . , no relevant experience that is, so I am getting the brush off from recruiters."

"It might look like that but if you really want a job I will say don't give up. You'll be surprised all the informal experience you have that you take as nothing, just take your time and see how things pan out."

"Yeah, thanks. I'll make a move on now. Thanks for your help."

"Anytime . . ."

Ray assisted Ola as she got up off the chair. He waited for her to go through the door and they shook hands at the entrance as they parted ways.

"Mm . . . mm," sighed Ola who suddenly felt hopeful about her chances of finding employment. Though nothing had physically changed about her situation, Ola was certain things would work out fine. They had to Ola swore vehemently . . .

Chapter Fifteen

A MONTH LATER AND OLA still wasn't any closer to achieving her secret plan. She could not find any other source of income but to keep relying on Deji. Some people blamed her for her present predicament but Ola knew it was not all her fault. She knew it wouldn't have been this way if Deji had not urged her to stay at home when he joined her in Ireland. She questioned how it happened that she always just went along with Deji's plans . . . ? It could have been due to her lack of personal aspirations but Ola knew deep down that the reason she went along with the plans was because she saw her aspirations fulfilled through Deji's achievements. She thought that if he was doing well that somehow their family would be okay. . . . how wrong she had been, so, so wrong an assumption because all Deji was now into was himself with a capital HIM which left Ola on her own . . .

There was unease in the house that kept everyone on tenterhooks especially the kids. Ola was able to manage with him as she was already used to his mood swings but her major difficulty was how it was affecting the children. Very often, Deji's presence had everyone scurrying to put the house in order. As if on cue, Ola heard the sound of Deji's car in the driveway and her heart started racing as she took in the messy state of the house, immediately making a lie of her claim that she could manage Deji! She knew the way he reacted to an untidy house particularly as he always found a way to make his displeasure known. He'd start shouting from the door and kicking things around to emphasise his point. But Ola was in no fit state for him today so she doubled up the kids to put the house in order like soldiers in a military cantonment. "Michael, please pick your sister's toys off the floor. Quickly your dad is back. You know how upset he gets when he comes home and sees Alicia toys around the place."

"Hmm . . . ," mumbled Michael

"Go on quickly." Ola shouted at him as he dragged his feet to show his reluctance by moving as if in slow motion. She gritted her teeth as she resisted the urge to push him to hasten his pace! Ola was desperate to avoid any confrontation with Deji today especially as she needed to ask for some money.

"Heck . . . ," Ola swore under her breath as she realised she could not take out her apprehensiveness on the kids. She knew it was not fair on them.

Ola dillydallied around until just before Deji went to bed before she finally decided to take the bull by the horns and ask for the money she needed. It would be an easy assumption to make that it was one big amount the way Ola was fussing about asking him but with Deji, everything was a big deal. It was as if he delighted in humiliating her for every little thing. Ola wished she had listened to advice all those years when she was told to ask for a specific monthly allowance from Deji. She was wearily thinking that if she had done it then, maybe they would have had a system going by now. However, with the benefits of hindsight and knowing Deji the way she did, Ola knew he never would have agreed. He would bend backwards to block anything that gave her any form of independence or power.

It made her remember when she asked him to teach her how to use the computer and Deji kept putting it off and coming up with all kinds of excuses. Ola chuckled as she recalled being told by him how complicated the system was and how it would be hard for her to learn until she went and enrolled for one of those mother and toddler groups where they took care of the kids while the mother learnt a skill. It was very fortunate for her to get that computer class at the time . . .

She knew there was no point in moaning . . . *very soon* she reassured herself taking solace in her secret plan. Her day was coming soon, but right now she had to bide her time and make her request to Deji.

"Deji, there is no gas in the car, please can I have some money to buy some petrol?" Though Deji heard her, because she was standing an arm's length from where he was sitting, he acted as if he didn't hear her.

"Deji . . . did you hear me?"

". . . Why don't you come and jump on it! Now you know how to say please and to talk to me respectfully. If my black arse was banged up in prison where do you think I would get money to give you? I have told you though I am here you must assume I am not here. I don't exist for you anymore."

"Deji, this is not about me. I need gas to be able to take the kids to school and their weekly activities."

"Walk if you have to! Just look around the house no one is able to pick up after themselves. We have toys all over the place, uniforms . . . books on the floor . . . everywhere. You are doing my head in I tell you." With a long sigh he walked away without giving Ola any opportunity to respond.

". . . argh," Ola shook her clenched fists at his retreating back snarling in frustration. Deji had a funny way of reducing her to feeling like one of the kids. He spoke to her like a father admonishing a recalcitrant child, but Ola refused to be drawn into a fight with him . . . not now. Her plans required keeping her head down till she was able to act. Ola had resigned herself to a week of scrimping and saving to put gas in the car so she was quite surprised as she walked out to the living room to see that Deji had left a twenty euro note on the living room table.

"Oh well thank God for small mercies." Ola went and added the money to the growing pile she had been saving up. It wasn't much yet but she was confident that it added up and as the advert claimed ' . . . every little helps.'

Once Deji was gone out the door, Ola went back to her search . . . she has been looking for a new place that was affordable though she worried about how the kids would react to moving house. Ola's financial situation made it obvious that she could not afford the same size of the house they had now, with landlords asking for a month's rent and another month's deposit which Ola definitely couldn't afford. She would have to downsize her search to a one bedroom flat and a place that was close to the children's school. Most importantly Ola had to keep it all to herself so she could not ask friends for support. She couldn't be too careful in case one of her friends betrayed her plans to Deji. She was sure he would kill her if he even thought she was planning on taking the kids from the house. Deji usually used money to maintain his authority in the house so if he even knew about her plan he would make sure he left her with no money at all.

". . . No," Ola resolved to continue as the dutiful little wife so she could carry out her plan. She turned the computer back on from the hibernation to continue with her search working as fast as she could as she only had till the kids came back from school.

Ola was hopeful as she set up two viewing appointments to see two flats. One of them was actually quite hopeful because it had a back garden. She hoped they would allow her pay just the rent because she definitely could not afford a month's rent and deposit at the same time.

Just for once, Ola wished things would go smoothly for her considering the mess her life was in. . . .

It really made her wonder why things had to always be so hard for her. She could not understand it. How things for other people went easily and she had to struggle to get anything. Even if they said something was free for everyone, from experience Ola noticed that it would quickly change just before it became her turn. It might seem like an exaggeration but that had been her experience in the last few years . . . no actually as far back as Ola could remember!

Maybe a slight exaggeration she scolded herself but not too farfetched if she considered a few of her mates. It showed her life as one big struggle. She knew better than to compare herself with others but she was human and sometimes one only knew what was missing in their life when they saw what others could have freely. She thought of some of her friends who were not even half as pretty as herself yet their husbands took care of them . . . taking them out, on holidays, dinner and even buying presents for them! Even her friend Rita who already earned well in her job was presented with a car which her husband bought for her at a surprise party he'd arranged for her birthday! And here she had to beg for money to put gas in her old banger of a car.

Many people have the *'if I came back to life moment'* when they are old and dying, but Ola thought regretfully that if she came back to life again, she would definitely look carefully before she said "I do." Unfortunately, her case was not any different from many of her friends she realised. She was getting to the dreaded marriageable age and she had waited and waited for Mr Right and at his continued absence or maybe her impatience, Ola settled for Mr Available.

"Hah," Ola derided herself. It wasn't as if Deji had been her only suitor at the time—some fourteen years ago. He just seemed the most likely to be successful and he was actually quite nice to her when he was wooing her. He took her out, paid the bills and he spoke politely to her though the truth be told, some signs were there. Ola remembered the way he always spoke about women's roles . . . , he seemed hung up on it. When Ola visited him over the weekends he always had a very visible pile of washing which she always gladly cleaned for him—*mug* that I am thought Ola!

It even seemed to get worse once they got engaged, though in retrospect, Ola didn't see it as getting worse she saw it as being accepted into the wifely role in his life. Their engagement translated to visiting Deji over the weekends, cooking enough soup to last him for the week, cleaning his apartment then and helping him iron enough of his clothes for the work week. She knew what happened at the time. She was trying hard to show him she was good wife material and that he had made the right choice in selecting her as his fiancée. Well seeing where it has landed her now . . . a glorified slave with the title of wife Ola wished she had taken heed to the Nigerian proverb that *'what you will not tolerate as a rich person you should not tolerate as a poor person.'* She wished she knew then what she knew now that *'whatever someone did to get a relationship they have to keep doing it to maintain that relationship'.* Maybe she would have been more cautious . . . maybe not . . .

———⁓⁓◦◦⊙⥥⊙◦◦⁓⁓———

After four weeks of meeting different landlords, Ola was at her wits' end. No one was ready to give her a house without two month's rent, one for the rent and the other as security deposit. Ola walked briskly into the coffee shop where Rita had arranged to meet her during her lunch break. From her vantage position inside the shop, Ola admired her friend

Rita as she sauntered through the door, elegantly dressed in a black skirt suit with a rose-coloured camisole. Rita was always hard to miss even in a crowd as she was usually smartly dressed. Even the clicking of her stiletto heels going click clack as it sounded on the wooden floor made it more difficult to miss her.

"Hi love," Rita said cheerfully hugging Ola.

"Hi yourself,"

"How are you doing? I haven't seen you in a while. You know how I worry when I don't hear from you," Rita carried on in her mother hen way of being.

"I am sorry, I just got swamped with so many things and really, I have reached my own decisions and I didn't want anyone to feel responsible for them or to even try and talk me out of it."

"Ok . . . , that sounds . . . I don't know. Maybe you better tell me from the beginning."

"I just went to get a letter from my solicitor stating that I have applied for legal separation."

"Ok . . . ?"

"Well, the good thing about it is that I can now go and apply for some form of assistance from the state till I am able to get a job."

"Is this what you really want, I know how much you talk about 'your home and doing the right thing"? Rita asked cautiously.

"I have had enough Rita, I am afraid that one day Deji is going to accidentally kill me and say that I fell down and broke my neck or some other lame excuse like that. I think it is time to go before they take me out to the morgue on a stretcher!"

"I cannot say that I blame you. You have a responsibility to yourself and to your children to be safe and to be alive to care for them."

"My biggest challenge is that I cannot find a place on what I have."

"Do you want me to loan you some money?"

"No! . . . no thanks. What would happen next month and the next and the next . . . , I prefer to do something that I can afford."

"Okay. How is the situation at home, are you guys mending bridges?"

"Hmm mm . . . Sweetheart, it's like the gulf war with the emphasis on gulf, so wide, it's a surprise there is a building still standing. We are not talking to each other, he is not eating my cooking, he barely gives me any money to buy food for the house at least for the kids. So I have been managing the kids on less than nothing while he seems to be enjoying eating out and having late nights out."

"That can't be good for the kids. Do you want to come to mine till you sort yourself out?"

"Thanks ore—my friend, your house is already full, two adults and four children, you don't need my mess."

"It's not a mess Ola and you are not alone."

"Thank you my dear friend, thank you."

"Look, Deji is not being hostile to you is he?"

"Not really, just that it is a bit worrying that we are sleeping in the same room and I can feel the vibes of his anger from across the bed. I can hear him whispering on the phone, text messages come at all hours and he answers them and now because of how things are I cannot ask him about it and I cannot even voice or show my anger or objection to such carryon!"

"Ola! You mean you are sleeping on the same bed with a man who is not talking to you, not eating your cooking, oh that sounds scary."

"Why . . . ?"

"What if evil enters his mind and he snaps one night and kills you while you are sleeping. I am sorry to think like that, just that so many things have gone on between you that I am afraid there is too much hurt and hate on both sides."

"I don't think that Deji can be a cold blooded killer. I am just afraid that in the heat of the moment or in the heat of a fight he might hit me stronger than he intended."

"Ola, I am not happy about this at all, it is either you want to make up with him or you move out of there. If you are hoping he will miss you and want the relationship then you can make the first move but I think it is a dangerous thing to just be hanging on the edge like that and tempting fate, please!"

"You don't need to be afraid for me. Deji is a good man it's just that he feels that by beating me he will make me afraid of him so that I don't question him. You know, it is his way of clipping my wings to make sure I am not too forward."

"Ola, listen to yourself, please, you are not a bird, you are a grown woman, an adult, please don't leave yourself at risk, I can lend you the money for the deposit. I'm sorry I have to go . . . my lunch break is over. Please let's talk later. Go and sleep in another room or sleep with the kids on the floor if you have to. Don't tempt fate, please."

"Ok . . . ok, I'll do something about it" Ola murmured to satisfy her friend and make her leave

Ola hugged Rita as she walked away miming "call me."

"I'll be fine." Ola mimed back though she wasn't really convinced that she would be. Her GP had just increased her blood pressure medication because for the past few months she had been having dizzy spells and her blood pressure was very high, I mean very high Ola thought with a grimace. She didn't tell Rita about it as she was worried enough and there was not much she could do. Ola saw it as a problem she got herself into and she would just have to get herself out of it. Ola promised with a determined nod.

"I hope you are not going to nod off into a faint this time."

"Ambulance guy! . . . Sorry" Ola apologised as she quickly corrected herself, ". . . Ray . . . I mean. What are you doing here?" Ola asked self-consciously as she recognised the African paramedic who had attended to her at the house and when she'd had that annoying panic attack on the street."

"Good to see you are doing okay and not bumping into anyone today," Ray said teasingly.

"I am thanks. What are you doing in this neighbourhood?" Ola asked again just a bit flustered and at a loss of what to say.

"I am here on my lunch break away from college."

"Oh . . . ? Are you still studying, I thought you were already qualified?" Ola asked with a confused look.

"Don't panic" Ray said reassuringly. "I am fully qualified, I am presenting lectures on Occupational first Aid at the college down the road and I wanted some thinking space."

"Well, don't let me disturb you," Ola said as she made to leave.

"You are not, please stay and have a cup of tea."

"I had one already, I met a friend for coffee."

"Then please stay for a few minutes."

"Ok," Ola agreed as she sat back down a bit uncertain about what to say to Ray.

"How are you doing?"

"I am okay, thanks."

"I am not just asking a polite question, Ola, I genuinely want to know how you are doing and if there is anything I can do to help?"

"It must be my day for receiving help or is there a sign on my head that says needy woman?" Ola snapped sharper than she intended to.

"Okay . . . , I see I have touched on a raw spot. So are you going to tell me? Are you in need?" Ray asked more directly this time.

Softening her voice to throw him off Ola replied quickly

"No, I am okay, I apologise about my tone, it's been a crazy day or few days more like" Ola added.

"You know you can talk to me. Sometimes, it is safer to talk to total strangers."

"No, thanks, it's nothing and it will be sorted."

"Please let me help," Ray pleaded softly as if he really cared.

"It's no big deal really, I have just been looking for a job but I also need to up skill and take a course in retail."

"You should go and see them at the college where I teach, they are actually interviewing for new intakes."

"Okay thanks for that," Ola could see Ray hesitating with a questioning look on his face. She was sure he was on the edge of asking how things were with Deji and her but he didn't and she was very happy about that. She really didn't want to share her private business with him though he seemed really easy to talk to.

"I have to get going," Ola said looking for her escape.

"Here's my card . . . look, just hold on to it," Ray insisted as Ola tried to resist and return the business card.

"You never know when you might just need a paramedic so hold on to it," Ray insisted.

". . . and please go to the college, it's a good school," he added quickly as Ola was about to resist some more.

"Thanks, I will. . . . it was lovely bumping into you again." Ola stammered dismissively as Ray stood up and took her hand politely in a very formal and proper handshake that made her want to giggle.

CHAPTER SIXTEEN

OLA KNEW WHAT SHE WAS about to do was wrong and even cruel, but it was the only feasible option left for her. Anyway, she had lived with so much cruelty she too had learnt to be cruel. ". . . No," Ola said shaking off the last shreds of conscience telling herself Deji had none when he dealt with her so she too had to learn to deal with him without any. This had to be done and it had to be done now, no looking back . . .

Ola stood on tenterhooks as she went about like the dutiful mother preparing Alicia and Michael for school. There wasn't much to do for Michael in the mornings at his age and he was a really good boy if you turned a blind eye to his clothes scattered all over his bedroom floor! He got himself ready on school mornings, made his own breakfast-cereal or toast and he usually had his bag packed ready and waiting for Ola. Today was no different—at least from the kid's perspective as she mechanically went through the motions of getting them to school in good time.

Ola knew she would have to wait for Deji to go to work so she could commence her plan! Excitement and fear mingled in her mouth as she imagined what she was about to do. Ola's mind strayed to her conversation with Rita the day before and her chance meeting with Ray at the same coffee shop. What were the chances ehn . . . , but it felt good to talk to people who were thinking of her own interests for once. It was a completely alien feeling for Ola to sit and talk to a man who listened and waited till she was done before he spoke! The most amazing part

Ola reminisced were the few minutes of not being apprehensive, not worrying about saying the wrong things and just being able to speak without having to analyse the other person's mood first!

Sighing in resignation and defeat

". . . oh well," continued Ola in her musing, "this is the bed I have laid for myself, I have to lie in it." . . . she knew she couldn't go on this way . . . , there was no way she was going to let things continue. Ola was at this point certain something had to give but her fear was that if she didn't do something now she would be the one to give.

Contrary to what she told Rita the previous day, Ola wasn't sleeping . . . she couldn't remember the last time she had genuinely laughed or indulged herself in any luxuries. The recent warning from the GP about her blood pressure levels was one of the scares that had motivated Ola to take these drastic actions. Her blood pressure was constantly too high and worse of all, she was supposed to be on blood pressure medication but of course Ola couldn't even think of that as she could not afford the tablets. Ola despaired of life . . . she had no health insurance, no medical card and no savings to buy essential medication, nothing to her name.

"What a life," muttered Ola shaking her head. She was ashamed that at this stage of her life when she'd thought she would be established and maybe even built something . . . , a career or a business using her entrepreneurial skills, all she could be proud of . . . all she had was the story *"I am living abroad"*. She was disheartened that she was living worse than some of the friends she'd left back home in Nigeria some thirteen years ago. She remembered how they envied her—some still did especially when she chatted with them through social media. But the truth was that they only saw what she wanted them to see. She only told them *"the living abroad story"* they all seemed eager to believe! How could she tell someone that she didn't have health insurance . . . , she couldn't afford necessary medication of only €79 or that she had to ask another human being at over thirty years of age for money to buy sanitary pads because they were cheaper than tampons! Ola's mocking laughter changed to tears as she reassessed her life. She realised she was having to live by faith just like most Nigerians did back home. It could be funny to those who could afford expensive treatment but when you had no money back home, you had to believe in what they called divine health where first you pray not to get ill and if you did get ill, you prayed again till you got well!

Sometimes when Ola moaned like this people ignorantly asked "why don't you just go back home . . . , go back to Nigeria". Ola laughs at them as they didn't understand, because going back home was not that straight forward. After thirteen years living abroad, those at home had expectations of her, she was supposed to be this *big woman* who had come back to Nigeria . . . they would expect her to have her own house the minute she arrived. She would be expected to have a brand new car, the type they called *tear rubber*! Meaning you were the first owner as in you took all the plastic covers off the seats of the brand new car.

"No . . . !" Ola exclaimed they didn't understand, that she couldn't just pack up and go back home. What about the kids, who have lived all their lives here, it meant that if she took them back to Nigeria she would have to put the children in private schools. One of the average ones in Lagos or Abuja was about half a million Naira a year for a primary school child which was equivalent to €2500! Where would she get the money to give them the level of education they were getting here in Ireland back in Nigeria?

"Hmm mm . . . no, people don't understand." She laughed when she heard Irish people say, "if Ireland is so bad, then why don't you go back home?"

Where is home? Would she after thirteen years go and start struggling for the kind of jobs she left behind all those years? Would she go back to being the Personal Assistant to her classmates and friends who now had senior political appointments?"

"Ah," there was no way that was going to happen and that's why many continued to stay even when it was killing them.

Ola was saddened that she had joined those trapped in the living abroad story . . . too scared and too broke to go back.

"What a life!" she lamented, piqued by her limited choices. Ola had reached the end of her tether and she'd had enough! She was scared but she was still going ahead with her plan B. Ola knew getting a place of her own was out of the question now as she could not afford it without having to borrow from friends. Though Rita was willing to loan her the money, the truth was that from the way things were now, she knew she would not be able to pay her back, at least not in the near future. Ola cherished her friendship with Rita so much she didn't want to create anything that would make her too embarrassed to call on her.

Ola decided it was better this way and with her resolve firmly in place, she picked up the phone and called the locksmith.

Ola could not contain the mixture of excitement and apprehension bubbling in her heart as the time got closer to 10am. She could not believe she was actually going to do this. Just waiting for Deji to go to work was nerve wracking as she listened to his every movement from the bathroom to the bedroom. He appeared to be in no hurry as he usually resumed work at 11am on Wednesdays so he took his time getting ready. Ola could hear him filtering through the cupboards maybe looking for his hair comb. Her excitement was so palpable . . . it was unreal as Michael would say in his youthful way. Ola had to literarily stop herself from telling Deji what she had in store for him.

". . . Nahhhh . . . !" Ola decided, that would be too easy and it would take away her element of surprise. Anyway, knowing Deji, that would definitely put a stop to the plans because he would stop at nothing to turn the tables on her. Ola knew she had to hold on to the upper hand and act with the element of surprise.

She was aghast at the circuitous nature of the plan and it really shocked her to see how devious she had become but it wasn't enough to stop her as she banished all thoughts of remorse by focusing on keeping herself and her children safe. What's that thing they say about . . . *desperate situations requiring desperate measures . . . ?*

Finally, Ola heard the sound of the closing door, with a sigh of relief she ran to the window to watch Deji drive off. Ola's heart pumped with excitement mingled with fear as she took his departure from home as her cue to move into action.

First Ola called the locksmith to confirm that their appointment was still okay and at eleven am he arrived and proceeded to change all the locks in the house. Ola gave him one story about how she lost her bag with her keys in it and details that showed her house address so for security reasons she was changing the locks.

The nice old locksmith changed the front door and put bolts at the back and side entrances to keep the cost low. That done Ola proceeded to the courts to seek for an immediate baring order or whatever fancy name they called it. The hospital and her GP had been very kind. They agreed to give her a report on the number of hospital visits she'd had. Even the Garda gave her the number for them to confirm the number of calls and reports from her house. Ola hoped that this would work as she was determined to stay alive.

"I will not allow one man to kill me here . . . I want to see my children grow up . . . ," Ola repeated this over and over to herself every time she faltered. It helped to harden her resolve because she was certain she didn't want to die. It all seemed so clear to her now that she wondered what she had been doing stuck with Deji all these years allowing him to treat her like rubbish.

"It ends now," she vowed "it ends today . . . !"

With each stroke of the clock Ola's heart seemed to beat a little faster especially as it went past six. Any minute now Deji would be home and he was in for the shock of his life. Though it felt scary it also tasted good at the same time. Sweet revenge thought Ola, no wonder they called it sweet. Ola had sent the kids to Rita because knowing Deji, he would not let this happen without a fight and a good one at that but hopefully she had the law on her side this time as she had spent the whole day putting procedures in place.

Pound! Pound! Pound! Ola could literarily hear her heart pounding. She was actually scared because she didn't know how this would end.

"God help me," Ola sent up a silent prayer . . . so far from home, no family, no one to support her or help her out. At times like this when Ola needed some support, it increased her feeling of loneliness so much that she too asked herself what she was doing here in this Oyinbo land.

The loud thud of Deji's fist against the door was the first sign that he was home. She could hear someone banging loudly against the door post.

"Oh my God . . . he's back," Ola whispered shakily, suddenly feeling like the kid in the Home Alone movie. Unfortunately she didn't have any of the setup to trip him up if he tried to harm her Ola managed to joke in the midst of the unfolding chaos.

"Olaaaa! Olaaaaa!"

She could hear her name being called as Deji alternated between shouting her name and banging on the door. Running down the stairs in panic in case he broke the door down, Ola grabbed the phone to call the Garda.

"I have changed the locks of the door and you have to go to the Garda to get permission to come in and pick up your stuff," Ola informed Deji coldly across the closed door keeping well away from the entrance as if he were going to be able to walk through the door.

"Ola, what are you talking about?"

"I am sorry Deji, we cannot continue to live here together and right now this is the only thing I can do. You have an income and you can get another place."

"Ola, open the door" he said calmly but Ola wasn't fooled by that voice.

"I am sorry Deji, I have a barring order in place and the court is ready to enforce it. You can go and live with the women you want to kill me for."

"Ola! Are you out of your mind? Will you open this door now before I lose my temper?"

"I am sorr . . . ahhhhhhh!"

Smashhhh . . . the loud thud against the sitting room window had Ola jumping back in fear.

"Deji! What are you doing?"

"What does it look like? I am doing exactly what you have done, remodelling the house."

Smash, another big thud against the door galvanised her into action. Running up the stairs and dialling 999 at the same time.

"My husband is breaking through the window, I am afraid he will kill me."

"Calm down please, do you need an ambulance or the police?"

"I need the Garda," Ola shouted. "I have a baring order against my husband and he is trying to break into the house through the window, please hurry."

"Can you give me your address?"

"Please hurry, he's going to kill me" Ola shouted as she reeled out her address to the emergency person. Ola's heart jumped at the splintering sound of glass as it seemed the window finally gave way to Deji's force.

"Oh no, no, no . . . ," Ola panicked.

"What am I going to do . . . ?" She hadn't envisaged this happening . . .

"Oh please, help me," she whispered a silent prayer to the big man up there.

"This is it . . . ," she knew as she began to say her final prayers like a person on death row. Running back towards the sitting room in a confused haze, the sight would have been hilarious if it was not so scary but Deji trying to force his 6 foot 2 frame through the sitting room window was enough to clear her mind and let her know coming back to the sitting room was a wrong decision. Making a hasty dash for the door, for a split second Ola was caught in-between trying to decide the best route for survival! Run upstairs and still have possession of the house because if Deji succeeded in getting her out that would be the end of her . . . or run out the back door and throw herself at the mercy of the neighbours for protection . . . ?

Deji's growl of pain as he fell to the floor littered with broken glass in the living room was her answer. She picked up speed as she ran up the stairs taking the steps two at a time. As Ola finally entered her bedroom, she had only one thought in her mind which was to secure the locks behind the door.

Ola gave a sigh of relief behind the closed doors suddenly feeling like Alicia, playing hide and seek . . . or maybe the home alone guy was a more apt description of how she felt.

"This is my house you bitch, you better run, you hear me . . . you better run," Deji shouted making Ola move quickly away from the door. The venom in the words made her blood curl in fear of what Deji would do if he succeeded in getting his hands on her before the Garda officers arrived. Ola was sure all he needed was one minute alone with her and she would have the marks on her body to remember this day for life—that was if she lived to tell the story! Picking up the phone Ola began calling the Garda again praying "please come now, please come . . ."

Ola's heart was beating erratically as she heard Deji running up the stairs really fast and loud. This is what they should call fast and furious Ola thought as her situation flashed before her eyes.

"You have two seconds to open this door before I break it down, Ola . . ."

"You have to leave please. The police are on the way."

"Open this door now, Ola, open this door."

"Please leave . . . ," silence from the other side of the door had her a bit worried but she knew he was still there as she hadn't heard any movement on the stairs. Anyway, knowing Deji, he never backed down from a fight!

"Ola, you have proved your point, open the door, let's talk about this," Deji's cajoling voice didn't fool Ola at all. She knew it was just a ploy to get her to open the door. Yet it didn't stop her from longing for what they once had and what being with him represented for her. The softening in his voice made her heart melt a little as she remembered the gentleness which Deji seemed to be able to switch on and off when it suited him.

"Let's talk in the morning, please Deji. You know things have not been okay between us and we have to do something about it. It is unhealthy for the kids to live like this!"

"Where are my children?" Deji asked quietly. Ola's reply was stony silence because she knew that anything she answered to his question would probably aggravate him.

"I said where are the kids?" Deji asked more sternly.

"Yeah," said Ola to herself, she knew that quietness was only a ploy as his real disposition seemed to be coming out. She knew him well enough to know that he could not suppress and keep calm for long.

"Is this the way you want it to be ehn . . . ?. Is this the way you want to play the game? . . . ok, as you lay your bed so you lie on it." Ola heaved a sigh of relief at the retreating steps on the stairs. Her relief was however short lived as Ola heard the creak of the stairs again . . . and oh my God! There was a key turning in the lock.

I am dead! Was it . . .999, 911 Ola wasn't sure as she hit redial on the phone.

"Where are they?" It seemed like so long since she made the first call.

"Oh no, no, no . . . , they never come when you need them." Ola was confused and at her wits' end as she could not think of anyone else near enough to call in the face of the impending danger.

"Who can I call now . . . oh God, who can I call . . . ?" Ola cried with shaking hands and watched as if in a trance as the door moved back on its hinges . . . ! Revealing Deji, it seemed her nightmare had just begun . . . one she urgently needed to wake up from! She had completely forgotten about the spare keys for the rooms. She hadn't thought beyond changing the outside locks for the main doors to keep him out of the house. Deji must have found them in the kitchen cupboard.

"So you want to inherit my house while I am still alive, you bitch."

"Please let's talk about this."

". . . Oh, so now you want to talk, now you want to talk!" Ola managed to sidestep him as he lunged at her with raised hands open wide as if to attack. Ola began running blindly heading straight into the bathroom. She got there and managed to push the door close behind her but . . .

"Oh my God!" screamed Ola as Deji's foot beat her to it.

With his right foot in the door, Deji didn't need much effort to push the door open . . .

Whack across the face was the first contact Ola had from Deji. He spent the next few minutes hitting her everywhere his hands could connect so full of rage he could not even utter a word.

"So you want to kill me, you want to take over my house while I am alive, you ungrateful woman!" Deji ended each word with a forceful blow like a professional baseball player who never missed his target.

"Please! I am sorry, please, Deji, you are hurting me."

"You don't know what hurt is, you useless woman, you are finished you hear me, finished. If you have a death wish you have come to the right place because I will help you die." Grabbing his shirt Ola began pulling him getting into a full scale fight with Deji. She had just had enough and decided that at least if she was going to die, she was going to go down fighting. Her plan was to leave him with enough marks on his body that he would not be able to claim she killed herself or that she fell down the stairs as he usually said.

Big mistake! Ola realised too late, her biggest mistake ever as Deji grabbed her by the scruff of the neck, aiming for her throat. Deji easily used his grip on her neck to lift Ola off her feet. By now, Ola was sure her end was coming making her even more determined in her struggle motivated by the fear of never seeing her children again. Ola knew she had to stop him anyway she could, that was the only way out! She bent her head down towards his neck, opened her mouth wide with the scream of the pain and closed her teeth over a huge chunk of Deji's neck muscles like a pit bull without his muzzle!

". . . aaahhhh!!!" Deji cried out in shock and pain giving Ola some temporary relief until he grabbed her head, twisted her lips tightly and the next minute her head was pounding with pain as he began hitting her head against the bathroom wall tiles. Ola knew she was dying as she slowly began to slip out of his arms unto the floor.

She cried at the turmoil in her mind as the start of the day replayed in her mind. Ola remembered not saying good bye to the kids properly . . . and Michael . . . he just ran off when he left. She didn't hug him or even kiss him when she left him off at Rita's place after school . . . Ola knew she should have insisted on a hug if she knew that was the last she was going to see him . . .

As her life was flashing before her eyes Ola sent goodbye greetings to the kids . . . then she remembered her mum.

"Oh no . . . , my mum will be gutted," Ola panicked as she felt some dampness on her face, but she calmed down when she realised it was hot, sad tears flowing down her face—she was crying and she didn't even know it.

The kick of Deji's shoes into her sides sent such pain into her body she could feel it at the back of her brain. In a split second she made the decision to play dead hoping he would stop. After two more kicks where she lay hoping the Garda or someone would come, Ola kept her eyes tightly closed without moving, holding her breath and hoping to God he would stop. "Please God make him stop. Please God . . ."

After a few seconds it seemed to dawn on Deji that her body was not moving . . . that she was still. Ola continued to lay as motionless a she could and truly it wasn't difficult to do because she was probably one leg already on the other side. Then she felt the tip of Deji's shoe cautiously dig into her side between her rib cage and her hip as if to get a reaction from her. Ola allowed her body to roll with the push of Deji's shoes and comeback down again as he removed his foot as lifelessly as she could muster. She continued holding her breath as he poked at her again with his shoes a second time . . . still nothing.

"Ola! Ola?" she could hear Deji's voice rising in panic. It would have been funny if the pain at the side of her head didn't feel so much like dying.

"Ola, you think you can stay there and pretend? I will just leave you there so you can die slowly. Look at you . . . you are a wicked, evil woman. For you to lie there and pretend you are unconscious shows the kind of wicked woman you are."

Ola could not imagine what Deji was going to do as she remained unmoving listening to his rants and curses at her even when he felt she was unconscious.

"Ola, get up, this is not funny, get up now before I make you," Ola could not believe the cheek of him that he was still threatening her even when he felt she might have fainted or worse still be dying.

"What am I married to?" She lamented quietly as she agonised over her situation. She held back the tears not to give herself away as at least the beating seemed to have stopped. Suddenly, Ola felt Deji's arms behind her head and knees as he gently lifted her off the floor. Sometimes he seemed not to be aware of his strength. Ola imagined how strong he must be to easily lift her off the floor.

In the midst of all that pain, Ola remembered another time when Deji lifted her off her feet and let her body slide down against himself that she could feel the strength of his manhood as he welded his body to hers. Sighing inaudibly, a heaviness and sadness descend upon Ola as she returned to reality. She felt the mattress give way beneath her as Deji dropped her on the bed. Ola waited expectantly wondering what Deji was up to . . . , and softened as she realised he was probably getting some water for her face to try and revive her. She lay there waiting in her pretend state of unconsciousness for the splash of cold water.

Finally she heard the patter of Deji's shoes as he seemed to walk back towards the bed, then she felt his arms pull the covers over her shoulder . . . , and then a clicking sound from the switch of the bedside lamp as the light went off bathing the room in the gentle orange glow hanging over Dublin City from the rays of the fast disappearing sun behind the clouds. Under the cloak of darkness, Ola cautiously opened her eyes curious about Deji's next move. She couldn't believe it but he was walking out the door! Out of the room shutting the door behind him.

"Oh no! no . . . , no . . . , no . . . , come back," Ola whispered stunned by Deji's actions.

"I am a dead woman," she cried, she could not believe it . . . , she could not allow her to mind imagine the implications of what this man had just done or would have done if she were really unconscious!

This person she called her husband . . . , her supposed protector . . . , her defender! Ola was dumbfounded and shocked. She could not believe Deji had left her like that to die! She would never have agreed she was living in a dangerous place but this was the height.

"I have been living dangerously and I didn't know it." To say Ola was shocked at what Deji was capable of doing was a mild understatement.

As realisation dawned on her, she heard the door bell ringing. She hoped it was someone with authority who could enter the house to rescue her. Ola who always thought of herself as independent knew that right at that moment, she needed rescuing. She was too beaten . . . , too deflated to help herself. Maybe the Garda are finally here she hoped as her heart began to race in hope of help . . .

"I am living with an animal . . . ," that thought played over and over in her mind. She knew she needed help as the thoughts of Deji finishing the job he started swamped her mind. Ola crawled around on her knees as she tried to retrieve the phone to call the Garda again.

"Why are they never here when you need them?" Ola grumbled dejectedly. She could not contain the thought that if she had truly lost consciousness, she would be sleeping in her own death bed. This was what Rita was talking about the previous day at how easily a woman could get killed! Ola managed to dial the police number again with shaky hands at the same minute she heard Deji coming back up the stairs. For a split second Ola was confused like a little girl with her hand caught in the cookie jar. She took in the picture of herself on the floor where she had crawled to the middle of the room to get the phone. She would have made a mad dash for the bed to continue to feign being unconscious but she was in too much pain to move. Suddenly she released that no . . . , Deji had lost all rights to any consideration or gently thoughts towards him.

"Ola? Ola!" she could hear some panic in his voice as he called her name louder probably uncertain if she was still unconscious or not

"You are an evil man Deji . . . *ika ni yin!*-you are a dubious man! You are wicked and evil! You mean you left me on the bed like that without making sure I was okay or not . . . ? You are a murderer. *Akpa ayhon ni yin oh*—you are a murderer. Anyone who can do what you just did can kill," Ola accused Deji as he stepped back into the room.

"You are the wicked one, Ola, pretending to faint is something only a wicked woman like yourself will ever do. I have told you that you are an evil person but you have just proved it again. I am not here to argue with you, the Garda officers are here, they want to see you."

"Oh! So that is why you came back upstairs, not even to check on me? Ah! Deji, God will reward you according to how you have treated me. God will reward you in this life. You will get your reward," Ola shouted hysterically.

"Don't start your drama, now you know the Garda are here. I didn't do anything to you and you know that. You provoked me . . . behaving like a senseless woman, who has no regard for her home. They want to see you now. This is your chance to come and tell them the lies you have been concocting."

Pulling herself together refusing to change out of her ragged clothes, Ola mustered up enough energy and got off the floor with every part of her body protesting in pain.

"Go and wash your face before you go there looking like if someone has killed you."

"I will not Deji. You want me to go down pretending everything is okay as if you have not beaten me almost within an inch of my life? I will not pretend to cover you up anymore. You have shown me the type of animal you are," Ola's rant seemed to goad Deji who as if by reflex action lifted his right hand in reaction to hit her.

"Make my day . . . you just make my day and hit me. I swear you will do time for it. Just hit me one more time," Ola boldly dared him.

"That's what you want isn't it."

Ola decided not to answer but reserve her strength for the journey down the stairs as she pushed past Deji.

"Are you okay, we had several calls from your house? It has been a really busy evening at the station."

"No, I am not okay" Ola's voice broke as she recounted the events of the evening to them.

"First Mr Peters, we have a baring order from the court which we have been mandated by the court to hand deliver and enforce. You are to move out of the house effective immediately, we are to wait for you to pick up your stuff and you are not to come anywhere she is until your hearing in court on the 18th of February. If you have any queries you can address them to the court." As the male Garda Officer continued talking to Deji, the female Officer looked Ola over and asked if she should call for an ambulance as she was bleeding from the side of her head. But she was just too tired . . . , she just wanted all of them to leave so she could get some peace.

"Peace," Ola laughed in derision, what peace was that . . .

CHAPTER SEVENTEEN

. . . BACK TO SQUARE ONE. Life for Ola was as if she was starting all over again. She looked back over the last three weeks without Deji. Everywhere in the house felt really empty even inside her, she felt empty. Ola couldn't help smiling as she remembered the last time she saw Deji depart with one last sullen look at her over the head of the female Garda Officer.

It wasn't what she had hoped for but Ola was settling into a pattern with her life revolving around the children and their needs.

"I want a story mummy," Alicia's tiny voice broke into her thoughts.

"Okay, what story do you want love."

"I want daddy to tell me a story."

Every time Alicia asked for her dad, Ola was hit with pangs of guilt for depriving her of her dad's love. Even when Ola knew there wasn't much she could have done otherwise, it still didn't stop her from wishing things had been different. She wasn't left with much of a choice but Alicia was too young to understand and Ola made sure she shielded the kids from the brunt of Deji's behaviour to her.

Ola told herself firmly that it was either he went or she got sacrificed in the name of peace. "No," she said resolutely "it was better this way . . . , lonely but definitely better this way." Pulling Alicia close, Ola tried to calm her down.

"Hey princess, don't cry, daddy will come and see you on Friday. You know I explained to you that daddy and mummy are spending some time apart to help us understand each other better."

"Maybe, daddy doesn't understand me too . . . , maybe I have been a cry baby. Michael says I cry too much. Maybe daddy is not here so he doesn't have to hear me crying."

". . . shhh, don't say that my love. That's not true. You are the sweetest and most loving girl and daddy and mummy love you. And you know what, you don't really cry too much. You only cry when you are hurt and even mummies cry when they are hurt as well so you are never, ever the problem. Ok? I love you my little princess."

". . . then when is daddy coming home, I want to see him?" her soft plea just broke Ola's heart in many pieces.

"Your Daddy will come and see you on Friday."

"Promise . . ."

"I . . . I . . . you know love . . . , daddy said he will come and see you we have to wait till then," as much as Ola wanted to reassure her she could not as the last three visits arranged for Deji to meet her and take the kids out had all fallen through. Ola had waited and waited the previous week, his phone had been switched off and he didn't come to the centre where she had arranged to meet with him.

"I will call daddy tonight to make sure he comes on Friday."

"Thanks mum."

"Goodnight my princess, sleep tight."

Ola knew for the kids' sake she would have to make proper arrangements with Deji. She could not stand watching Alicia hurt like that. Michael was indifferent or at least he acted like he didn't care so Alicia was the main problem. Ola decided to place a call to him to see if he would be taking the kids on his Friday visit.

"Hello . . . Deji . . . ?"

"Sorry, who is this?" answered a female voice

"Can I speak with Deji, this is his wif . . . tell him Ola," her heart began to beat erratically as she swallowed the word wife and said Ola instead. She was not even sure if she had the right to call herself his wife! Ola was riled that Deji, who would not allow her to even see his phone, was actually allowing a woman answer his calls!

"Sorry, he is in the shower, he will call you back later," said the woman very briskly as the line went dead even as Ola's heart also went dead.

Ola was disgusted that Deji was openly living with another woman. He was making no pretences and he was not even sorry.

"Shit head!" Ola swore violently suddenly feeling numb as the reality of her situation seemed to hit home.

"Ahhhhh!" she screamed in frustration throwing the phone on the table wishing it was Deji she was throwing that way or better still his new fancy woman. Ola didn't know who she was but she hated her. She hated her so much she wished all possible evil to befall her and a boil to hit her in her private parts for taking another woman's husband!

Ola sat in the kitchen for over an hour just staring at the wall until finally her heart stopped racing and her mind became too numb for thoughts. The heaviness in her heart seemed to have numbed her thoughts. She wanted to continue to think, she wanted to cry or maybe she even curse him . . . but there was nothing. Just a blank . . . her thoughts had gone blank. Like a zombie, Ola picked herself off the chair and went up to the room she had shared with Deji all these years and lay on his side of the bed staring at the ceiling till she woke up with a start to the sound of the alarm clock.

Ola realised she must have dozed off but her head was pounding so hard she thought it was going to explode. She knew she needed to be strong for her children, she couldn't afford to be ill. She was a bit worried as her vision was more blurred than usual, she might have to measure her blood pressure again soon . . .

"Help me please," Ola prayed . . . "I just need to be strong for my children now . . . and yourself," a gentle voice reminded her.

It was Friday and Ola was expecting Deji to come and pick up the kids for his visit time with them. She stood in front of the mirror adjusting her clothes and makeup acting like a bundle of nerves! Ola was impatient with herself as she didn't really know what she wanted. She felt freer without Deji in her life but she found it really challenging knowing that he was with someone else. She wished he were by himself, lonely and unhappy. She wished him to be so miserable he would come back begging her to forgive him and take him back promising that he had changed and learnt his lesson. Deep down Ola really yearned for that to happen. She knew how crazy it sounded, in fact she could not tell this to anyone least of all her friends and family most of whom thought she was crazy for leaving her husband in the first place! Ola laughed at herself as her situation seemed to fit what people meant when they said '*it's complicated.*' Her desires were difficult to understand, even she didn't fully understand them herself. After all she had been through with Deji . . . she thought she should be called the world's best Idiot, giving up on herself.

"I better get on with it," she decided

"Alicia, Michael are you both ready, your dad will be here to pick you up in a few minutes."

"I don't want to go." Ola rolled her eyes as she got ready for the argument with Michael.

"Look Mikey, we've been through that already, you have to go. I need you to make sure that Alicia is okay and she wants to see her dad. Please let's do this for her, please."

"Let's see if he will come today, he said that the last two visits and he didn't show. I wonder why you won't just give up."

"Don't talk like that Michael, he's still your dad."

". . . hm mmm,"

Ola grimaced. She was sure if he had the vocabulary to give meaning to that sound it could very easily be interpreted as 'sperm donor' and truly in the last few months, Deji had taken on the role of really nothing more than a donor! Ola was miffed and could not understand why she was still bothered or even why she was making any effort.

"Hello!" Ola answered in her coolest sounding voice as Deji's number showed on her phone.

"Ask the children to meet me outside," Deji said curtly.

"Come on, your dad is outside," Ola was a bit excited at the prospect of seeing Deji again. She had made special efforts to look beautiful, maybe if he saw what he was missing . . . she hoped. After all they did say absence made the heart grow fonder. Ola wasn't actually sure why she was doing all these things—she reckoned that maybe her head was probably messed up.

Her excitement was however short lived as she opened the door and they were greeted with the sight of Deji in his car with another woman and two kids in the back seat. For a few minutes Ola's eyes saw red and she just wasn't sure how to react. Her gut instinct was to take the children inside and refuse them going with him. She knew she couldn't do that without making it obvious she was angry that he was with another woman.

"Can you have the kids back at 7pm and if you can call me ten minutes before you get here as I am on my way out. I have a date and I want to make sure I am here when you bring them back." Ola didn't have a date and even if she did, Deji didn't seem bothered! Ola berated herself for her feeble attempt to make him jealous.

"Okay," that was all he said in reply. He didn't even do the polite thing and introduce the lady. Ola wondered if she had the right to insist on knowing who her kids were going out with. This was all new to her as she had never been in this position before. Ola never in her wildest imagination envisaged that this would happen to her. She and Deji were supposed to be forever! This was supposed to be forever raged Ola watching Deji and his fancy babe helping the kids into the car. Ola imagined that if Deji were ever to leave her, it would be for a younger model but to see that he was leaving her not even for a younger person but an older woman with two children made her furious!

"Come on guys, let's go and have something to eat. This is Jonah and Elizabeth, you can call her Betty." Ola had to walk away as she could not listen anymore to Deji being so nice to another woman's children right in front of her house.

"Damn it . . . !" Ola cursed angrily.

Her day was ruined, her mind was in turmoil and there was nothing she could do. For the next few months that was the routine apart for missed visits and then one grandiose visit where everything was supposed to be all right.

Money was still one major problem for Ola as she tried to manage with what she had from the state support and the supposed maintenance from Deji which he paid whenever he wanted after a number of missed payments. She was lucky about the house as he had to keep paying the mortgage. Anyhow the payments went from his salary account so that made it easier for her. Ola had tried getting a job again and had still not made any head way and was beginning to think of starting her own business. The main problem was what product or service she would sell? She had returned to minding kids for friends but it was not enough unless she wanted to do it professionally. The problem with that was that it was not a steady supply of work as some days the parents could just cancel at the last minute.

While she was trying to reason the business side out, Ola decided first to make Deji responsible for his family. If he had enough money to take care of another woman he should have enough money to take care of the children he fathered! Ola fumed ready for a fight as she prepared to call him.

"Hello Deji, please you need to give me the maintenance money for the kids for the month if not we will have to go back to the courts. I am not asking for anything for myself just your responsibility to your kids."

"You can go back to the court if you want, I don't care but remember, you have not applied to immigration for naturalisation, you have no job and so when they do Garda clearance it is your loss because all the court cases will come up. So do your worst and see who will be affected by it."

"Deji, it is Christmas, you cannot leave these children without anything, no food, no presents, nothing, you know Alicia is still young and Christmas is still very big for her."

"Well, you wanted this . . . , you wanted to be a single mother so as you lay your bed so you lie on it or should I say as you lay *my bed*. You have the nerve to ask me for anything when you are living in my house and I have to share with people like a man with no home."

"What kind of a man are you Deji, when did you become like this?"

"I have to go."

"Deji . . . ! Deji!" the line was gone.

Ola did not know whether to follow through on her threat of going back to the courts, but he was right, when she wanted to renew her stamp 4 visa, all the police palaver might all come out. Michael's birth made it possible for both herself and Deji to change from student visas to stamp 4 which meant they could both work full time without needing a work permit. That was great on one hand but every time they needed to renew their visas, they had to prove to the immigration officers that they were economically viable and of good character especially if you were from Nigeria, even worse as your details were doubly scrutinised! Ola remembered the story of the family which made the rounds of how their visas were only renewed for three months instead of three years as the immigration officers wanted them to prove that they had made attempts to either work or go to school. Instances like that made Ola think twice, even when it was not the norm or the experience of everyone she wasn't willing to take chances.

"Oh heck . . . ," Ola swore becoming angry with herself for swearing. For a woman who hated cursing she seemed to be doing it a lot these days.

Thinking about Deji just seemed to bring out the worse in her. It left her genuinely baffled as she didn't know what to do anymore. It had been really difficult feeding the house, paying the bills and Michael being in secondary school and his books so costly she was literally going from hand to mouth spending everything she got on one waiting need.

With tears streaming down her face she bumped into a solid wall or so she thought until two warm, strong arms reached out and steadied her. Ola looked up in embarrassment with a ready apology and her embarrassment doubled in fact it quadrupled as recognition dawned on both of them.

"We must stop meeting like this," Ray's deep sounding voice broke into her shocked silence. Oh no, it is Ambulance guy again . . . , not today . . . , not now Ola prayed.

"I . . . I am sorry . . . , I wasn't looking where I was going."

"It can easily happen, are you all right Ola . . . , that is your name isn't it, Ola?"

"Yes, I am sorry about this," they both bent down at the same time to pick up his papers and smack! They banged their heads and she nearly fell over as those strong arms reached out again and steadied her.

"Why don't you let me get these," he bent down and hurriedly picked the sheaves of paper together.

"I am sorry for being so clumsy."

"You are not clumsy and I came round the corner too fast, but I am happy I bumped into you again." Ray said with a mischievous smile.

Ola was surprised by the funny butterflies feeling she felt in her stomach. She twiddled her thumb self-consciously feeling excited and guilty at the same time.

"Let me buy you a cup of tea . . . or coffee to apologise"

"I should be the one apologising." Ola insisted.

"I will let you apologies if you agree to have a drink with me."

"Sorry, I don't drink."

"We all drink, you can have water, tea, anything, just have a drink with me to apologise, that is the apology I chose."

"Okay."

"I kept hoping to see you in college. Did you start in another school?"

"I didn't. I got swamped with so many other issues."

"Okay . . . , you do know we all have to try and make space for the things we really want don't you?"

"You don't understand."

"Then help me understand . . . ," Ray invited her as he steered her to a quiet corner of the café.

Ola did not understand why but she found it really easy to talk to Ray. Maybe because she met him in a helping role she wasn't sure, it was just great to share with a stranger who didn't seem intent on judging her.

"I got separated from my husband and the kids are finding it really hard to settle down. I know I might be over compensating but I am trying to be there for them as much as I can."

"I am sorry to hear that things didn't work out for your relationship . . . It might be hard but maybe it's all the more reason to try and find some space for yourself . . . , for the things you want that can help you be better placed in life. I . . . , I can't say I know it all . . . but I have sisters and . . . it's the same issues they are struggling with. In fact it's one of the many reasons I am not very anxious to settle down into a relationship"

"What is your story anyway, are you married?" asked Ola boldly

"No . . ."

"Why . . . ?"

". . . Just never found the right woman."

"Never . . . ?"

"Well . . . once I thought I did but we had different dreams and I was a bit younger, no job, not much happening in my life and I guess she made a good choice. I was a loafer and her jilting me was one of the best things that happened in my life. I grew strong from it. I got my act together and went back to college."

"I see . . ."

"I hope you do Ola . . . I hope you do. Look . . . you can make something out of your life, you can turn your situation around but you have to make sure that you are not coasting through life if not you'll wake up one day—how old are you now?" he stopped half way to ask the dreaded question.

"Thirty sss . . . , hey . . . , didn't your mum ever teach you that a gentleman never asks a woman her age?"

"That's for people who play games," reaching across the table Ray touched Ola's hands lightly without holding onto her. For a fleeting moment he let their hands remain connected before breaking the contact and letting his hand rest gently beside hers.

"I like you Ola, I genuinely like you. I feel . . . hmm mm . . . , no . . . , I know you are in the middle of your own stuff so I will not ask you for anything just that you allow me help you get your strength back up. When I look at you, I see a strong woman who life has given a few knocks but the strength, the life in you is electric. I think of you for days every time I bump into you."

Ola was shocked by his sincerity and willingness to lay himself open.

"I am sorry Ray, I don't . . . , hmm mm . . . I don't want anything and I cannot be anything to you. I am . . . , I'm a complete mess right now and I think that somewhere inside me I want to get my husband back," as the silence stretched between them she became so self-conscious . . .

"I am sorry, I know that is not what you want to hear and I know I sound like one of those silly women . . ."

"No . . . , you sound like a good woman. The kind of woman I think you are . . . and you have nothing to apologise for . . . , nothing. It's just my loss that I didn't find you many years ago." Ray's quiet words lightened the mood and broke the awkwardness that Ola dreaded was going to develop.

"Ha ha . . . you probably wouldn't have liked me then," she added jokingly. With a very serious look on his face, Ray reached out again for her hand in a gentle touch . . .

". . . Don't! . . . don't put down yourself Ola. Let me be your friend, just a friend, no strings, no demands . . . no commitment. I would like to help and talking to you really brightens my day."

"I don't know what that means or what it entails but okay. . . . I'll like you to be my friend . . . maybe a brother."

"I won't go that far but let's start by doing something about that not too expensive training that can provide the knowledge and qualification you need to start looking for a job and maybe get some financial freedom. As your supposed brother anyway that's my advice, the same one I would give to my own sisters."

They both laughed at the face he made when he referred to himself as her brother. Brother indeed! Ola continued laughing.

"So we'll start tomorrow by getting you on the training programme. The last time we bumped into each other, you were supposed to make enquiries about a course, months have gone by and you haven't done it. So I am making myself your self-appointed career guardian. So where do I meet you tomorrow?"

"Sorry . . . ?"

"You know—the business marketing course. I will pick you up tomorrow or if you don't want that we can just meet up at the college . . ."

"Hmm . . ."

"Can you translate that for me please?" Ray said barely trying to conceal his laughter which showed off his perfect set of teeth that made Ola wonder if he did some work on them.

"I am just thinking of how best to answer you," answered Ola joining in the laughter

". . . aaand," Ray said trying to prompt an answer from her. He had this way about him that made her wonder why Deji couldn't treat her with the same level of patience or joviality. Ola couldn't help comparing the way her relationship with Deji was and how effortless it was to have a conversation with Ray. If this was Deji, by now he would have shouted at her and walked off. Insisting she was not interested and that she better forget it! All words he would have said with annoyance.

Ray's gentle movement beside her reminded her he was still waiting for an answer.

". . . Okay," she said slowly, sounding like a shy school girl "let me meet you at the College, that might be better." Ola hedged as she didn't want him coming to the house with the kids there and Deji . . . who still seemed to be a big part of her life.

"Brilliant! Will you give me your mobile number . . . just in case we miss each other at the gate," he added quickly as he seemed to read the uncertainty and reluctance on her face.

"Okay" she backed down and reeled off her number "see you tomorrow then," she added with a bit of excitement at the prospect of seeing Ray again. Walking to the counter Ray paid the bill for their teas and they left the café together.

As they walked out the door Ray reached out and touched her hand gently "Take care."

CHAPTER EIGHTEEN

OLA HAD BEEN SO CONSUMED with her problems she had lost contact with a number of her friends. After her chat with Ray the day before she realised she had been living a lonely life by not keeping in touch at least with some of her proper friends. Maybe she'd give Ronke a call she decided considering it was nearly Christmas and her family normally had a Christmas party.

"Hello Ronke, long time no hear . . . , what's up? I haven't seen you in a while."

"Ola Babes, I am so sorry. I have been really busy."

"Too busy for your friend ehn . . . ?"

"You know the way it is, between family, kids and their school work no time at all for anything else."

"Does that mean you are not having your traditional Christmas party this year?"

". . . hmm mm . . . we are actually," Ronke stammered hesitantly.

". . . eh, that's great, at least one fun thing to look forward to. I didn't get my invitation yet oh. Are you not leaving the invitations too late?"

"Look Ola . . . , there is no easy way to say this. You know the way you are separated . . . , that means I cannot invite you. Hmm mm . . . , you know how it works. You know you are my personal person but as it is now I cannot invite you. My husband only relates with my friends who are married."

Ola could not keep the shock out of her voice as the words from Ronke, her friend of over ten years left her stunned. Ola could not reply for a few seconds though it felt like long minutes.

". . . you are joking right!" Ola squeaked choking with emotions.

"Ola, I am sorry, there is nothing I can do. You know how it is, when you leave your husband—and in your case . . . you sent him out of the house and if I keep associating with you my husband is going to get angry. You know how it is," Ronke added apologetically sounding as helpless as Ola felt.

". . . No Ronke, I don't know how it is, tell me. So I have become a bad person because I said Deji cannot kill me? Tell me what is wrong if I say that instead of killing me he should leave me? So you would prefer me dead or maimed?"

"No Ola . . . , stop twisting my words. What I am saying is that you know these men, when you stop talking and give them what they want they will not hit you. You know that. You have to know when to stop."

". . . so in others words I should not live? I should be like a zombie? I am a robot . . . *bah*? Well thank you for your support at least now I know my friends!" Ola screamed as she put down the phone broken hearted.

"Ola! Ola!" she heard Ronke shouting her name pleadingly as she dropped the phone.

"Oh well, what did I expect?" Ola seethed. At least now she had her answer. She had been wondering why she had not heard from a lot of the end of year groups who usually invited her for events. Ola was really upset, she felt as if she was being punished first by Deji now her friends and family seemed to be helping him punish her.

Maybe she was a glutton for punishment, Ola wasn't sure but she had to find out why the other groups had not sent her their invitations. She just didn't want to believe they were being that small minded . . . they definitely couldn't be judging her . . . could they . . . ?

Ola wanted to call the women's leader for their kparakpo-the ethnic women's group she belonged to. On second thoughts, she decided to check the Facebook notifications and invitations because the group usually created a group invite and conversation on the page. There was usually an end of year activity for the women.

"Oh no . . . !" Ola groaned at the number of notifications and messages on her page. She had been so taken with Deji she had kept away from any public contact. As she trawled through the messages on her page, Ola noticed there was nothing from the group for her. She decided to go to the group page as there might be some information there. True as she thought, the advert was on the page for the 29th of December. Ola scrolled down the list of invited guests, and her heart dropped with each move of the arrow as it went on to confirm what she already knew.

Ola was piqued that her name was not on the list of invited guests. She could not believe it because she was instrumental in starting the group. To think that they felt it was okay to cut her off! Ola stomped off in search of her phone. She wasn't about to throw a fit on her own. Someone needed to hear this and she was prepared to give it to them. Ola dialled the new Chairperson who took over from her after her one year tenure.

"Let them tell me to my face that I cannot attend," Ola dared them angrily.

"Shola, what's the story?"

"Hello to you too . . ."

"Cut out the sarcasms! How come you are organising the end of year activity without me?"

"Ola, calm down, you know the way the group works . . . you have been there long enough. You know that any woman who is divorced or separated cannot attend the programmes or hold a position. It is the rule of the group."

"So it is a crime to be single eh!"

"No, not being single and you know that Ola. Single women are welcome but you know we have always closed the door on divorce or separation. It is important for us that our leaders are women who can hold their homes together. Women who can put their own needs second and place the family first . . ."

". . . even if she has to die . . . ? Even if it kills her you mean?" interrupted Ola

"Look Ola, try and stop being melodramatic, it is really nothing personal at you. You are only feeling it now. We have cut off a number of divorced women from the group before and we have done that for many years. If not many husbands will stop supporting their wives to come for the programmes. You know we get more support from our men because we are pro marriage."

". . . because we are stupid you mean?"

"Ola I am really sorry you see it that way . . . I am genuinely sorry, but you know the rules."

"Okay, I wish you all the best until of course it becomes your turn."

". . . look Ola, don't take it like that. We are friends first before any group or committee. Let's meet up and we can talk about this face to face."

"No love, there is no need. Your actions have shown me already where you stand. My only shame is that at one time I was just like you. I hope you and the others like you will be able to stand over the deaths you encourage!"

". . . Ola? Pleasssee . . ." she could hear the exasperation in Shola's voice but Ola was past caring.

No . . . she decided . . . everyone should mind their space from now. They had caused her enough pain. Feeling miserable about the turn of events, Ola resolved not to allow her pain show. If they didn't want her, then she sure didn't want them she decided. . . . or at least she wouldn't give them the benefit of letting them know how much their decisions had hurt her.

"No worries mate! Have fun and enjoy your good life!" Ola could not be bothered to keep the anger and frustration out of her voice as she reverted to a kind of western drawl to emphasise the sarcasm. with as much force as she could muster, Ola clicked the off button on the phone and promptly broke into tears shaking all over.

Ola was overwhelmed. She felt like a salted freshly scratched wound full of raw pain. She didn't know how much more she could take. Containing her muddled thoughts was a bigger problem for her. It felt like her head was going to explode as sharp pain went through her left eye up one side of her head and settled at the front of her head.

She couldn't stop crying from internal and physical pain. Who had she offended . . . , Ola cried reverting to Yoruba to ask the gods what crime she had committed.

"*Ta ni mo she*—who did I offend oh . . . ?' She wiped her eyes as her superstitious side crept out. She wondered if this was HT . . . maybe she should stop treating everything as normal occurrences when maybe some spiritual forces were working against her. She remembered that back home such continuous misfortune was called home trouble which the locals nicknamed HT!

Ola's eyes twinkled as she thought of her situation, maybe it was HT with capital H in her case. She didn't think it was true at least not in this case but at this moment Ola was frustrated enough to believe anything.

The sound of her mobile phone ringing broke Ola's concentration on her misfortune.

"Hello?" she answered the call cautiously as it was a number she didn't recognise

"Ola . . . ? It's me Ray, what happened . . . , I thought we were meeting at the college."

"I am sorry, something came up and I couldn't make it," she sniffed

"Are you okay . . . , are you crying . . . ?" Ray asked cautiously

"No, I just had something in my throat. Look I am sorry about today but I can't come out and I will try and do this on my own."

"Ola . . . , let me help, please . . ."

"I can't Ray, I am sorry and I appreciate your offer. I am sorry but I have to go there is someone at the door." Ola fibbed as she quickly got off the phone. She was afraid of breaking down and spilling it all out to Ray. She couldn't handle any kindness right now. Ola had a rethink about receiving help from Ray. She just wasn't sure if depending on others to do things for her and make decisions for her were not the things that got her into the kind of problems she had with Deji. No . . . , she decided, I'm going to learn to do things for myself, enough of dependency on others.

"Pull yourself together girl," Ola reprimanded herself coming to the conclusion that crying wasn't going to help, but only make her sad and depressed. The chiming of the cuckoo clock in the hallway reminded her it was nearly time to pick up the kids from school.

Ola was grateful for the distraction that took her mind from feeling so sorry for herself. She realised she had no food at home as well so she would need to stop over at the store for groceries. Dragging her tired bones out of the house Ola made time to pick up Alicia and Michael from school.

Alicia was very chatty as usual, as she tried to tell Ola in great details every single thing that had happened in school, at least as much as she could remember and for a six year old. It just seemed she remembered a lot to Ola, who could have done with a bit of quiet with the kind of day she'd had.

"Hey love, how was you practice for the school nativity play?"

"It was very good Mummy. We have to bring our costumes to school. I am acting as Mary in my class," chirped Alicia cheerfully.

"No problem love, we'll have it ready for you to take in on Monday. Did your teacher send a note of what is required?"

"Yes Mum, there is a list of things to bring in my bag."

"Michael love, how are you?"

"I'm okay mum, school was great. I am in the break-dance team for the end of year activities," Michael responded with a contagious excitement on his face that made Ola forget the misery of her life for a few moments at least.

"That's great love. I need to pick up a few groceries from the shops," Ola added quickly as she saw Michael lift his brow in query as she took a different turn for the house.

Michael wasn't too fond of shopping with Ola as she was a kind of manic shopper going from aisle to aisle turning simple shopping into a long tedious process. He usually just went to the kids section while Ola rummaged through all the discounted shelves looking through the products with a best before date of a day or so. She usually got better deals at less than half price, that way her limited funds was able to buy more.

"Come Alicia, let's go to the vegetables section. I need some potatoes and fruits," turning around to the trolley where Alicia had been doing her best to push it around with her, Ola nearly lost her mind as Alicia was gone . . . she was not by the trolley. Looking around in panic . . . a thousand thoughts flashed by her mind in the same instant blinding her. Alicia was a complete mummies girl, she would never go on her own away from Ola in a shopping centre.

"Alicia!" Ola called out in a low voice trying not to sound alarmed.

"Alicia!" she called again slightly louder this time.

"Daddy! Daddy!" Ola saw Alicia the same minute she heard her screaming and running in the opposite direction down an aisle at a right angle from where she was.

". . . Oh no . . . , don't tell me," groaned Ola as she prayed fervently that it wasn't Deji. She didn't want to believe that he wouldn't have the decency to go to another shop when he knew this was her local. But no . . . , no such luck. As Ola rounded the corner she saw Deji with a woman . . . the same one he came to the house with the last time and the same two kids. Ola could not believe her eyes. Deji was actually shopping for groceries with a woman and he was pushing the trolley! Wonders would never cease she thought at this totally unbelievable sight.

"The same Deji? . . . mm mm," Ola looked on amazed that the man who claimed to be too busy to even stop by and pick up milk, ordinary milk on the way home . . . , the same person who got angry at the thought of being asked to go anywhere with the kids because he claimed they messed about . . . and ran around the place, here he was actually holding the hands of the younger child and pushing a trolley dutifully!

Ola was gutted by the picture of the perfect family on a day out shopping that they painted. 'My man . . . !' she fumed. 'It must be me then,' she concluded berating herself . . . '. . . there must have been something wrong with me to make Deji behave the way he did to me.'

As Ola got beside them, her embarrassment doubled and she took the anger out on Alicia for coming this way. She definitely would have gone to hide in the toilet than to allow Deji and his new woman see her this way. Ola groaned as she looked at the pathetic pile in her near empty trolley with most of her purchases having the yellow sticker for discounted goods while the other woman had a big trolley that was over flowing!

Alicia was tugging at her Dad's hand to get him to pick her up while at the same time she was trying to tell him all her news in the few seconds she was there.

Without saying a word to either of them, Ola grabbed Alicia and pulled her away.

"Come on, love we have to go."

"I want my daddy, I want my daddy!" Alicia cried.

"I will come and see you later," Deji said to Alicia. That finally pushed Ola over the edge and she walked back to him leaving Alicia beside the trolley where she was sobbing her little heart out. They always did say the kids suffered most. Walking right up to Deji, she looked him straight in the eye warning him.

"Don't you go making promises you do not plan to keep . . . you hear me? You don't make promises to my child . . . , you do not do that!" Without giving him a chance to reply Ola flounced off in anger.

Rounding up Michael and Alicia she ended her shopping abruptly and made her way out of the shop paying for the few things she had selected. Ola was really upset that she was buying almost out of date goods to feed his kids while he was busy playing the big man and filling a trolley that should have been hers for another woman! Ola couldn't help herself as she cursed him hoping he would be rewarded painfully!

". . . You will get your reward . . . ," she hoped he would be rewarded for how he had dealt with her and the children. Ola was incensed that Deji had repaid the good things she did in his life with bad things . . .

CHAPTER NINETEEN

The following week started out badly for Ola. She was constantly snappy and irritable and she couldn't understand why. Worse still, Ola was constantly crying. As if on cue tears just flowed down her face.

"Oh oh . . . ," cried Ola, because she was doing it again, crying for no reason . . . The ringing bell stemmed the tide of tears overflowing from her eyes. Ola wasn't expecting anyone and she rarely got any visitors these days at her door.

"Deji . . . ?" Ola wasn't sure if that was excitement, anger or fear as she called his name questioningly sounding just like Alicia.

"What are you doing here?" she asked

"Are the kids about?"

"You know they are back in school after the Christmas holidays, after all you have a readymade family so you are aware of the school calendar!" Ola could not help adding the dig which Deji wisely refused to rise to.

". . . Let's not go down that route Ola, I just brought some food for you as I went to the African shop, I thought you might not have had the time to drive that way."

"When did you start caring?" Ola asked in a daze.

"If you don't want it or if it is a bad thing that I have done I can take them away."

". . . no, thanks," responded Ola. Deji went back to the car and brought in a bag of rice, a carton of chicken and some plantain.

". . . just a few things, I wasn't sure what you had already, but I know the kids like their plantain."

"Thanks," she said in a voice laced with suspicion uncertain how to react to this new Deji.

". . . why are you not at work?" She asked as her mind started working again.

"I am off today . . . , can I get a cup of tea?" Deji asked politely.

Ola was at first hesitant. She wasn't sure really what he was up to but she decided to oblige and make him a cup of tea reasoning it was harmless. They sat like two old friends and he asked her safe questions about the kids and she didn't mention anything about his readymade family or his fancy woman. After about thirty minutes, he got up to leave.

"Thanks Ola. Well, take care and I will pick the kids next week."

"All right, bye," she sat for a few minutes confused at this turnaround from Deji. It felt good, it felt exciting but she was still a bit sceptical about Deji's agenda and what it meant. She knew her Deji too well . . . he never did anything without a motive that was not to his benefit.

———————

Ola was at a loss for adult company. It was as if her life had come full circle back to the time when she was expecting Deji to join her. She remembered how desperate she'd been to be reunited with him that she had been prepared to do or bear anything to make it happen!

She didn't seem to have friends any more. The ones Deji didn't like were long gone as he made sure she didn't attend their functions or if she insisted on going, he delayed her so much that she was embarrassingly late! Even the kids when they were invited to parties by her friends he didn't like he insisted she not take them. At that time, Ola was big into the rule of obedience and submission as a woman's act of service. On lonely days like these when Ola looked back at her life she was full of regrets as the very thing she had borne all the control and discomfort for still happened.

"Guess who is paying for it now?" she asked herself . . . "Me . . . , yes me!" Ola answered her own question. "I am the one who has no friends."

Why she was thinking all these depressing thoughts Ola wondered scolding herself. But try as much as she could, they wouldn't go away. Ola could feel the onset of a pity party where she went on the bend feeling sorry for herself. It was a good thing she was expecting Rita if not she would have gone into an annoying dark mood that stayed with her sometimes almost for a week.

Ola went about as she started cooking the soup she had offered as a bait to tempt Rita to come over for a visit—though Rita didn't really need much tempting. Ola was preparing one of her delicacies, Ola's specialty really—Okra pepersoup. She was quite confident about it and Rita who loved the taste of it so much never ceased badgering Ola to invite her for lunch whenever she prepared it. Even cooking it now had Ola salivating already from the aroma as it filled the kitchen. Stirring the soup gently and lifting each catfish to avoid the fish breaking in the soup, Ola reduced the heat and allowed the soup to simmer. All that was left was to make the pounded yam. Ola was grateful at how life had changed from many years ago when people, mainly women had to physically pound yam in a wooden mortar. Now with industrialisation, the yam had been processed to a powdered form like a powdery mashed potato so that with a kettle of boiling water, a spatula and a microwavable bowl Ola had the food ready just as Rita rang the bell.

As usual Rita was looking gorgeous in her casual outfit as they exchanged pleasantries. She didn't stand on formalities with Ola and she got right down to it and asked for the food immediately.

"That aroma is killing me Ola, bring the food now . . . I can feel my stomach growling," she added as she pretended to hold onto her tummy as if feeling real hunger pangs.

"Come on don't exaggerate . . . you," Ola joked as they both settled to the real business of eating pounded yam the proper way with their fingers.

"Oh Ola, that was terrific, my . . . my you are a really terrific cook. That man is missing, I tell you."

"I don't think so. You know the way they say the way to a man's heart is through his stomach?"

"Hmmm"

"Well, I obviously wasn't a very good cook or the saying was a lie because Deji still left and he seems to be doing okay while I am struggling," Ola's mood dipped the minute Deji was mentioned.

"Hey come on Ola, don't let things like that change who you are. You cannot think less of yourself. You are a brilliant cook. If Deji decided not to stay you cannot take the responsibility for his actions. Deji is an adult and what he does is not a reflection on who you are or what you are not. That is dangerous ground to walk on my friend . . . really dangerous ground."

"I hear what you are saying but I cannot help but think that something is wrong with me. I really feel maybe it's me."

"Why do you think that?"

"Oh I don't know . . . , I saw Deji a few weeks ago and you won't believe it, he was shopping and pushing the trolley with another woman and her kids. The same Deji who refused to go out with the kids and all because he said he could not stand children running around uncontrollably."

"So you think that it is you . . . ? Why isn't it him who took advantage of your gentleness and generosity?"

"Oh I don't know, he seems to be quite different now, you won't even recognise him."

"Really . . . , is he picking up the kids at the right time now?"

"Yeah and more! I mean he came over a few times in the last three weeks, once he brought me a bag of rice, another time he brought me some meat and a carton of chicken. He drops by some evenings and brings me some food for the house or the kids."

"Is that what you want?"

"It is better than nothing . . ."

"Instead of bringing you food why is he not giving you the allowance or is he doing that as well?"

"Em . . . mm, not really," Ola stammered

"I don't want to speak into your relationship but you have to very careful because it seems he is warming his way back into your life and giving you stuff instead of the resources to get what you need. That puts him in control again and that can sway anyone's judgment."

As Ola began to look shamefaced Rita seemed to notice and soft pedalled from her initial position.

"I don't know Rita . . ."

Rita interrupted her quickly as if anxious to speak her mind before she changes it completely.

"Look, I don't want you to feel bad okay . . . , I just want you to be smart, to take care of yourself. If you want Deji back then make sure you guys talk to someone first. See a counsellor, seek help first because you didn't just leave Ola . . . , Deji was violent and things like that don't just go away. The next time you might not be so lucky."

"I don't know Rita. I miss him. The kids miss him . . . at least Alicia misses him. I feel so alone and I met someone who I really like. But I have these kids and it complicates things so at the end of the day I don't think I am going to go into a relationship with another person and I told him that much. But . . . , the thing is . . . why should I now allow another woman to reap what I have sown? She gets to enjoy Deji while my kids and I are broke and alone. Honestly Rita, you don't know what it's like."

"I don't my friend . . . I don't. Look . . . , I am sorry I haven't been there as much as I could have been. Work has been demanding combined with family. It doesn't leave me much time for other things," said Rita moving closer to her on the chair in a comforting motion. Ola knew she hadn't changed her views and she was rightly sceptical about her allegiance with Deji but she could see the wheels turning in her head as she seemed to change course and back down from her point. . . . yet, Ola could still see the objection in her eyes very clearly.

"I actually promised myself I wasn't going to use our time today talking about Deji and what did I do? Exactly that! You probably have used up all the energy in you on his issue again!"

"It's okay, after all if that is what is on your mind then there is no point treating it like the elephant in the room. I hope you understand and the very last thing I will say about this issue is that you have the chance now to reorganise the way you relate with Deji. You are not the 20 year old girl he met years ago. You are a mother now, a woman, an adult in your own right. Don't fall into the mistake of exchanging your natural parents for a spousal parent. Maybe I should give you a copy of the book I read recently titled *Becoming Unforgettable*. One of the principles I enjoyed the most is where the author said 'don't complain about what you permit'. It doesn't allow you to make excuses but it encourages its readers to take responsibility for their lives. Why is Deji doing things for another woman he wasn't doing with you? Look, We have a funny way of letting the other person know what we will bear or tolerate maybe they instil fear in us, but usually, it is because they have studied us so well that they know what they can get away with. Okay. I will shut up now, I am sure you get what I am saying."

"Thanks Rita, I'd love to read the book. It sounds interesting."

"It is actually. But enough about managing Deji, so who is this person you say sounds interesting?"

Ola updated Rita about Ray, but somewhere within herself she knew she could not take up the offer . . . she couldn't go out with him. She just wasn't ready yet . . . She had been separated from Deji just over ten months . . . but she still had hopes that things would improve.

Ray had become a really good friend. He had been really helpful and encouraging. She had almost completed her course and he had been providing Ola with some help with applying for work and preparing her resume. Though Ola was worried about stringing him along because she knew what he wanted, she was very reluctant to send him away as right now Rita and him were the only true friends she could count on.

"I wish . . . , I wish . . . No!" Ola rejected the thoughts. She told herself she couldn't afford wishes . . . , anyway, wishing was for young dreamers . . . , for the unsoiled and the undamaged!

"As I am now I won't wish me on anybody . . . ," Ola concluded

"Ola! Where are you . . . , you seem miles away?" Giving Rita a sheepish smile she evaded the question by using diversionary tactics!

"So when am I coming over to yours for one of your special delicacies. I want to give you the opportunity to retaliate," Ola joked flashing her teeth and making a funny face at Rita.

"Hmm mm . . . ," Ola sighed audibly. It's been a long time she relaxed enough to laugh spontaneously . . . but images of Ray broke into her thoughts making a liar of that claim. . . . truth be told, talking with Ray was undemanding and refreshing . . . it left her feeling refreshed rather than drained and pulled on every side.

"Come on, it's time for school run," Rita interrupted her thoughts more determinedly. Moving the dishes into a washing bowl, she adjusted her clothes pulling her woollen jumper over the smart brown trousers she had on. Ola looked at Rita who was always so psychedelic, it was hard to believe she was a mother of four and working full time!

The girls hugged as Ola expressed her gratitude for Rita's support and friendship. Ola thanked her lucky starts for their friendship as she had become a sister, mother and friend all rolled in one.

"Thanks for being there for me."

"Hey madam, none of this mushy stuff! I know you would do the same for me," she said minimising all the support she had given to Ola.

"No, really, thank you. I know I don't say it all the time but your presence has kept me sane many times. So please . . . let me thank you."

"Accepted . . . don't fret yourself too much love, this too shall pass, honestly, think about it, everything that comes to us always passes, you know the way one day gives way for the other I believe this bad patch will give way to refreshing times." Smiling at each other they both picked up their car keys and rushed for their children's schools . . .

Chapter Twenty

Deji's visits were becoming more and more frequent and Ola didn't know how to handle them neither did she know where they were leading. At first she thought he was coming because of the kids but she noticed he was dropping by during the day when the kids were at school. This left Ola confused and uncertain what to make of it. She knew she had to talk to him about it in case he was just trying to mess with her head.

Ola knew Rita was right and that she hit the nail on the head when she warned her to be mindful of what she was permitting with Deji. . . . but on lonely nights and lonely days, she couldn't help missing Deji . . . his touch . . . some of it anyway. When he was gentle . . . she thought she missed him . . . Ola admitted to herself annoyed by her display of weakness where Deji was concerned.

"Maybe it wasn't Deji she missed . . . , maybe she missed being in love," Ola laughed uncertain if there was a difference between the two.

"Ohhhhh . . . !" Ola roared giving vent to her mounting frustration . . .

Less than a year . . . , was all it had taken for her to be reduced to a wanton simpleton! She couldn't understand how in less than a year her mind and thoughts were clouded with thoughts about Deji . . . the same person who made her do repulsive things that made her feel downright dirty . . . like a whore.

. . . maybe hers was a case of *half a man is better than no man . . . !* Ola quizzed herself as her body had been sending her messages that were messing with her head and emotions. Grasping at every excuse she could find, Ola wondered if her ovulation period might account for the intense feeling of sexual tension. She really couldn't explain it. Some days were so bad she was afraid to watch even a simple romantic movie as it made her body tingle all over and kept her up all night staring at the ceiling feeling frustrated. Some women did things to themselves but Ola's faith didn't allow her to go down that route. Ola wondered how people never talked about these seasons and how to handle them.

If in less than a year of being without a man . . . , without Deji, she felt this bad, Ola cringed at the thought of permanent separation. The difficulty loomed ominously large before her eyes as she thought about the consequences. Did that mean she would never have a relationship again? Her religious beliefs saw divorce as bad . . . , her parents, family, even almost all of her so called friends had been onto her to reconcile with Deji, though there wasn't much she could do anyway as he hadn't actually asked her for reconciliation!

Ola put all the silly thoughts down to her hormones. She was sure that's what was clouding her mind or maybe just being apart from Deji and the bleak feeling that this was the end. The thought that she would never feel sexual pleasure again was scary . . . , really scary for Ola. It wasn't as if she was a nympho or something as intense as that . . . she thought defensively, she hoped it was all part of being a red blooded human being with normal human feelings.

"Hmm mm . . . ," Ola sighed deciding to occupy her mind with other things. Thinking like that didn't help, in fact it made her feel hornier.

Ola decided it was definitely time to get dressed and go to college for her training. At least that would take her mind off any debauchery! Ola was attending a business management course and she had promised to meet Ray for coffee during her break. She was enjoying being back in college which had turned out to be a brilliant choice with fantastic lecturers. Ola was also working with a phone company in the City Centre to fulfil the work placement component of her training . . . The ringing of the doorbell startled Ola as it broke into her reminiscing . . .

"Oh no . . . !" Ola mouthed as she looked out the window from the upstairs bedroom and saw Deji's car outside the house. It was as if thinking about him so intensely that day had conjured him up. Ola was a bit panicky about Deji visiting today because she felt a bit vulnerable. She was worried that it would not be an ideal time for a visit, not just because she was running late for college, but her emotions were kind of all over the place . . .

Pulling a brush through her hair, she looked at her face in the mirror. She didn't want Deji thinking she was suffering or anything. Ola grabbed her bag and car keys and headed for the door just as the bell rang the third time with more insistence and for a longer period.

"Yeah . . . that's my man! That commanding pressure on the bell was so like him." Putting her shoes on, Ola walked hurriedly to the door practicing her surprised look.

"Deji . . . ! Hi . . . I didn't know it was you," she feigned surprise visibly jingling her keys to let him know she was on her way out.

"Are you going somewhere?" Deji asked in a gentle voice that made her almost want to shake him and say return my husband because she didn't recognise this soft spoken alien she joked privately.

"I . . . I have a date," Ola said but as soon as the words left her mouth, Ola regretted it. She knew she had no reason to mention that especially when she was actually going to college. Ola was repentant about playing such cat and mouse games with Deji. She wanted him to be jealous that others found her attractive, but she knew this wasn't the way. If he couldn't see her as attractive nothing was going to make him do that.

"I see . . . ," was all he replied to her.

Ola made a conscious effort to avoid his eyes which seemed to have deepened in contemplation. Ola asked the very next question that popped into her head without thinking.

"Did you want something?"

"I brought some stuff for you. I bought a carton of yams and plantain and I thought you might want some for the kids. I'll go and get them."

Rita's warning words were running through Ola's head the whole time Deji was outside. She watched him silently as he put the tubers of yam and plantain on the kitchen floor with a carton of malt drink.

"Thanks Deji . . . ," she said with a suggestive hint that the meeting had ended. Deji didn't take the hint at all. Pulling out the kitchen chair he sat down without invitation as he asked for some drinking water.

Ola pulled open the kitchen cupboard and automatically reached for Deji's special drinking glass before she realised what she was doing. She wanted to put it back because he was no longer the head of her home and serving him with that glass seemed to her to be saying otherwise. However, she decided against returning the glass as he had seen her take the glass out. Hopefully he didn't read the same meaning she had. As she stood by the kitchen sink running the cold water Ola heard the chair scrap against the floor but she stood still and resisted the urge to turn around as she heard Deji's movements on the cream tilled kitchen floor. He sure moved gently for a big man thought Ola. She could feel Deji standing behind her trapping her between his strong torso and the kitchen sink with the hardness of his manhood fully pressed against her but she said nothing as she suddenly felt choked with emotions . . .

Say something . . . , speak . . . , anything . . . , anything . . . ! Ola prodded herself and still nothing . . . , not even a squeak.

Ola was appalled by her inability to act and wondered why she was opening her mouth yet none of the words in her mind were coming out . . . ? Fear . . . , or excitement . . . probably a mixture of both she wasn't sure.

Reaching around Ola with a strong hairy arm, Deji turned off the kitchen sink, took the glass from her shaky hand and without relaxing the pressure behind her back he drained the water in one big gulp then gently dropped the glass on the dish drainer at the sink.

The sound of the glass against the aluminium of the kitchen sink jolted Ola into action and she made a feeble attempt to come out of Deji's arms that circled her so easily.

"I have to go Deji. I have an appointment."

"You are my wife Ola. You cannot give what belongs to me to another person. I will not allow it."

Ola was surprised that Deji had noticed when she mentioned she was going on a date earlier, but that soon changed to irritation as she realised he seemed to think he had a right to lay down the rule for her life even when he was not taking the responsibility of being a husband to her or a father to his children.

"Is it one rule for you and another rule for me?"

"We are different Ola, I am a man and you are a woman," he said logically as if that explained it all . . .

"I . . . I . . . have to go."

"I want you."

"Deji, no . . . nooo . . . We are separated . . . ," Ola whimpered struggling to get the words out of her mouth as Deji began to fumble with her breast and with the other hand he grabbed Ola by her crotch and lifted her closer against his hardness.

"You are my wife, Ola . . . you are my wife. You hear that? You belong to me and you cannot go to another man. I will not allow it. You hear me . . . do you hear me?" he said insistently with his voice hardening but remaining level as he spoke with that deep authority Ola found really hard to challenge.

"Okay Deji," the more he spoke, the more excited he became and Ola could feel him become harder against her thigh. Ola was excited that he was jealous enough at the thoughts of her being with another man to react and she had missed male contact. Even when it wasn't good fun for her at least the build-up to the actual act had moments of excitement sometimes . . .

"Now say you want me . . ."

"Please stop this . . . ," Ola protested half-heartedly. She wasn't sure if she really wanted him to stop that very moment. She thought maybe for a moment, maybe for now she could just forget all the troubles they had and enjoy the moment . . . Deji himself didn't make it easy for her to resist as he seemed to be able to read her body and the battle of wills raging within . . .

"Come on Ola, you are my wife, you hear that, you are my wife. You are the only woman I married," he whispered over and over into her ears in a gentle sweet-talking voice as his hands grabbed the helm of her skirt, gently pulling it up around her hips.

"Deji . . . ?"

"Shhhh . . . ," he cooed at her.

Ola's mind and body both seemed to be conspiring against her better judgement as they reeled her into Deji's fold. Ola stood on the brink of indecision swayed by the fact that Deji was still her husband—wasn't he? She asked to no one in particular. It was one of those questions that didn't demand an answer. Why should she allow another woman have him while she became the woman with no husband . . . she rationalised as her body of its own volition seemed to relax into Deji's touch enjoying the feel of him.

Ola was suddenly startled by the pressure of Deji pushing his hardness into the wrong channel in her body bringing her to the present out of fantasy land. Realising what was happening, Ola gently shook her bottom to help him readjust and find the right channel, but he seemed not to be getting the message.

"Oh no!" Ola despaired about how to address this small detail without embarrassing Deji. The increased pressure and pain however made the decision for her as she spoke up immediately.

"Deji . . . stop! That hurts . . . can you . . . you know . . ."

"Hmmm . . ." Deji reached out for her hand and stopped her feeble attempt to physically disengage herself from him. "Shhh . . . sh . . . . ." he said over and over.

"Deji . . . not there . . . , that hurts."

"It's okay Ola, I am your husband. You'll like it. It's more fun. It is tighter. You know after two children it's not the same. We have to explore other channels for fun. That's one of the reasons this marriage was breaking down, we were not giving each other enough fun."

Ola was shocked and disgusted because she had assumed that it was a mistake but Deji's words confirmed his original intent. Fear and pain propelled Ola to resist more but Deji wasn't listening. He had only one goal and that was to stamp his possession over her and maximize his fun anyway he could!

"Deji, please stop! I am not enjoying this, please . . ."

"Shhh . . . relax, just loosen up woman and stop acting frigid. Relax okay . . . , just relax babes, this is . . . ahhh . . ." Deji broke off mid-sentence as his breathing seemed to accelerate. That moment she knew it was a lost cause. She knew Deji would not stop till he got his way. Flinching in pain Ola tried to make her body go limp to ease the pain but the tearing pain made her cry out as he forced himself more into her.

"Stop please, stop . . . ," Ola cried out as she began to struggle again. This time Deji lifted her up easily holding her bottom firmly against himself without breaking their body connection. He walked over to the kitchen table, pushing her face down then he pushed harder into her holding the back of her head against the table top.

The coldness of the table against her face was like the final slap that woke her to the reality of what Deji was doing to her. She cried out as the pain tore through her body and the tears rolled down her face silently.

"Why me of God . . . , why me?" Ola cried angry at life, angry . . . , Ola lost herself in thought as Deji had his way with her.

I hate you . . . , I hate you . . . , I hate you . . . , you sick pervert, you rapist, you sodomiser . . . I hate you . . . I hate you! I hate you! Ola screamed hysterically over and over and the voice was getting louder and louder, she suddenly became scared the neighbours could hear and know her shame and what had happened to her. But Deji's words penetrated her world.

"Thanks Ola . . . , don't cry, look it's like the first time you had sex as well. It gets better you'll see. The next time it will be better and you'll really enjoy it." He said in a placating tone.

Ola was dumbfounded . . . , her body was wracked with pain and full of shame. She dropped her weight into the chair in a daze saying nothing as she realised her screams of hate had all been inside her head.

Ola stared disbelievingly at Deji with tears streaming down her face all the while saying nothing . . . she watched him clean himself up as he prepared to leave.

"When will I learn?" Ola cried in self-recrimination. "Deji had just raped . . . , no," she thought, shaking her head. He had sodomised her and she could not even say a word to him, even worse she knew she could not report him . . . to whom . . . that what . . . , how would she? What would she say . . . ? She despaired as a new wave of tears flowed faster down her face.

Ola could not even imagine saying the words out to another human being not to mention admitting it happened to her! She felt so dirty . . . , maybe like the people of Sodom from the story from centuries ago? Ola wondered if she deserved it . . . like they said. After all . . . , she had let him into her house. She wanted him to be jealous, maybe she drove him to it . . . she argued feeling defeated. She was grateful when a strong angry voice in her head answered back . . . *did I make him cheat on me . . . did I make him hit me . . . did I?*

From the corner of her eyes she saw Deji picking up his keys strolling unhurriedly around the place as he ambled his way over to her. She couldn't decipher what he was saying because she was so numb, he dropped a placating kiss on the top of her head, tweaked her cheek and patted her on the back. The next thing Ola was conscious of was the sound of the closing door.

Ola did not know how long she sat like that until the persistent ringing of her phone annoyed her enough to get up. By the time she got the phone it had stopped ringing, but she could see the name flashing on it. Ray . . . twelve missed calls. She had forgotten she was supposed to be meeting him after her class in college. Ola couldn't be bothered that moment. She was done with men.

Slowly coming out of her hazy state she realised she had missed her class and it was over three hours since her fiasco with Deji ended. She realised she had just been sitting down and staring into space. Ola knew she would have to pull herself together as the kids would soon finish school.

"I have to be strong . . . , I have to be strong . . . I cannot fall apart . . . not now" Ola consoled herself as the cold phone in her hand began to ring again. It was Ray . . . again . . . sliding the on button she answered the phone without saying a word. She really had no energy left in her.

"Ola? Ola . . . ? Hello Ola!" The pitch of Ray's voice increased probably in panic but she was past caring. He was a man . . . another man trying to control her life Ola reckoned. She'd had enough. Though he wasn't the source of her problem, heck he wasn't even a part of it but she couldn't help herself as she thawed a little and her anger bubbled over.

Ola did not know what came over her or what motivated her as she opened her mouth and spewed out the first words that came out.

"What is it, what is it? Do I owe you? Can you stop calling me . . . , please, can you stop calling me. Stop calling me you hear me? I hate you. I hate you! I hate you men!" with that Ola threw the phone as far away from her as she could and fell back on the chair as she gave in to a renewed bout of tears.

Becoming Mad-Angry Mad

The cold chased away my strength
The dark room mirrored my mood
The howling wind blew away my dreams
How did I become . . .
Mad—Angry Mad

A tightly wound ball ready to explode
A rolling stone out of control
A roving panther fully agitated
How did I become . . .
Mad—Angry Mad

Full of words but no voice
Wanting to speak but no sound
Needing to say but not able
A scream, a shout, a silent cry
How did I become . . .
Mad—Angry Mad

Surrounded by darkness
Nowhere to turn
No one to talk to
No one who understands
How did I become . . .
A ball of Mad—Angry Mad

By Ebun Akpoveta

CHAPTER TWENTY ONE

OLA WAS AMAZED AT HOW she had changed from the confident self-assured woman she used to be to this jumpy nervous wreck before her very eyes. As if fate wanted to confirm it, the doorbell rang startling Ola that she almost tumbled off the chair where she was sitting.

Ola had come to dread people knocking unannounced on her door after her episode with Deji confirmed that her worries were not groundless. Thinking of Deji, Ola suddenly realised she hadn't locked the door after him when he'd left earlier. She had been too deflated to move. Ola quickly wiped the tears from her eyes as her heart beat accelerated and she began to shiver in panic. The thought that it could be Deji coming back so soon increased her agitation. Ola considered calling for help but then the bell stopped ringing.

She almost flew out of her skin in fear as the caller seemed to have only abandoned the ringing to begin knocking insistently on the door. Like someone in a trance Ola knew what was going to happen next as the knocking ceased and she saw the handle of the door slowly turn. The intruder seemed desperate to come in she reckoned. Ola picked up speed to try and lock the door but it was too late as the door opened and was slowly swinging back on its hinges.

Ola stopped trying to blend in with the wall as she looked in trepidation wondering who was walking into her house. The silhouette of a man with a large frame filled the door way with the light behind him casting his face in a shadow.

"Ola . . . ?"

"Ray . . . ? Ray Johnson?" Ola recognised the intruder's voice as Ray's as he called her name and his face became clearer. The presence of a big dark skinned male seemed to be her undoing as the events of the day flashed through her mind making her hands shake in panic.

"I am so sorry for coming into your home. I know you said I shouldn't come to yours but I was worried . . ." Ola stood frozen in the corner with her breath coming in fast bursts as she continued holding on to the banister in the hallway staring at Ray with her eyes wide open looking like a cornered rabbit

"Ola, are you okay? . . . You sounded really distraught on the phone let alone all the things you shouted at me." Speaking gently Ray took some tentative steps further into the room and noticed her tear streaked face. He stood in front of Ola for a long time as he watched her cry her heart out. He made no attempt to touch her or to stop her from crying. He just stood silently and watched her till the tears slowly ebbed away. Ola became conscious of how she must look with her hair in disarray and her makeup smudged and running down her face. In embarrassment, Ola dropped down, crouching into the corner hiding her face in her hands as she was engulfed in a new wave of tears.

"Go away Ray, I don't want you here," she cried out in a muffled voice coming from between her sleeves with sobs making it difficult for Ray to understand. The next thing she knew, Ray was down on his knees beside her. Ola prayed he would not touch her because one more touch would just tip her over the edge. It didn't matter whether this touch was with care or not she just couldn't stand the thought of being touched by anyone . . . not now . . . maybe not ever . . . and began to sob some more at the thought . . .

"Are you hurt . . . or did you lose something? Do you want me to call the Garda . . . ambulance . . . ?"

"Ummm . . ."

"Is that a yes or a no . . . ?" Ola knew she would have to pull herself together if she didn't want Ray charging in and insisting she needed to go to the hospital.

"I am sorry. I am just in a bad place."

"Is there anything I can do . . . ?" Ray asked as he reached out his hand to take her hand. The feel of his hand suddenly brought the pain back to Ola who flinched and jumped up quickly . . . maybe too quickly as she lost her balance and toppled over falling right into Ray's arms who reached out to steady her.

"Take it easy!"

"No! No! Get away from me . . . , get away!" Ola screamed as she struggled within the circle of his arms, kicking, punching and pushing as hard as she could.

"Ola, Ola! It's okay, I'm not going to do anything to you. I promise. I am only trying to stop you from hitting your head on the floor in a fall . . . unless you'll rather have the fall . . ." he added as a lame attempt to joke.

"Steady . . ." he said as he gently let her go keeping his hands loosely close by for a second longer till he was sure she wasn't going to fall over again.

"I'm okay now," Ola said slightly sharper than she intended to. Ray straightened up at the sharp rebuke in Ola's voice.

"Whatever it was Ola . . . don't take it out on me . . . It wasn't me! You hear that? It wasn't me. I want to help . . . please let me help . . . ," he pleaded in a gentle voice. For such a big man he spoke so gently it was so unexpected especially in Ola's world and fresh tears started to roll down her cheeks.

"Don't Ray . . . , please don't say kind words to me. I can't handle it now." As the silence stretched between them, it was obvious Ray was looking for a way to say something, he looked like he was testing in his mind what he wanted to say and how best to say it.

"Did something happen with the children . . . ?" shaking her head from side to side, Ray got the answer to his question and he continued with another one.

"Did . . . did something happen with their dad?" he asked tentatively. At the renewed flow of tears Ray kind of got the answer even as she nodded cautiously.

"Did he say something . . . ?" Ola shook her head

"Did he do something . . . ?" though Ray was getting too close to the truth, Ola just could not talk to him about what happened because he would say it was her fault. She could not even bring herself to answer him as she turned her face away to hide her shame. After a long silence where Ray listened to the sound of her tears he seemed to pick up the questions again in a different direction or so it seemed.

"Did you see him . . . , today . . . ?" Ola nodded

"Here . . . ?" The tears flowed more freely as she nodded again

"Did you have a fight with him . . . ?" first she nodded, then in the same instant she shook her head and she suddenly seemed to be nodding and shaking her head at the same time continuously until Ray reached out and gently stilled the movement of her okay.

". . . Its okay . . . ," Ray dropped his hands from her again as he remembered her last outburst but he stayed as close to her as he could manage without sending her into a panic again.

"I . . . I can't tell you what to do Ola, but you should not live in pain or even fear in your own home. The law is there to protect you . . ."

"I know . . . I know . . ." she responded

Ray continued as Ola reacted in protest at the thought of contacting the police.

". . . I see this every day in my job. I carry dead women out every day . . . , I carry bruised women every day and sometimes it's the children I carry. Ola, what I am saying is that some women are fortunate to be alive to answer questions. Many times, it's the dead bodies we carry by the time we get there. If something has happened, you have a barring order and you can get help . . . ," when she still said nothing he continued.

"Okay, I've said enough" Ray said out loud probably cautioning himself. "Is there a girlfriend you can talk to if you can't talk to me . . . , can I call someone for you or maybe drop you off somewhere? I don't think you should be alone but I also don't think you should drive in this state." The mention of driving reminded Ola she had to go and pick up the kids from school.

"I have to pick up the kids . . . look I am sorry . . . ," she rushed on as he looked set to say something, maybe offer to take her but she didn't want to have to introduce him to the kids, not now . . . maybe not ever.

"I am sorry I didn't come out to meet you today . . . I couldn't but it is difficult to explain . . . I can't even explain it to myself . . . but thanks for your help and I will manage . . . I have to manage." Ola moved to the door taking charge of her emotions again. Ray had no choice but to follow her to the door as she seemed to be dismissing him.

"I am sorry if I spoke out of turn . . . I care and I worry about you that's all. That's what friends do . . ."

"I appreciate it and I have to take charge of my life now but I really appreciate it, Ray. Thanks . . ." Ray seemed set to protest as he stood between the open door "I have to do this on my own, for me, by myself . . . you understand . . . don't you . . . ?"

"Okay, call me if there is anything I can do. . . . Please keep yourself safe," Ray added as he conceded to Ola's wishes and left.

Two months passed since that incidence with Deji and no . . . , Ola didn't report it . . . she couldn't report it. She couldn't even repeat the story to anyone and say what . . . ? Even her bessimate Rita could not get it out of her. It was her pain that she was going to take it to her grave but the problem was it was eating a hole into her heart as she was living in constant fear. She wasn't sleeping well from constantly being woken up from a nightmare where a big steel rod rolled off a moving truck cutting a neat hole in the windscreen of her really small car. The rod always found its target—her chest, like a well-aimed javelin cutting into the ground. It then pierces through her chest, coming out at the back pinning her to the seat of the car.

In the dream she would be waiting to die because there is blood everywhere. Any minute, she was going to take her last breath and meet her maker . . . but the cars around her would begin tooting their horns urging her to move. They would shine their light in her face as she struggled to come out of the car but the rod would hold her down. Ola's panic would increase as the urge to get up increased with the lights and horns but the force holding her down would be too strong. She would shout and cry out for help and suddenly a sea of faces would surround her car asking why she couldn't move . . . urging her to move . . . then it would dawn on Ola that they couldn't see the rod holding her down. She'd grab the rod to pull it out knowing that if she did the hole from the rod would kill her . . . so she'd wait for death to take her but the horns and noise kept death away.

"Help . . . ! Help . . . !" She'd scream till she awakened drenched in sweat. That usually marked the end of sleep. Ola was suffering from sleep deprivation not because she didn't want to sleep but because she was afraid to sleep. Even when sleep came she woke up from the nightmare at about 3:45am. From then she'd count the hours in bed thinking until it was time to get the kids ready for school. She always got caught up in the same old dream!

Ola had not seen or heard from Deji since their last encounter if she could call it that or since her life turned over and she was just at the point of deciding what to do. Deji had reverted to his usual gimmicks of not paying the maintenance for the children, he didn't pick them up and Alicia kept asking for him while Ola was running out of excuses for why her dad was not there to read bedtime stories to her and why he was playing with other children and not her . . . the poor darling. Ola somehow felt it was her fault that the kids were suffering because she couldn't manager her relationship with Deji.

As if thinking about Deji conjured him up, there he was again at the door . . . at least the kids were home this time and she wasn't going to be left exposed to him on her own.

"Why didn't you let me know you were coming?"

"Hello to you too," Deji replied. Ola was uncertain how to answer him, if he spoke in sarcasms or humour, anyway, it didn't matter. He couldn't just do stuff to her, disappear and waltz back into her life as if nothing had happened as if '*time healed all wounds*!' Ola guessed those who said that had never been wounded like she had been.

"Don't go there Deji, please state your business and leave."

"Is this the way to talk to your husband, the father of your children . . . ? I thought by now you would have gotten back to your senses Ola. Look . . . ," he said lowering his voice as the children could be heard in the living room "if you leave this too long, things can . . . and they will happen. It will make it very hard and near impossible to patch things back together . . . do you understand?"

"Are you threatening me now, are you resorting to threats too now Deji? You wanted out, you decided we were not enough for you. You needed more women so what are you saying . . . ?"

"Daddy! Daddy . . . daddy!" burst in Alicia screaming with joy. Turning in her direction Deji swung around and lifted her high up in the air giving her a big twirl that her pink pastel dress blew big circles around her hips as she screamed in glee.

"How is my little Princess?" Deji asked softly with a smile on his face as he flashed his well-set teeth at her. All the hardness was completely gone from his face as Deji turned on the charm for Alicia. Ola fumed silently as she watched the display between father and daughter, thinking about the innocence of being a child.

"Daddy, where have you been, when are you coming home? I promise to be a good girl and Mummy promises to be good too, please daddy . . . Pleaseeee! Pleaseeee! Pleaseee daddy, say you will come home . . ." Ola couldn't stand the heart break in the little girl's voice anymore. She excused herself and went into the bathroom for a few minutes to pull her emotions together.

"You are always a good girl my love and I'll be home soon. I am just doing some work and things that take me away more . . ." Ola was vigorously shaking her head at Deji as she heard his part of the conversation . . .

"Go and get your brother." Ola watched Alicia as she skipped out of the room in a happy mood

"Don't say things to her that are not true Deji. I already told the kids things are not working out between us and you are living somewhere else now. Don't make promises you can't keep, you hear me . . . don't make promises." Grabbing her hand he pulled her closer that she could feel his breath on her face as he bent towards her and spoke in a whisper.

"I mean it Ola . . . , this is my home, I am your family. Don't let the Whiteman's land and law fool you. We are married in the African way. I am your husband and your head. Do you understand me? I am only out there now because I want to be and I think it is time we cut out this mess. I can continue if you want but there is no going back after a while and if you think that you are free to go out there, you are not. I am a traditional man to the core. I paid your bride price and so you belong to me."

"You don't own me Deji? I am a free agent just like you. After all you are living with another woman so what gives you the right to dictate to me?"

"We can marry more than one wife or are you so westernised now that you have forgotten our tradition"

"It is not our tradition Deji, it is greed . . . you cannot hide being a cheat under the guise of tradition. It won't wash. I am not the silly clinging, gullible girl I used to be, you hear me . . . I am not."

"So because I brought you abroad you have grown wings Ola, you are a big girl now you say . . . First let me tell you, I have put Magun on you. You know I travelled home the last time, well I put Magun on you and you cannot sleep with another man. So unless you want to condemn yourself to celibacy or you want the man to die trying to have sex with you then carry on. I have told you Ola, you belong to me."

"You are joking"

"Do I look like I am joking ehhh . . . do I?"

"Mum! Are you okay?" asked Michael as he came into the room and saw his dad holding Ola by the arms and shaking her vigorously. Using the surprise moment she broke out of Deji's arms and gently caressed her elbows which was hurting from the pressure of Deji's hold. Sometimes it was as if he didn't know his own strength!

"I am fine love . . . have . . . have you said Hello to your dad?"

"Hi dad," Michael replied in a robotic way. His resistance was so palpable!

"Is that how to greet your dad? Just standing there looking me in the eye? Did you not teach him how to greet elders in the traditional way?" Deji raged at Michael, and then turned to Ola including her in the outburst and somehow making her responsible despite the fact that they had raised the children together in the same house all these years. You would almost think he had been away from the house since the kids were born and not the miserable twelve months that it had been.

"Ekaro Sir" Michael said, using the traditional dialect meaning good morning to greet his dad. He didn't' wait for more conversation with Deji, he just turned around and headed towards the kitchen exit.

"Michael . . . !" Ola called out to him. She didn't want an exchange between them. Deji was always impatient when it came to Michael and he was always quick to use his fists to correct him. He called it discipline . . . Ola was sure if the welfare officers found out they would call it something else.

"Here, take the car keys and bring the food from the booth of the car."

"I'll help." Ola quickly jumped in

"No, it's okay . . . it's not so much. I am sure he can get them." Michael took the keys off his dad and continued out the door with a sullen look on his face. That was when Deji noticed a scared looking Alicia in the kitchen corner. She had always been an over sensitive child. She got really worried at raised voices.

"Come on love . . ." Grabbing Alicia's small hands which she was nervously wriggling together, Ola cautiously walked outside to help Michael take out the food from Deji's car. Ola did not understand how the roles changed and it became okay for Deji to live with another woman and still waltz into her life as if he never left, freely controlling and even intimidating her and the kids. She knew she wanted change but somehow she was certain this wasn't the one she wanted . . .

CHAPTER TWENTY TWO

OLA COULD NOT SEE THE light people usually promised at the end of the tunnel because hers was a Y shaped tunnel! She had to make choices that took her in two completely different directions and if there was one thing she hated with a passion it was making choices. She told herself she wasn't good at it and she usually wished someone would just take the responsibility off her and tell her what to. Unfortunately, the choice Ola was faced with now no one could make for herself.

Sighing, she stood with the freezer door wide open, trying to see how she could make a good meal with what she had. It was either she remained an M.R.S. Mrs—somebody's wife never mind if she was abused, raped, threatened, manipulated and plain old punching bag and dumping ground or make the separation permanent and have a life where she was treated like someone with the plague! . . . Because that was where she would end up. She grimaced as she remembered all the women's groups and meetings that she was not invited to over Christmas. While Deji was free to go around being *the man*, no one dared tell him to his face what they really thought of him or his actions.

Ola wished she were a different kind of woman . . . , one who could say what was going through her mind rather than fuming and suppressing her thoughts and feelings only to end up suffering from sleepless nights, raging thoughts and a banging head! Her body was beginning to show signs of sleep deprivation as she was constantly tired these days with very low energy levels.

Ola sighed regretfully as she thought about the kids. She knew they deserved more, she wished she could give them what other kids had. Thinking like that never failed to draw tears from her eyes. She wondered if all the tears she had cried in her life with Deji could speak, what they would say . . . , how they would describe themselves . . . maybe sad and angry?

Ola saw a call coming through on her phone saying mum. It was her mother from Nigeria. She approached the call with excitement and apprehension because most of the calls from home usually meant some problem or other they wanted her to solve. With Deji gone now and her job still only an internship she was not able to help herself not to talk of helping another person.

"Mum, oh mum . . . how are you doing? Is everything okay . . . is the old man okay?" Ola rushed one question after another as her mind went into overdrive wondering if something had happened for her mother to call that early in the day.

"Ola, why are you doing this . . . you want to kill me is that it Ola?" cried her mum.

"Mummy, what is it, please Mama tell me if something is wrong, please?"

"Why all these years Ola, you made us proud now you want to bring shame to the family?"

"What do you mean mama?" Ola's voice cooled a bit as the wheels in her head began to spin and she was putting two and two together.

"My daughter, you know all the people in the town are calling you names as Deji's mother is going about saying very serious things about you . . . my daughter, I am not well, this kind of thing can just finish me off. Ola my child, what is happening, what has gotten into your head? You have driven a whole man from the house now he is living on the street. Ola my child, has the Whiteman's lifestyle confused you so much you have forgotten who you are and the values of our family . . . ehnn Ola . . . ?"

"Mummy . . . you don't understand, it's not like that."

"How is it my child? What has he done that men have not done before ehnn my child? Do you know how many things your dad did to me that I still forgave him and till today we are still living together . . . ehnn? My daughter, you want me to die for you, you want me to die on your neck Ola . . ."

Ola was moved by the tears of her usually very complacent mum. It was proving too much for Ola especially today when she was feeling really raw and in a bad place. Ola had actually been thinking of calling home to get some TLC from her family, but that was not to be as it seemed Deji's family had already gone to her parents with all kind of stories!

"Mummy, you have no idea what I have been going through . . . what Deji has been doing to me mummy. Deji is not the man you see oh . . . he does things . . . really cruel things."

"My daughter, my heart cannot take this, I am really sure this will kill me, please my daughter . . . , please help me. Married women don't follow other men, it is forbidden in African culture"

"Mum!" Ola protested outraged by the insinuations.

"You are completely mistaken. It's not me you should be saying these things to. . . . it is Deji! He is the one living with another woman in her house with her children. Women were phoning my house and he was doing funny things on the computer. Mummy there are many things I didn't tell you because I didn't want to worry you but Deji has . . . done very evil things to me." Ola tried to emphasis it without giving too many details.

"My dear, all I see from here is all this going on in your life means my early grave. Please Ola my child, please. Remember, divorce is not good. . . . don't let me die like this . . . I am begging you!"

"Mama, I will call you later to talk. You know . . . things are not as straight forward as you see them . . . you don't know what Deji is like . . . ," sobbed Ola in frustration and confusion as she grappled with how much she could safely reveal to her mother. Ola's main fear was that giving her family details of how troubled her marriage was might result in them disrespecting Deji if they were to ever get back together. But it was really hard to hold on with the emotional strings her mum was pulling.

"My dear, what I see is that *'you do not send a thief to watch over rich peoples purses'* make up with your husband my dear. If your husband is weak where women are concerned then you now think the best thing you can do is to send him straight into their hands? Please do not let me die because of the shame you want to put over my head . . . please oh my daughter," Ola's mum pleaded with one last gust of energy.

"Thank you Mama . . . please take care of yourself. It is well and things will sort themselves out."

"Don't disappointment me my dear, please do the right thing! I am counting on you."

What was the right thing, Ola questioned inwardly.

All night Ola tossed and turned in bed. She woke up from the same nightmare with sweat pouring down her chest as her breasts rose and fell to the rhythm of her accelerated heartbeat. Picking up the phone she called her friend Rita.

"I am so sorry to bother you, but I am stuck . . . really stuck and I need to talk urgently. My mom is threatening to die if leave Deji. I am confused and lonely. I am so tired of being alone and you know the way it is, many people within our community don't wants to touch me even with a foot long pole! What am I going to do Rita . . . what?" Ola let her frustration out as she cried noisily and inconsolably. She was at the edge and it felt like her life was tipping over in slow motion.

"Calm down Ola, please remain calm. There has to be another solution."

"Tell me Rita because I can't see it"

"Do you think that things have improved between you and Deji? Are the issues which made you ask for separation still there or do you think they are gone and won't happen again?"

"Honestly . . . , I don't know any more. Deji has done things . . . , terrible things to me that I cannot even tell you . . . but what choice do I have? I say no . . . he doesn't hear me . . . I say stop and even the sound of that word rolls off him like water off the back of a duck . . . I try to resist and that is like a drug to an addict as it excites him even more and exposes me to worse treatment. What can I say to you Rita? How do I explain it?"

"Hmm mm . . . ," Rita sighed

"I am sorry . . . , I know I sound like a silly women, I just don't want my mother's blood on my hands. She has high blood pressure and you know the way medical treatment is back home . . . you have to pay so much to get a good doctor. No . . . but there is only one thing I can do." Ola seemed to have finally reached her own solution.

She however did not have the time to put her decision into action as three days later she got a phone call from three of the known leaders from their community group asking her for a suitable time when they could come and visit her. To tell the truth, Ola was dreading the visit. She knew what to expect, in fact she was one of the team who went to the Adegbete's residence the last time the couple were having problems, so she wasn't too thrilled about the impending visit. Unfortunately for her, the closer Thursday loomed the more apprehensive she became . . .

Going through the sixth set of clothes, Ola had to admit to herself that she was as nervous as a scared rabbit. Her head seemed to be all over the place and nothing she wore seemed to portray the image she wanted. The black jacket looked too serious as if she were going to work. The turtleneck jumper which she normally loved on cold mornings she thought made her look unapproachable. She picked out her black and white polka dotted chiffon top with black skinny jeans, no, no no . . . she again took it all off as the dots made her look fat and the tight jeans making her look like what they would call a loose woman. For such people it was bad enough she was separated, for her to be dressed looking too good would just confirm their thoughts that she was either playing around or searching for a man. Guilt about her friendship with Ray Johnson flashed through her mind momentarily . . . he had been so kind and helpful. In fact he had challenged her these past months to be ambitious for herself. Ola was impressed with a man who was not intimidated by her success, a man who was interested in her succeeding and making something of herself.

". . . oh well," Ola thought and gave up on the idea of Ray telling herself nothing was going to come of it. Ola was conscious that separation was not as widely accepted among Nigerians as many of the western world. The names one got called, the stigma of being with another man after your first marriage stayed with you all your life. What about the children . . . who would they call daddy . . . ?

"Ahhhh," exclaimed Ola. "No!" She said out loud making a weary face to her reflection in the mirror, there was nothing she could do about that. She had to settle for a life without . . .

Ola finally settled for a long flowing olive green caftan with wide sleeves and a fitted bust line and headed for the kitchen. She had prepared some roast Turkey, coleslaw and Jollof rice. That was one Nigerian dish one never went wrong with she laughed. With the food set, Ola had time to resume fretting about the meeting. What would she say . . . and really just how much could she reveal without embarrassing herself? The problem she had with these types of interventions was that anything you said would be remembered for such a long time and so to try and protect herself and even Deji who in her mind did not deserve any protection she had to be careful how much she revealed . . .

The sound of the ringing bell signalled the arrival of the troop! It sure felt like facing a firing squad . . .

"Good Morning Ma . . . , Sir," Ola greeted them bowing her knees respectfully as was expected in many Nigerian settings.

"My dear . . . how are you?" asked Aunty Favour putting her hand on Ola's shoulder in a soothing embrace.

"Fine Aunty, thanks for coming Ma," Ola answered leading the guests to the living room. "Please sit down Sir, Aunty please have a sit."

"Thank you my dear," they choroused. Ola offered them some drinks first and then sat down at the edge of her sit waiting to see which of them was going to start the talk.

"My dear . . . ," Uncle Charles started, signalling he was the chief spokesman for the group. "We cannot say that we are not aware of what has been happening but since you didn't call me, your husband even did not call me or my wife, we felt it was best to leave things for you to manage on your own. However, it has come to our notice that the situation is not being resolved, rather it seems to be getting worse to the point that you are going to drag yourselves through Oyinbo courts. That is completely unacceptable Ola."

"Sir . . . , Aunty Favour, I am sorry I didn't contact you when the situation between Deji and I worsened. I spoke to Aunty privately at the early time but as you said, I thought it was something we could resolve ourselves and we did for many years, but somehow, they turned worse and even became life threatening and I had to take action."

"I appreciate that my dear, but at the same time, you know us men. It is not easy for you the woman to resolve the issue yourself and when it gets to that stage we try to bring another man in to try and talk some sense to him. That is what we normally do. But my dear, you did bad oh . . . you sent the man to jail even if it was for a few hours, you sent him out of his own home and he is now squatting with people. You cannot resolve anything with a man by using so much force. How did you forget about what we call treading gently?"

"My dear . . . we are not here to blame you or to apportion blame," interrupted Aunty Favour as she could see Ola preparing to explode! She knew this was how it was going to go and she just blanked out and remained silent as she allowed their words to go over her head. You can't win at such talks as a woman Ola knew.

". . . so we have asked him to come at 2pm . . . ," lifting her head immediately Ola reconnected with the conversation . . . *what is she saying . . .*

"I hope it is okay with you . . . I know it is a surprise but for us to resolve the issues, it is important that we have you and Deji at the same time. We spoke with Deji last week and he told us the things which he said were not working in the relationship for him and he is really interested in keeping his family together."

"Emm . . . emm . . . is Deji coming for this meeting?" stammered Ola trying to clarify what the woman was saying.

"Is it a problem my dear . . . ?"

"No Ma . . . I am just surprised that is all . . ."

"My dear, we have heard all the things you have described and we know all these things but remember, this is your home . . . this is your family, do not throw it away with your own hands. If someone out there is trying to take my husband, do you think I will sit down complacently and allow her take him away? He is the father of my children, my head, my covering . . . ," Ola sat down silently listening to the talk . . . she knew, it wasn't about justice or what was right, it was about maintaining the status quo. They were going to tell her how it was done . . . that was how men were . . . blah . . . blah . . . blah.

"When will it stop . . . , where does it stop . . . , who stops it anyway when everyone has to dance to the same tune, no one challenging or facing the truth that it was wrong for a man to beat a woman in the name of marriage when it was not a life sentence or slavery . . . ? Ola knew she was fighting a lost battle. She did the easy thing and nodded in agreement to everything the female spokesperson in the group said.

Saved by the bell or rather bring on the next level of the show . . . Ola was not sure which as she was certain it was Deji at the door. She wondered why he had even agreed to attend the meeting.

"Hello . . . , Madam . . . ," shaking hands and all the pleasantries done, Deji sat down beside Ola on the long couch. She realised that it must have been part of their plan because she had offered the couple the couch when they came in but they chose the single sitters and Mr Adeniyi—had been rather quiet throughout the discussion Ola realised. Anyway he chose another single sitter so she found herself sitting on the long sofa which she was now sharing with Deji. She knew she had just been had!

"Thank you all for taking the time to intervene in my family situation. It is not a very comfortable position that I find myself but I appreciate your effort and time. We spoke last week and I have taken on board all that you have said and I am prepared to work forward from here." Listening in disgust, Ola felt that the well-rehearsed speech Deji had made completely put her in her place and made it difficult for her to say anything without looking like the trouble maker or as the cantankerous one! One point for Deji she conceded.

"Thank you Sir," Mr Bamidele or Uncle Charles as he was affectionately known said in response to Deji's speech.

"So Ola, how do we move from here, we have heard all you have said and your husband is prepared to let bygones be bygones, so what do you say?" continued Uncle Charles directing his next statement to Ola. She felt all their eyes pinned on her.

"I don't want to sound like I don't appreciate your help but the problem was not just . . . you know . . . all the surface things. Deji hit me and I was afraid for my life, Deji is going out with other women and those are not the things I want to continue with . . ."

"We have spoken to Deji and he is going to make sure he doesn't use hitting as a means of communicating again and he said he is also calling off anything he has with any other person. So we have to appeal to you as well to try and not be provoking him . . . if you are angry about something, try and keep your mouth silent as much as possible because you cannot be hit for saying nothing." Aunty Favour interrupted and took over the counselling baton.

"My dear, don't reply violence with violence, remember a good woman builds her home and if you don't want to be hit learn to keep silent. I promise you it works all the time. Ehn . . . satisfy your husband in bed and you know he will not have enough energy for other women ehn . . . , you understand what I mean . . . ?" They left Aunty Favour to do this part of the woman to woman talk. Ola saw this as the part where she was told that to have a successful marriage meant to be *'stupid'* only they did not call it stupid they called it *'wise'*. Ola smiled wearily at the thought. She was always intrigued that the more women did such things the wiser a woman they are called, some even called you a good woman! Some people think it's only women from the developing world who have this problem, but living in Ireland for the past thirteen years, Ola was beginning to see that it was every woman's problem . . . black, white, tall, short, educated, wealthy . . . every woman's problem.

"So what do you say Ola?" asked Mrs Bamidele. Without waiting for Ola's answer she moved over to Deji.

"This must be her own style of brief therapy" Ola smiled. She wished she could be bold enough to really say the things she was thinking that he was not a lover but a rapist, he was not a man but a dog open to everything in a skirt . . . but of course she couldn't say any of that and not be branded an evil and difficult woman to live with. They would just conclude that she was the quarrelsome woman. There was a saying about it being better to live on the roof top than with a quarrelsome woman. Ola knew what she had to do . . . she had reached that conclusion after she spoke with her mum. It was a hard decision but she believed she could do it . . . , she was going to have to do it to have any bit of dignity or life . . .

"Deji . . . do you love your wife . . . , do you love this woman who is the mother of your beautiful children . . . do you love her?"

"Of course I love her. I would not have married her otherwise. She is the mother of my children as you say."

"So can I ask if you are prepared to make things work and move back home if she agrees?"

"I don't have any plan to have different families . . . this is my family."

"Ola, you have heard the man, he has humbled himself, he has declared his love again for you and the children . . . , so what do you say? Do you want to make this work?"

"I want my marriage to work Sir, the only thing I am saying is that I want to be alive enough to enjoy it."

"Ola, you know that in African culture, the younger person is the one that has to make the first move. It is not about who is right or wrong."

"Yes . . ."

"So what I am going to ask you to do is not about whether you are right or wrong, it is the order of families."

"Yes Ma."

"Okay, so I want you to go to your husband now and kneel down and apologies to him as your husband . . . the head of your home."

Ola stood up from her side of the sofa, she knew there was no going back if she did this now she would have sealed her fate. Ola moved directly in front of Deji and shook away any last vestige of resistance in herself. She dropped to her knees keeping her eyes firmly fixed on Deji and asked him for forgiveness.

"Deji . . . , I know things have not been the way they should be and things are not perfect, but I am sorry for the part I have played in reducing our relationship to this point. I am sorry, please forgive me." Ola almost withdrew her apology at the smile on Deji's face. He looked like the cat that swallowed the canary!

"Ola, I am sorry too for all the wrongs I have done in this relationship and I love you and I want to be the head of this home with our family." Deji stretched forth his hand and lifted Ola to sit on his lap! Ola felt embarrassed in front of the guests. She wasn't sure if this was all a show or how much of it was real but it was obviously a good enough show for the three guests who clapped their hands commending themselves for the successful outcome.

"*Come oh* . . . Madam, the first duty you can perform for your husband now while we are here is to feed him . . . ha . . . ha . . . ha. So it is time to bring the food out," chuckled Mr Adeniyi at his own joke. Ola took the cue from that and served the food, serving Deji first and sitting him at the head of the table.

CHAPTER TWENTY THREE

"WHEN ARE YOU MOVING BACK home?" Ola asked as Deji was coming in everyday for his dinner but going back out at night. He still wasn't spending the night at home. The kids were happy to have him around . . . at least Alicia was but Michael had had a sullen face since his dad came back home. He just seemed constantly angry and short with everyone. It had been two days since Ola reached the agreement with Deji to let things in the past go, but she still wasn't sure if she had done the right thing.

"I told you that I had plans already for this week and by the weekend I will be home fully. I am in a planning phase with some friends. We are planning some business together but because we all work, the evenings are the best times to meet and I had agreed to go over to theirs as I didn't know our situation was anywhere near changing. I will see you after work tomorrow and I'll move my stuff back in on Saturday. Is that all right?" Ola had no choice but to accept his explanation even when she somehow knew it was a story . . . what was the option she asked herself again? What would she gain from it . . . ?

"Okay, see you tomorrow and have a good rest," pulling her close Deji patted her on the bottom as he walked out the door. Ola's suspicions were aroused but she didn't know how to deal with them. What if he was still with that woman . . . was that what he wanted now . . . to be with both of them at the same time? Ola knew the problem was that they didn't address the main issues between Deji and herself. She was mandated to forgive apologies and move back together. This was what Rita meant about resolving the core issues first to avoid future problems.

Ola was worried and she couldn't hide it. She hatched a plan to check up on him to see if he would answer her call. She hoped that the background noise would give her an idea where he was. So at 11pm, late but not too late, Ola placed a call to Deji's mobile making her number unknown. The phone rang twice and then a woman's voice answered the phone.

"Hello, hello?" without saying a word, Ola disconnected the call. Ola was disgusted with herself that she had become the telephone stalker she hated so much. But it told her what she wanted to know!

Deji wasn't at any meeting, he wasn't meeting any lads and there was no business anywhere. This was Deji all over again. Ola cried asking herself when she would learn? If in the first few days of making up he could not even keep it zipped up . . . what hope did they have ehn . . . what hope? She asked herself in despair. She needed to just talk with someone if not she was going to explode. Ola was very reluctant to call Rita again but she always helped her calm down.

Picking up her phone, Ola dialled Rita's number but the phone rang out . . . Maybe she was on duty . . . , she tried two more times then gave up. Ola desperately needed to talk to someone as her thoughts were literarily driving her up the wall . . . maybe she could call Aunty Favour . . . or Margaret . . . maybe Margaret would be willing to talk. It was getting really embarrassing for Ola now with everyone knowing her business as if she was the only one who had problems . . . who could not keep her home. It made seeking for help difficult for Ola. Even with that she was conscious of people who didn't really want to talk to her anymore because they were tired of hearing her issues. People definitely got tired of talking to you because it was one trouble situation after another.

"Hi Margaret, how are you, do you have a moment?"

"Am okay, how are things with you . . . and Deji, how is he settling back in . . . ?" Ola was silent for a bit as she tried to think of the best way to answer without sounding like a whinny or a moan bag . . .

"Ola . . . ?"

"I am sorry . . . , I know you are tired of me by now."

"Don't be silly Ola, you know we can't do much but even if it is to listen or offer you the space to talk . . . , what is happening, is the settlement with Deji not going ok?

"I really don't know what to think, Margaret . . ." Ola recounted the situation with Deji ". . . and I don't just know how to go with this."

"I am not an authority on relationships or anything, but you look like you are walking straight into the same situation you were in before. You are doing detective work, following his every move . . . you can hurt yourself emotionally and even your physical health. Many of us who appear as happy women, well the truth is we have decided to turn a blind eye to certain things so that peace can reign in the home. If not we would all leave our husbands and then those . . . women who were not there from the beginning . . . women who didn't suffer with us will now take our place and reap the rewards of our labour. At the end of the day Ola it is a choice. Either turn a blind eye or see everything and be man-less."

Ola's despair seemed to deepen at the bleakness of Margaret's message.

"It seems so unfair. I hate being alone but I hate even more having to pretend I am okay with something when I am not. It sickens me inside and sometimes I feel as if I am the living dead just going through the motions of life. Will it ever end, is there a way out . . . ?"

"I don't know what to say to you Ola, you seem to be getting idealistic . . ."

"What is wrong with that? I mean what is wrong with having standards and values and expecting the same values you hold for yourself to be held by others? . . . anyway, I am only talking it's not as if I can do anything about it. Look don't mind me, I'll be okay."

"It gets better Ola, women have been in these situations for years and years."

"Maybe it is time for someone to do something about it. . . . my fear is that if we all keep silent, put our heads down, what legacy are we going to leave for our children, what kind of life will my daughter Alicia have? Will she not grow up confused where now we encourage her to think and be her own person, we teach her to have a mind and know herself then she gets to marriage and she is then subjected to a relationship where another human being can decide he doesn't like her friends and demand she doesn't see them anymore? Or she will earn her salary from working hard and one man will take it off her to entertain another woman . . . ? Look Margaret, I can't do it for me, I don't even have enough energy to fight for myself but this little one and every other young one coming . . . don't they deserve to live a fulfilled life rather than at the whim of another human being just like themselves . . . ?"

"Ola . . . , our mothers went through this and they survived it but between you and me silence is the best resort or you lose your man . . ."

"Maybe it's not about another person but about what I want or what is good for me . . . rather than thinking of losing my man. Yeah Margaret, maybe that's what I have to start thinking of . . . what I want, what is good for me. Is that too much to ask . . . ?"

"I guess only you can answer that because only you know what you want, what you can or cannot bear but it is always about the consequences of our actions," Margaret cautioned Ola.

"Thanks . . . thanks for taking my call."

———∿∾⟨⟩⟨⟩∾∿———

Ola was dreading going into college on Friday because she knew she had to have a conversation with Ray . . . Ray Johnson . . . , he had become an ally these past months helping her with college work and even challenging her to reach higher in life . . . Though there was nothing going on yet between them, Ola knew that Ray was hoping she would at some point become available to his affections. . . . but Ola knew that as long as things were still up the air with Deji there was nothing she could do . . . Ray in the few months had shown her that it was possible for a man to respect her as a person and for her to have a conversation where she didn't get shouted down. In fact she had almost forgotten what it was like to talk to have a two way conversation with an adult male until Ray. He really made her feel so valued . . . , Just thinking about it, Ola knew that what she would miss the most from putting some distance between Ray and herself was that he simply made her feel . . .

"Hey Ola, how are you. I almost called you on Wednesday after my class when I didn't see you because I know you ordinarily don't miss classes." The worried look on Ray's face made Ola's heart drop at the news she had for him. She knew he was hoping that soon they would be more than tea mates or coffemates she grimaced.

"I am okay, just some urgent things came up and I couldn't make it to college. Do you have a minute to talk?"

"I can meet you in twenty minutes. I need to pick up my notes from the staff room," Ray said looking at the leather strap watch on his wrist.

"Okay, see you at the café," holding onto Ola's hand longer than he needed to, Ray reluctantly left her after a minute of prolonged silence. He probably had a premonition that it would be something he wouldn't like . . .

"I'll see you in a few," he reiterated as if to reassure himself.

All Ola could do was nod as her throat seemed to be clogged by emotions.

Ola made her way to the café and found a quiet corner after ordering her tea which she sat nursing looking miserable.

"Tell me . . . ," was all Ray said as he arrived at the café and sat opposite Ola in the half full shop. "What is it?" he prompted as Ola seemed to be hedging and was focusing a lot on her hands with a long face.

". . . Ola, just tell me, what is it? I can clearly see that something is not right. Are you ill or did something happen again?" Lifting her head in one brave motion Ola jumped in . . .

"I can't see you again . . ." Ray reeled back sharply as if he had been struck in the face.

"What does that mean . . . can I ask why?" he asked trying to get his head round Ola's bombshell.

"There is really no easy way for me to say this . . . but you know how things have been with Deji and I . . . ," as Ola slowed down Ray urged her on

"Yeah, go on . . ."

"Look, I am sorry but we have had some family intervention and I have decided to give Deji another chance." Ola said the words quickly before she could chicken out of addressing the issue. Ray held her gaze as if to read into her soul. Though he didn't say anything for a few minutes she noticed the tightening around his knuckles which he kept firmly together on the table.

"Is that what you want?"

". . . I think it is more than what I want . . . it's more like . . . , oh . . . I don't know,"

"Are you happy with him . . . I mean . . . really happy Ola . . . ? Have you ensured that he has done the work on himself not to put your life at risk again . . . ?"

". . . I . . . I," Ola tried to articulate a response to the very questions she had been asking herself but Ray interrupted her quickly as he charged on in full steam!

"You deserve to be happy . . . , you have rights to have expectations as well . . ."

". . . you don't understand what it's like . . . what it has been like . . . the challenge of being a separated woman, the stigma in our community of being a single parent. I have been treated like a leper with a contagious strain!"

". . . but you are alive . . . , you are alive to tell, to bear to be a part of your life . . . to witness it. You are alive damn it! . . . I never told you this but I lost a sister in a domestic brawl. I never forgave myself for not doing anything. We all encouraged her to stop being too bold and mouthy. Twice she was carried naked bruised and battered by her husband to the hospital. I don't know who she was angrier with, her husband or . . . her family. She blamed us till she died for not rescuing her from him. She always blamed us for not challenging him on her behalf. She never could understand the brand of love we said we had for her when someone was beating her to the point of losing consciousness and we still welcomed him and treated him as our in-law! . . . I have never forgiven myself for that."

". . . I am sorry, I didn't know . . ."

"It was a long time ago and I was only sixteen then."

"Ray . . . I have to do this, I have to try. I have kids with him already. They miss their dad and I just never saw myself as a woman having kids from two different relationships. . . . I'd like to have one more child and . . . I had a miscarriage once and . . . look Ray it is complicated. I am so sorry. I appreciate your friendship. It has held me, but I hope you understand. I . . ." Ola stammered and seemed to run out of steam. Looking sad, she dropped her eyes from Ray's piecing gaze.

". . . I can't stop you, I will not even try to stop you . . . not because I think this is right but because I value the family unit and I guess you have to satisfy yourself if there is still something there for you." Reaching across the table, Ray grabbed her hand turning it over in his without saying a word for a long time. Finally Ray stood up slowly, pushed back his chair and dropped a kiss on the top of her head as he whispered "Keep safe . . . keep yourself safe . . . ," and he was gone. Just like that. Just as quietly as he came into Ola's life and came to means so much to her . . . he was gone . . .

Taking a tissue from the table Ola wiped the tears from her eyes as she thought of what could have been . . . and the pain he must have been carrying for his sister all these years. So much for a sixteen year old to have to carry. One never knew the impact of such things on others. Many times people saw the obvious person who suffered . . . the woman, yet there were so many others who suffered . . . wiping her eyes she walked blinded by more tears out of the café wondering what life had in store for her . . .

CHAPTER TWENTY FOUR

AT NUMBER 44 WHERE OLA lived, it was business as usual—as if Deji never left the house.

It was two weeks! Just two weeks and Ola's life was exactly where it was before he left. She was back to tiptoeing around him and meeting his every need but now Ola felt constrained by the unspoken threat in the house. She wasn't sure if it was done deliberately but Ola absolutely loathed the warning look Deji seemed to enjoy giving her whenever she had an opinion different from his. He seemed to be able elicit respect and compliance by what Ola mockingly referred to as '*the look*' which seemed to say 'have you forgotten so soon". It was a look veiled with silent threats of what he could do if provoked!

Ola found she could not argue or have a different opinion from Deji's and her obedience had become an unspoken rule in the house. She was very upset when she heard Deji boast to his friend over the phone about how peaceful his house was now and how she obeyed his every desire.

This was the choice she had made and even if it killed her Ola wasn't going to complain to anyone anymore. She noticed that her friends were now always 'too' busy doing one thing or the other . . . or they were rushing off somewhere when she called. Some even let her calls ring out.

No . . . , Ola couldn't blame them, as she knew she too would have been tired hearing continuous complaints about the same relationship.

This was her choice, she would have to live with it as best as she knew how.

Ola had been given a lot of advice and to avoid being used as a punching bag by Deji she decided to resist less and agree more with most of what Deji said. It was annoying but it eased the tension. Ola saw that spending more time apart helped a great deal so even when she and Deji were home at the same time, she deliberately reduced the time they shared by staying in another room on the pretence of giving him space to do his work, watch his programme or whatever . . . not that he seemed to mind or even notice as long as his needs were met promptly Ola realised. She even welcomed him whatever time he came back home with no questions asked and she always . . . always had a hot meal ready for him. For the bedroom department, Ola had learnt to supply on demand sex which seemed to resolve a lot of angry looks!

Sex . . . , hmm . . . Ola thought pensively because that's what it had become. It was no longer making love—there was no making about it except maybe making pain, hurt and humiliation that could not even be mentioned to another person and still have any dignity left. It took all of Ola's concentration to go through the motions of her life that the skin along her cheek bones was so tightly stretched it felt like porcelain about to crack. Gone was any hope of carefree conversations or spontaneous laughter. . . . sighing and exhaling deeply Ola picked up the washing and headed up the stairs with the laundry.

Later as Ola sat down she realised the crick in her neck reminded her that her tiredness was not from the hour she had spent working on her final essay for college but from the hours of house work she had to do before she could settle down to complete the essay. As the key turned in the lock signalling Deji's arrival, Ola hoped she could be excused out of the usual routine of preparing a hot meal for him as she was going to miss the extension submission deadline for the essay.

"Hi honey, how was work . . . ?" she asked giving a cursory look at the clock over the kitchen shelves 9:05pm. Ola was sitting with the laptop at the dining room table with only one thousand words done for an essay of two thousand five hundred!

". . . Okay," Deji's answer reminded her she had asked him a question in the first place!

"I am just struggling with this essay . . . it's not easy at all . . . ," she added by way of conversation. ". . . Your dinner is in the microwave and the table is set if you can just heat it up for two minutes. My brain seems to be working well now so I want to continue till I have most of it done at least before I lose my concentration!" she joked as she returned her attention to the essay. The silence from where Deji was standing made Ola look up again.

'Oh no . . . !' Ola mouthed in apprehension as she suddenly noticed that familiar look on Deji's face which he normally had when he was working up a rage.

"Oh no, not tonight, please not tonight . . ." Ola offered a silent plea as she was not ready for a fight. The assignment had to be in . . . but Deji's face was like a dark cloud with his brows almost meeting in the middle and his checks firmly ridged and hard.

"Is everything alright hon . . . ?" Ola asked tentatively as she tried to defuse the mood.

". . . So I come home now and you are too busy to even look up and talk to me?" Deji's calm but ominous sounding voice heightened Ola's anxiety.

"No honey, it's not like that. I . . . I am just trying to complete the essay for college. You know the one I mentioned to you I . . . I am undertaking a course and these are the assignments for my final exams."

"So you are the first to do exams, that my house has to ground to a halt? Now you are sitting there on your stupid arse asking me after working and bringing the money home to pay the bills and feed your fat arse . . . , you . . . , you cannot be bothered to make my meal?"

Pushing the computer away from her front, Ola tried to placate him.

"No Deji, I didn't mean it like that, I was just settling down to get this essay done as I had been busy with the children's homework and making the meal . . ."

"So that is too much for you to do, ehn . . . ? I knew I should have stayed where I was but you made promises and now only two weeks on you open your mouth and ask me to go and cook? You must really be sick in the head . . ."

"Honey, I am sorry, please don't be angry, I wasn't thinking," Ola apologised profusely trying to avoid a full bust—up.

"It has just been a difficult week . . . seriously, I am not asking you to cook oh!" Ola ended with the emphasis 'ohhhh' that is commonly added to the end of sentences in Nigeria to exaggerate a point.

"The food is already made . . . I am just asking if you could help me by put it in the microw . . . wave . . . ahhhhh!" The words were wiped back into her mouth as the force of Deji's briefcase landed against the right side of Ola's face, nearly knocking her off the seat.

". . . can you imagine this silly woman that you are . . . you are still sitting down there and you even have the audacity to repeat that I should go and cook . . . this single mother shit is really getting to your head isn't it?" Deji shouted at her enraged.

The ringing inside Ola's ears was so loud that it numbed her so much she couldn't respond at first.

". . . Deji! What did you do that for, do you want to kill me . . . oh my God, Deji. . . . what is this again? Do you want to kill me . . . what did I do to you . . . ehn . . . what did I do to youuhhhh . . . ?"

". . . Since your brain is not working, let me break that coconut head of yours and put the book inside it, dumb arse!" Deji shouted as he seemed to become even more furious. He reached for the laptop with both hands, grabbing it violently off the table with a murderous look on his face.

Ola wasn't sure what he intended to do but she wasn't taking any chances, she scrambled from the chair where she had slumped from pain . . . She however acted too slowly as the laptop smashed against her head, sliding down her back on impact and smashing on the ceramic tiles of the dining room floor. The stinging pain was enough to momentarily put Ola in a daze. In that disoriented state, she blanked out and couldn't move herself to react. Ola felt something like warm liquid rolling down the right side of her head. Still dazed, she lifted her hand to investigate the liquid and her hand came away damp with red stuff

". . . blood! Oh my God, I am bleeding!" She panicked. She couldn't understand it but once Deji got angry he seemed to act without thinking . . . , he seemed driven to inflict so much pain and he didn't bother with what or how he caused it. Thoughts of what he could do if she stayed in his path released Ola from the frozen state as real fear took over.

"Deji . . . you evil man, you want to kill me? What did I do to you for Christ sake . . . , evil man, you want to kill me ohhh . . . !"

A shouting Ola lunged for Deji and a frenzied deranged struggle ensued between them. Ola didn't have a plan. She didn't even know what she hoped to achieve by reacting to Deji's punches, it wasn't as if she could over power him physically if it came to that.

Enough . . . ! Ola thought, it was enough . . .

A slight movement caught Ola's attention as she suddenly became aware from the corner of her eyes of Michael and Alicia standing by the doorway. Michael was standing in front doing his best to protect Alicia from getting a full view of the room and the picture of herself and Deji locked in a tussle!

"Oh God . . . the kids, how much did they see, what did they hear?" Ola panicked. She hated the children witnessing their fights or even hearing the kind of weighty words they used on each other when they rowed!

Ola wasn't ready to release the grip she had on Deji's shirt which she had scrunched up in her fist to register her protest. She had actually forgotten the kids were home. She wondered what picture they made with their tangled clothes and arms. She feared that such images would leave long lasting scars in the children's minds creating a whole new circle of pain. Motivated and even more determined, Ola spoke directly to the kids while still maintaining her hold on Deji, . . .

"Alicia, play hide and seek with me again. Run upstairs and hide. Michael, go and help her hide properly." Alicia knew the drill and ran up the stairs as Ola listened for the patter of her tiny steps. ". . . Go Michael!" Ola shouted at Michael as he stood still refusing to leave.

"No! I saw it all already . . . so what is there to hide? . . . Why do you let him do that to you, why do you let him hurt you . . . talk to you that way as if you are nothing? Why did you even take him back? I would have taken care of you and Alicia, I am nearly 14 and I can get a job, why won't you let me get a job? Now see what he has done!" Michael's anger was very palpable and his passionate outburst broke Ola's heart just to look at him as his young jaw trembled tight with anger. It however had none of that reaction from his dad. One would have expected him to feel some shame or at the very least remorse but that didn't happen. It seemed to rekindle Deji's anger as he raised both hands and expressed his displeasure on Ola's face in the form of two criss-crossed slaps across her face and mouth, punctuating each blow with heavy panting and insulting words.

". . . So you have poisoned my son's mind against me so that he can talk about me like that ehn . . . ?"

"Deji, stop it . . . you are hurting me, stop it . . ." Ola screamed as she pulled at his shirt and tried to scratch at his arms and any other part of his body she could reach. Jumping on his back Michael grabbed at his dad shouting all kinds of four letter obscenities that shocked Ola. She didn't know he knew such words let alone used them!

"Leave her alone you . . . leave her alone . . . leave my mother alone you coward . . ." the force of Deji's wrath got directed at Michael as Deji grabbed him with his right hand, pulling him off his back. He smacked Michael across the face and pushed him against the wall. The chaos seemed to be escalating making Ola panic even more.

"Stop it Deji, you will hurt him, don't hurt my son! . . . don't hurt my son . . . , please, please . . . run upstairs now Michael," Ola commanded as she put herself between Michael and Deji like a human shield.

"I am calling the Garda. If she will not put you in jail I will do it because you hit me. I am going to call the police," Michael ran up the stairs in search of the phone.

". . . So you have turned my son against me, you have taught him to speak to me like that I will finish you in this country. I will kill you for your evil Ola. You are an evil woman."

Grabbing Ola by her hair extensions, Deji pulled her over to the kitchen sink making her cry out from the pain coming from the roots of her hair.

Ola's half crazed imagination started seeing Deji scalping her like in the prehistoric times and preserving it as a trophy.

"Where is the knife . . . where is the knife . . . ?" Deji shouted as he rummaged in the drawers throwing things all over the kitchen floor.

"What are you doing, Deji, what are you doing?" Ola's voice rose an octave to a thin shrill as her fear increased—as if that was even possible with the level of fear she was already feeling. Ola renewed her struggles to free herself at the revived image of herself being scalped over the kitchen sink in front of the kids.

Threatening words laced with venom poured out of Deji like a well-rehearsed plot! His words dripped with so much hatred that Ola's fear mounted and she was too afraid to speak. The feel of the thin edge of a cold kitchen knife against the side of her neck literally froze all the blood in Ola's veins!

"Stop . . . , stop . . . , stop . . ." Ola commanded her fluttering heart to slow down and stop beating. She stilled all motion so as not to aggravate Deji. She knew that all it would take was a simple push . . . even if he didn't mean it. She was sure . . . , no she hoped he just wanted to scare her by holding the knife to her throat but Ola was too afraid to take the chance.

She was saddened because Deji was right. Who would look for her if she were to die in this house? Even her family would not be able to come to Ireland to search for her. The last time they tried to visit they were not able to get visas to visit.

"Oh God," Ola cringed in fear "I am going to die like a slaughtered halal ram!"

"I am going to cut your fat veins and drain all your blood, down this sink till you dry up and beg for death. And you know what . . . , no one will look for you. The Irish government will be happy to miss you, at least one less mouth to feed, one less person who they have to give citizenship! Look at you, no one cares for you. I will kill you here and no one will bother to look for you, no one cares about you, you hear me? No one," leaning in towards Ola, Deji increased the pressure of the edge of the knife against her neck.

"Say you hear me, say I understand," shouted Deji

"I understand," Ola repeated obediently.

"Louder! . . . you stupid idiot," he shouted.

"I understand."

Reducing her actions to a motionless rag doll posture, Ola changed her strategy and began to plead with him. Her only thought was getting out alive. Ola was disturbed by flashbacks of all the recent deaths that ended inconclusive!

"I am sorry . . . please Deji," pleaded Ola who was by now desperate enough to promise anything to free herself.

"I love and respect you Deji, please, it will never happen again. I swear on my children's life, please Deji, I am so sorry, please . . . you are the head of this family you know that, we all know it . . ."

". . . do you get me now you lousy woman?" Deji screamed even more as he seemed to feel her energy abating and his victory so close.

"If you cross me again, this will not just be a threat it will be the edge of this knife going through that fat vein on you backside. I will drain your blood till you die and no one will ever know. In fact you know these white people, once they don't know something you can claim black magic and voodoo and they will believe it. I will tell them you started drying up in the house and one day you fainted and I couldn't revive you. Nobody cares about you. You hear me? No one! You are nothing but part of the statistics of unwanted black people in Ireland and you better obey the rules of my house or I will make you one less thing for the state to worry about."

The slamming of the kitchen door signalled the presence of another person in the kitchen. For a few minutes Ola was really happy not to be alone at home with Deji, then she realised she didn't want the kids to be lumbered with this memory of their parents or relationships.

"I have called the Garda, and you are going down this time . . . you are going down . . . ," reiterated Michael with so much venom in his voice the hatred was scary.

". . . I heard all you said and I put the Garda on the line while you were talking so they have you on record. You will not escape it this time. I promise you," Michael swore at his dad in rage.

". . . Give me that phone . . ." Deji shouted at Michael caught between holding on to Ola and going after Michael. He seemed to make a quick decision as he shoved Ola violently against the kitchen sink making her head reel. With outstretched hands Deji lunged at Michael.

". . . Give me that phone now . . . ," Deji barked in a stern no nonsense voice.

"Don't come near me . . . if you think I will let you continue to hurt this family like my mother does you are joking . . . ," screamed Michael as he ran out the door and up the stairs.

Deji appeared torn but he pushed past Ola and chased after Michael screaming at him to come back downstairs.

The pounding of feet up the stairs and the raised voices galvanised Ola into action and she took to her heels after the two men in her life. Ola blanched at the sight that met her as she pushed open the door into Michael's room. It was one that would remain etched in her mind forever making her remorseful about her decisions and the danger she had exposed her family to . . .

CHAPTER TWENTY FIVE

SCANDAL . . . ABSOLUTELY SCANDALOUS!

This couldn't be happening . . . , Ola wiped her eyes.

This just couldn't be happening! Her son, her Michael, her 13 year old baby should not be in a faceoff with his Dad, a man almost four times his age.

"What have I done?" cried Ola.

. . . Father and son were circling each other face to face with Michael welding a sharp hunting knife which he was waving menacingly in front of his dad who to Ola's dismay was in combat pose with his son . . . ! . . . his own son thought Ola holding onto both sides of her face to stop herself from screaming out loud and startling them into making a mad dash.

"Michael! Where did you get that from? Give it to me now, give it to me!" There was utter pandemonium in the room with everyone suddenly shouting at the same time.

Deji used that moment where Michael was distracted looking at Ola to grab him and father and son struggled for the knife. Deji grabbed his hand and tried to pry the knife from his son while Michael who seemed even more determined not to let go, tightened his grip. Holding onto his wrist, Deji increased the pressure on little Michael's hand shaking it vigourously in the air to make him release the knife.

Ola watched helplessly with her heart in her mouth and a head that felt light from fear it felt like she could faint!

Ola watched on in dismay. She could see Michael . . . her little baby weakening as the struggle got too much for him. With a final angry shout, Michael released his hold and the knife flew in the air narrowly missing Ola's face! The knife landed on the floor with a loud clatter bouncing back up and then rolled under the bed as both males rushed to try and get the knife again. Ola still filled with pain held onto her head in panic as she watched the scuffle between both males in her life.

"Stop . . . , please stop! Deji . . . , Deji . . . , what are you doing . . . ?" she cried sharply.

Michael and Deji seemed to suddenly hear her as they both stopped in their tracks with neither rushing for the knife.

"Okay . . . ," said Ola to calm the chaos as they all stood in the room eyeing each other while trying to catch their breath. Their sense of relief was short lived as the piecing cry of a little girls' voice filled the room. They all froze as the crying continued and they traced the sound under the bed.

"Mummy . . . ! Mummy . . . !"

Ola's heart literally stopped . . . she had forgotten about Alicia! Ola castigated herself for forgetting her.

"Oh my God! Oh my God . . . !" Ola cried in panic as she dropped to the floor. Ola had thought seeing her thirteen year old and his dad sparring with each other was bad enough but the sight under the bed was worse! She would never forget it as long as she lived—if she lived . . . , if she lived . . .

"Call the ambulance, call the ambulance now!" Ola screamed banging on Deji chest.

Ola was beside herself with worry. Alicia . . . , her Alicia was under the bed in her hide and seek place with the hunting knife sticking out from her chest!

"Oh God please . . . , please . . . , please . . . ," Ola cried over and over as she waited for the ambulance afraid to move her so as not to aggravate the injury.

"Michael and Deji were on the landline and mobile. She could hear their conversations explaining what had happened to the emergency number person but she was not listening to the details. Ola's eyes were glued to the knife sticking out of Alicia's chest and her cries had slowed to tiny whimpers as she seemed to be drifting off to sleep. In renewed panic, Ola lay on the floor parallel to Alicia and reached out for her small hands, rubbing her palm gently as she tried to warm and sooth her . . .

"Please honey, open your eyes, stay awake for mummy please, baby, stay awake for me."

"Alicia . . . , daddy is here . . ." Deji added his voice trying to sooth her but Ola was not having any of it.

"Get out . . . ! Get out . . . ! Get out before I pull out that knife and stab you myself." shouting like an enraged demented woman, Ola fearlessly grabbed Deji by the sleeves of his tee shirt, pounding on his back and pushing him out of the room.

Deji must have known the seriousness of the situation or maybe he too was in shock because he didn't resist Ola's punches and . . . with a dejected look on his face, he allowed himself to be pushed out of the room.

"I will go and wait for the ambulance," he said meekly to Ola's retreating back while Michael continued sitting on the floor in a daze, staring through the window.

Ola wondered how they were going to get through this . . . , how . . . , and Michael, she wondered what had come over him at the same time berating herself for exposing them to danger.

"Please don't die, my love, my angel, my princess . . . please don't die. I will do anything, go anywhere but please don't die . . . please . . . oh God please . . . ," Ola cried over and over in a small voice as she tried to keep Alicia awake and talking.

The blaring of the sirens signalled the presence of the paramedics with Deji on their heels running up the stairs.

"She is under the bed . . . please hurry she is not talking anymore," Ola told them.

"We have to move the bed first to be able to assess how to move her. Ray? . . . Ray can you give us a hand?" They called out and Ray Johnson appeared a few minutes later looking as agitated as Ola felt. Ray looked at Ola questioningly without saying a word, gave the room a cursory look as he moved towards the two paramedics trying to move Michael's bed. It was a very heavy bed, one of those that had attached cupboards over and around. Ola watched as the three lads positioned themselves and lifted the bed straight up without dropping it to try and avoid Alicia.

The sight of the pool of blood under Alicia's little body broke Ola's heart as she burst into tears again.

Reaching out for Ola, Ray pulled her out of the way as the team examined Alicia.

"Maybe you should wait outside while they assess her condition . . . Deji is downstairs with Michael and the Garda . . . Look I am sorry I came with the team. I was just going off duty when the call came through . . . and . . . and it was your address. I . . . worried that something had happened to you. Never in my wildest imagination did I think . . . it was one of the kids. You need to be checked out as well . . . there is dried blood on your head is that you or . . . ?"

"Me . . . Ray . . . what am I going to do if she dies, how will I forgive myself . . . why didn't I listen, why didn't I . . . ?"

". . . shhh, don't talk like that, I am sure she is a fighter . . . here . . . they are ready to go . . . her face is still open so that is a good sign . . ."

Ray's words were supposed to reassure her but they painted such a grim picture that Ola burst into tears again. Making arrangement for Michael to stay at her neighbour's till her friend Rita came to pick him up. Ola left with the ambulance as the Garda officers took Deji away for questioning. She had forgotten Michael had called them before Alicia's accident but Ola couldn't be bothered about Deji at that moment. He was the least of her worries not if there was a possibility that her precious baby might not . . . not . . . Ola shuddered as she couldn't even bear to think about it.

After two whole days of keeping vigil by Alicia's bed, Ola was at her wits' end. She had prayed, made all the promises of what she would do differently if Alicia was okay. Ola could not bear the thought of losing another child . . . , Alicia being in the hospital had unearthed all the pain of her miscarriage eleven years before . . .

"Mr and Mrs Peter's? I have some update for you about your daughter's progress," the doctor who had been monitoring Alicia's progress walked into the waiting room mistaking Ray for her husband.

". . . Oh no . . . , he is not my husband . . . ," Ola started protesting but then thought better of it as she was more interested in the news he had about Alicia than protecting Deji's position!

". . . but you can tell me please. How . . . how is she doing?" Ola stammered as she stood before the doctor fearfully waiting for his expert diagnosis.

"Your daughter is out of the woods, she was really lucky that though the blade pierced through, the force of the knife on impact was not so powerful and it missed any of her vital organs. We have been able to fix the damage, but she will need to take things slowly for the next six weeks. She can go home tomorrow after a further 24 hour observation but you will need to bring her in for check-up next week. But right now, we are happy with her progress.

The emotions of the past two days all came rushing back to Ola and she suddenly broke into tears—tears of relief which very quickly turned to worry as her thoughts drifted over the events that led her to that moment. It had been the worst two days of her life where Ola sat beside Alicia's bed keeping vigil refusing to leave her on her own. Ray had been very supportive, he was in and out of the children's intensive care unit, bring Ola food at different times including things to help her feel comfortable on her bedside chair, praying for Alicia . . . her precious little girl. She worried about Michael whom she had not seen since they brought Alicia to hospital. She was grateful to Rita her friend who had taken him in. Ola was worried about him but apparently so was Rita who mentioned that he had not been eating and at some point she'd had to insist he ate something. Ola recollected her last conversation with him which weighed heavily on her mind.

"How are you?" Ola asked Michael,

"Um umh," was his mumbled reply. She literally could not drag a proper answer from him. All she got were deep grunts which only he could understand. Ola was worried but she was still too stressed to have the head or emotional space to address Michael's own issues!

"I will call you later," she sighed in frustration and the line went dead immediately. That had been it, no goodbye mummy from him, no questions about Alicia . . . nothing.

Ola wished she could understand what was happening to her family as her shoulders drooped in distress and began to shake as she was wracked with sobs. Gentle hands pulled her close, engulfing her in some kind of careful warmth. . . . the type she wasn't used to getting. Ola was too tired to think about it as the tension of being on edge seemed to finally take its toil and she allowed herself to settle into the warm embrace for the moment. She dropped her head against the broad board covered in blue stripes in front of her face which seemed to have the ability to curve and become even warmer as if that were possible, but it did!

". . . sshhhh," the tiny cooing sounds coming from the curvy, blue board jolted Ola from her thoughts, as she heard Ray speaking to someone.

". . . thank, you doctor."

"We will keep her in for the next 24 hours for observation," and he was gone.

"What kind of a mother will he think I am?" Ola berated herself for not talking to the doctor. "First I let my daughter stay in a house where she has been stabbed with a knife . . . even if by accident! . . . and now I cannot even talk to the good doctor who has helped make her better. All I am doing is crying into warm curvy shoulders . . . !"

Ola began to push against Ray's shoulders in panic making soft protesting noises as he attempted to hold her still in comfort. She didn't want comfort

". . . I don't deserve any comfort!" Ola told herself vehemently. She felt guilty because she seemed to cause problems and trouble for everyone.

"It's okay Ola . . . everything will be all right, Alicia is going to be okay . . . you can let it go now," Rays words seemed as if he could read into her thoughts and the muddle of feelings raging within her.

"Ola!" The loud sound of her name coming from Deji's mouth was like her worst nightmare rolled into one scene. Ola had not spoken to Deji since the fracas in the house. She had refused to take his calls or the calls of his friends and family members. Now here he was, breathing the same air as her. Why was he not in jail . . . why did they let him go she wondered enraged even further? Ola was angry at the law and the system for wanting to go through protocols and bureaucratic procedures or whatever other gibberish they called it.

She was livid that Deji had been let go by the Garda. She wished they had at least called her to let her know that they were not going to keep him in. It was things like this that made it difficult for her many times to report some of the things that Deji did to her. Ola wondered how she was expected to process a case against Deji if they were both going to go back to the same house! Even the social workers were investigating Michael's call and comments to see if he was safe in the house! Ola wasn't sure with Alicia was out of the woods if they would not say the same thing. It never entered Ola's mind that she would ever be the woman whom the state might try to take her children from! As if she didn't have enough problems Ola raged directing her anger towards Deji.

Ray gently let Ola go while still maintaining a hold on her hand, a touch which did not go unnoticed by Deji who seemed to take in the scene with an angry sneer. Looking directly over her head straight at Deji, Ray locked eyes with him and the atmosphere became charged with tension.

"Do you want me to wait with you?" Ray asked Ola without breaking eye contact with Deji.

"Thanks, I . . . , I'll be okay," Ola stammered to Ray in a soft appreciative yet apprehensive voice. "I'll be okay," she repeated this time louder as she seemed to get some of her confidence most of which came from anger.

"I have nothing to be ashamed of . . . I have nothing to be sorry for." Ola placated her conscience. She was upset that it still bothered her how it looked to Deji to have Ray hold her hand. She could not believe why she was embarrassed for a man who had left her many times to go and be with other women . . . a man who raped, abused and threatened to kill her! . . . A man who put her daughter in hospital and turned her only son into a mumbling mess . . . Ola was so angry with herself she wished she didn't have to know herself!

Ola was disgusted with herself and wondered if it served her right to be treated badly by Deji. The more she thought about it the more she berated herself especially for still caring about what Deji thought. Finally sighing in resignation, Ola released her hand from Ray's feather light hold. Not before he gently squeezed the fingertips of her hands which seemed to give her some form of reassurance and energy to move.

"I'll call you later," she said to Ray as she ushered him through the door still ignoring Deji. He had done his worse already she reckoned.

"How is Alicia?" Deji asked immediately she turned around to face him

"She is not dead . . . no thanks to you!" she snapped at him.

"Ola, don't be like that, you know it was a mistake and I didn't know she was under the bed."

"There is no need to have this conversation because I have nothing to say to you. I am exhausted now. We can talk through the lawyers," she added moving out of his reach as he attempted to pull her into his arms.

"Olaaa . . . ," he drawled in that voice he used when he wanted to cajole her into doing things his way.

"No Deji, enough is enough. You almost killed me, you almost turned my son into a murderer, you almost killed my daughter! Do you think I am insane . . . ?" she ranted at him without giving him room to answer.

". . . How did the Garda let you out, what lies did you tell them? I promise this time, I will not cover up for you. You are going down for this. Even if it is the last thing I do, you've crossed the line this time . . . no don't touch me!" Ola shouted even more as Deji attempted to pull her close to himself. Not this time Ola reminded herself.

She had decided that even if she couldn't do it for herself . . . even if she were too weak to say no for herself, she knew she would have to say no for the kids. Just thinking that the kids deserved better was giving Ola the impetus to make the tough decisions she knew she had to make. Alicia and Michael did not ask to have parents like herself and Deji she reasoned. She knew she couldn't make them pay for it by continuously exposing them to danger just because she was afraid to be alone . . . yes, afraid, scared out of her mind of being alone. It sounded so final but she had to. She had to trust herself to make it. She had to be able to survive on her own . . .

"Olaaa, I love you," Deji's voice gently broke into her thoughts and she realised he had been talking to her and professing his love for her and the children.

"No Deji, you don't love me . . . , you want to own me. You don't love anyone, you only know how to love yourself but I am going far, far, far away from you. Enjoy your sad lonely life . . . but then like you said, there are women lined up waiting to take you in. Well, I am sorry for the next mug you find but this idiot is done being your mare!"

"Ola, Ola!" Deji called sharply, "keep your voice down, people can hear you and it's not like that. You are my wife, you are my family."

"Well, you should have thought of that before you decided to be god and decided when and how my life should end—at your command! Thanks but no thanks, you've done enough."

"Olaaaa . . ."

"Please go Deji, please go now before I scream this place down. I am almost losing my mind and the more time I spend with you the more I am losing it, go now please!" Ola ended her rant on a shrill note. Deji finally seemed to get the message as he looked at her for a moment, bent his head as if in defeat and walked towards the door. As Ola took a sigh of relief happy to see his back, Deji came to an abrupt stop and turned around and there seemed to be tears in his eyes. This really shocked Ola, who had never seen Deji cry or even show signs of weakness or obvious pain. She was more used to angry Deji, disgusted Deji or superior Deji who was always right . . . not this Deji with a contrite looking face, looking teary! The sight of him like that tugged at her heart strings, it made Ola long for a moment for that life, the dream she had of being with Deji, . . . together . . . forever . . . wondering where it had gone . . .

"I didn't mean to hurt anyone you know. I don't know what came over me," Deji seemed to gain more confidence as he noticed her weakening.

"It must have been some form of spiritual attack against me. I can't seem to help myself and everywhere I have been they say there is some kind of spiritual attack or generational curse that comes on us sometimes. Ola . . . you are an African woman and you cannot say you don't understand all these wicked home people and how some of them can use their witchcraft to affect people. You know they can be jealous especially when people are living abroad. Remember, Ola, even you have said it before that it is evil that is attacking my mind and body that is why I cannot control myself. Please Ola! I am prepared to go to anyone and we can pray about it and make it go away, we can overcome this together, we can bind the evil forces coming against our family. Don't let the devil win over us."

". . . the devil, the devil! Which devil are you talking about?" Ola shouted finally losing her cool. "You . . . you . . . you . . . you . . . you . . . you are the devil that has been sent to destroy my life. If there is any devil, then he is inside that jacket in front of me. You want to pray, then go and pray, get healed, then come and talk to me. But right now you are the devil that needs casting out. Devil indeed! Have you not heard that the devil is the thief and what has he come to do? Ehn . . . ? What has he come to do? Does the good book not say "kill, steal and destroy"? If I were to write your resume now and was asked for your personal profile, that is exactly what I would write. They say you should state your purpose in maximum of three words, well, I have yours sussed out for you to *'kill, steal and destroy'*. Tell me," Ola railed on, "which devil was standing over you when you held a knife over my throat, when you pushed the sharp pointed edge of a carving knife against the side of my neck. Which devil was holding your hand when you waved a knife in front of my face? You know what? If you have that kind of devil troubling you then I am definitely better off without you. Have you not heard that the companion of fools shall be destroyed? If I stay around a devil disturbed man I might just end up as part of the statistics of women who died in their own homes.

"No Deji, enough is enough. Take your psychobabble or should I say HT-home trouble babble and go away. There was a time when I was ready to try anything. I clutched at every straw, every excuse, every reason I could find for why you hated me so much, why you could not stay faithful to me. I wondered why you found me so undesirable. I tried to make myself sexier for you. I tried to jump as high as you wanted me to. I tried and I tried. The more I tried the worse it got. But you know what, I am done. I am past caring. You should have tried when I still cared. You should have tried before I started wishing for you to go out and never come back home. You should have tried before I realised that the children I was staying with you for so that they would not be without both parents were smarter than that and could see the messy sham we called marriage. They could see the hateful relationship we were lying about. Go now Deji before I confess all the thoughts in my mind concerning you."

Without saying a further word, Deji slowly walked out of the room, leaving Ola with the echo of the thoughts that had awakened in her head. She sat down in a huff as her heartbeat accelerated and she allowed her thoughts to wander into all the possible things that should happen to Deji as punishment for what he had done to her dreams, her life . . . her family. Ola cringed as her thoughts got darker. Burying her face in her hands she cried out for help.

"I am going to hell . . ." she cried out in self-recrimination ". . . hell."

———◦◦◦◦◦◦———

Chapter Twenty six

"Noooo . . . noooo, please Mummy, help me, help meeee," the familiar cry from Alicia broke into Ola's sleep. She groggily pushed back her covers and jumped out of bed making her way to Alicia's room. The sight never ceases to break her heart as it always did—Alicia crouching in the corner of her bed with her blanket and Pinky her doll tightly squeezed together. The surprising thing was that Alicia would still be asleep throughout the whole experience.

"Alicia, Alicia, come on my love, wake up, it's just a bad dream. Sshhhh . . . its mummy, mummy is here now, you are okay." Ola gently took Alicia into her arms, trying to surround her with her body warmth as she gently tried to open her clenched fist to release the blanket.

It had been a year since the knife from the tussle between Deji and Michael ended in Alicia being stabbed. It saddened Ola that the way children could sleep without a care was gone from her little innocent baby. She woke up every night, usually around 3am except for the nights when she slept in Ola's room. She now seemed to have developed a need for contact with her mother or another human presence to sleep through the night.

"Wake up baby, it's just a bad dream," Ola shook her more vigorously to wake her from the throes of the nightmare. Even the bitter cold nights of Dublin was not enough to put the fear at bay as Alicia was drenched in sweat. Slowly, her lids fluttered open with tears running down her face, which just broke Ola's heart all over again.

"Mummy . . . ?" Alicia's gently voice questioned the presence in her room.

"It is mummy my love, are you okay?"

"There was a bogeyman, he had big clothes and he tried to hurt me mummy, I was really scared . . ." Alicia said the last words as her voice broke in a sob.

"It was just a bad dream my love, just a bad dream. You know I am always close by and I listen out for you and I will not let anything hurt you."

"What if you are not there mummy, what if it happens by mistake? What if it happens when I am away playing like we were playing hide and seek?" Holding on to her emotions, Ola tried to reassure Alicia and help her to feel safe.

"You know what? We'll stay in my room together tonight and see how you feel in the morning."

"Thanks mum. I feel better when you are there." Lifting Alicia in her arms, Ola made for her room. She was such a big girl now it was getting more and more difficult to carry her in her arms, but this was not the time to say that. She needed some gentleness that moment. Gently depositing her on one side of the bed, Ola pulled the covers over her then said a prayer that put the bogeyman in a faraway place that he couldn't cross over to the side where Alicia and Mummy were because there was a big, tall wall between them. Dropping a gentle kiss on her forehead, Ola reached out to turn off the light but Alicia's cry of protest stopped her.

"Please leave the light on mummy. I can't sleep when the light is off."

"I will be here with you love."

"Please Mummy, I want the light."

"Okay, I will leave the small light beside the bed so it's not shinning into your eyes. Sleep now my precious and maybe we can draw the picture of the bogeyman the way that nice lady taught us and then we can burn him and throw him far, far . . . far way."

Waking up from terrifying nightmares had been on-going with Alicia who had even seen a child psychologist and all that, Michael as well. It was really only by miracle that Ola still had the kids. Social services had to investigate her role in the incident to ascertain if she and Deji were endangering the children's lives. The only thing that clinched it for her was her pledge to take the children away from the cantankerous atmosphere of their home and only allow supervised visits for Deji and the children which would to be regularly evaluated.

Ola also moved out of the house. She wanted a new start and that house and its constant reminders of Deji did not allow her to do that. With Michael, it had been one physical fight or other in school. He had become the recluse with loud outbursts and impatience with anyone and everyone, from his classmates to neighbours. In fact, after the last altercation with Deji, it was almost as if she was the perpetrator the way she got treated. The welfare officers came over and they spent hours and hours quizzing the kids, asking questions to ascertain if the kids were abused by both parents or if they were neglected. Getting into the bed, she gathered Alicia close to her warmth and she soon drifted off to sleep, while Ola was kept awake by the thoughts playing through her head.

At least one good thing had come out from her fiasco with Deji and the upheaval he had brought into her life. They had lived apart for about a year now during which period she had completed a number of short college courses The best thing was that with so much time on her hands she'd started baking for friends, for their children's birthdays, surprise 40th and 50th parties and even some wedding anniversaries. Ola felt so proud of her accomplishments that she had started working on how to get her business into the mainstream market and not just baking for the African community. Her main desire now was how to package the business to produce finger foods with some of the lovely African pastries she made. She was presently sharing a small work space with another lady who ran an African restaurant. Ola sang to herself as her confidence seemed to increase in her ability. Maybe somewhere under the dark clouds she thought, there might just be a silver lining. Joining in the song from the radio she allowed her happiness out.

"I will make it, in the nn . . ." Ola sang to Vicky Winnan's song playing on CD.

". . . Someone is happy," the sound of Ray's voice halted the next words of the song on her lips.

Ray! Ola exclaimed to herself. She had not seen him since that night at the hospital. She wondered how he knew where she was . . . , how he knew where to find her. One whole year had passed and not a word. The warm feeling that coursed through her body at the sound of his voice all of a sudden seemed to change to anger as she tried to work herself up to be angry so she didn't betray too much of her pleasure at seeing him but it was proving to be really hard.

"My . . . ," Ola uttered under her breath, thinking he was mighty fine! The guy sure knew how to turn a girl's head . . . Peeking at him from under her lashes Ola noticed Ray's well-groomed hair, and rugged shoulders firmly outlined under his black winter jacket.

Gathering herself together, Ola chose to play it safe and went on the attack to defend her emotions. She really didn't feel up to handling any man today of all days.

"Rrrr Ray . . . to what do I owe this August visit in November?" asked Ola as she stumbled over his name.

"Is that your way of saying you are happy to see me or . . . ?" Ray teased as he let his words trail away in a fashion that got her supplying answers to questions he had not even asked!

"I . . . I don't know . . . ," Ola began to say then thought better of it, but the words were out of her mouth already. "What do you want Ray?"

"I missed you. I have missed you so much that it took everything in me to stay away from you all this while." His direct answer seemed to leave her stumped and short of words for a few minutes. How did one answer that? It was what she wanted to hear, yet she was afraid to hear it.

"Don't talk silly nonsense."

"It's not nonsense Ola . . . I've missed you."

Every time he said those words the way his lips curled around the words were so suggestive Ola imagined his lips curling along the vein on the side of her neck. The same vein which seemed to be pounding so fast she was certain it was visible for all to see, making her drop her eyes in embarrassment. Her mind suddenly filled with thoughts of Ray's lips doing mind blowing things to her body sending tingles down her back, making Ola groan.

Moving closer to take a hold of her hands Ola jumped out of his reach. She wasn't sure she could handle a touch from Ray right now.

"You just disappeared," Ola said in a low accusing tone, making the light that surrounded his face to dull a bit as he looked pained.

"I am sorry Ola. It took everything I had not to come barging to your house after you left the hospital, but I knew . . . ," his face fell as his voice trailed off.

"Knew what . . . ?" Ola prompted him, anxious to hear what he had to say.

"I knew you were still in love with him. I knew that your emotions were all over the place with Alicia in the hospital and Michael . . . I knew it was a difficult time for you. But I also knew that you would not allow yourself to accept help from me . . . at least not at that time."

". . . Hum mm," was all Ola could mumble at his accurate sensitivity to the madness of what had been going on in her life at that time.

"How are you, I mean, really, how are you doing?"

"Exhausted, Ray, really exhausted," when he remained silent and said nothing, she continued talking. Just one of the things she'd missed about him in the past year. He never jumped into a sentence, he had so much control that he allowed her to finish what she was saying. He even used the silence to push her to say more. It always marvelled Ola how he seemed to get to her that she finds herself saying things she'd had no plans to say.

"I feel as if I cannot stop, as if I cannot slow down, if you know what I mean . . ."

"I saw on Facebook that you are having an opening of a cake and tasty treats store for the African meat pies. That is such a great idea I was too excited I had to come and see you."

"Yeah, it's only a small place and I am sharing with an already established eatery place so hopefully, it will draw some market . . . tt . . ." Ola's speech faltered as she suddenly noticed the intensity with which Ray was looking at her.

"What is it?"

"I missed you. I wish I was here to see your growth and this very confident woman standing before me with plans and a business to go. I am full of admiration for you and what you are doing for yourself."

"I. I . . . , I don't know if I can do this now Ray. I am still not okay, I am still so messed up. The kids, Dej . . ."

". . . Shhhh" Ray placed his index finger on her lips as he moved closer to her "I know you are *'not together'* as you say and I am not here to upset you. . . . But I like you. I really like you and I can't for the life of me get you out of my head—the truth is that I don't want to. I like you too much. I think of you all the time. I see you in everything I do. I tell you every good thing that happens to me during the day, I feel you beside me when I wake up in the morning. I really like you . . . you are in my head."

"I can't Ray. I am flattered that you know all the baggage I have and you still feel something for me but . . . , I . . . , I can't. I have been down that road of being with someone I loved whom I thought loved me but I am scared. I am . . . scared," Ola ended on a sob.

"Why . . . ?" was all he asked as his looks darkened. "Why?"

"Oh I don't know. No . . . , maybe I do know," Ola retorted. "I guess for once in my life I am happy to be living for me, by my rules. I go when I want, I come when I want. I am enjoying being free. I mean really free. Is that selfish? well that is what you Nigerian men have turned me into, a selfish bitch with no care for anyone but myself!

"Don't do that Ola, don't do that."

"Don't do what! That is exactly what I am talking about people just coming into my life feeling they have the right to tell me what I can and cannot do. Well you know what, I am sick and tired of it. I am Oladele Adegoke and for once I will not allow myself to be sucked in again by a lie." Ola reverted to addressing herself with her birth family name.

"This is not a lie Ola. What I feel for you is not a lie. The truth be told, what you feel for me is not a lie as well, if you will only let yourself and truly trust yourself as you have just said."

"That is just chemistry and I assure you that whatever reactions my body has to you will pass. I will make it pass. I know some people say the best way to get over one man is to get under another! You know what? I am tired of being under anyone. If my body refuses to respond, all I need to do is remember the knife held to my throat, or the knife stuck in my daughter, or a son who was so pushed to the edge he had a carving knife waiting, plotting the day he would attack his own father in defence of his mother. No way, Ray, no way. Even if I was tempted the N word for me is the final straw, a Nigerian man, never again Ray, never again. For me to get into a place where I am treated as someone's property there is just no way."

"Ola, you are making a big mistake, first yes I am a Nigerian man but I am not Deji. I have never been and I will never be. I have never in my life put my hands on a woman to hurt her physically and I never will. Yes Deji hurt you but all Nigerian men are not like that. Abuse is not restricted to a nationality type. Maybe certain situations and beliefs exacerbate it but it is really an individual thing. I should know because in the course of my work, I have seen abusers from different nationalities." He seemed to temporarily come up for air then continued softening his voice.

". . . Ola . . . , you cannot punish me for what he did. Worse still you cannot punish yourself for what he did to you. If you lock others out, invariably, you're locking yourself in. Then he wins Ola . . . then he wins. Every day you deny yourself happiness, he wins again and again . . . I love you, yes I do. Don't look so shocked, I love you. I would not have waited one year in the hope that you might have healed enough to even consider being with me.

". . . But I love you. These hands are big, yet they are not to hit, they are here to love and nurture you. These lips are not to wound, they are here to encourage you when you are weak, they are here to caress you when you are cold, they are here to praise you when you excel. I am Ray Johnson, I am not an abuser, I am here to love you and cherish you if you will let me . . ."

Ola opened her eyes and stared at Ray in wide-eyed amazement. She had never seen him literally lose control before. How she wanted to believe every word he said, how she really wanted to believe every word, forget about the past and loose herself in him. But she was scared. She had just found herself and she was scared to give that up again, so soon after Deji and all he'd put her through. She and Deji were legally separated now and he had wanted to file for divorce as well but he was told by his solicitor he needed to wait for one more year. Anyway, Ola knew he was living with someone else now and so he had no hold over her life. But she lived with the scars of her relationship with Deji and she wasn't sure if she could allow herself to love again. It was too much pain . . . too much risk involved! Though Ray sounded sincere, Ola knew she could not take him up on his offer. She knew she would regret this but she was too scared of losing herself in him. Dropping her head in defeat Ola tried to explain her fears to Ray, her loving hero who wanted to save her she laughed sceptically.

"I . . . , I . . . ," momentarily lost for words, Ola was shocked when Ray reached across the room for her, pulling her slowly as if happening in slow motion, Ray lifted her slowly against the hardness of his body. Slowly bending his head he angled himself till he blocked her view from the outside world and he held her that way for a few seconds but it felt like such a long time that she finally opened her eyes and looked into his. She was shocked by the raw emotions she could see on his face this close which sent tingles down her spine. It felt as if she could see the emotions in his very soul.

"Keep your eyes open because I don't want you to confuse me with anyone else. I am Ray Johnson and . . . , I love you." As his head descended to close the distance between them, Ola reached up and met him part of the way with her lips pursed waiting.

Kissing Ray was all she'd imagined it would be and more as his presence and aura surrounded her making feel safe. It felt so good she never wanted it to end. The moistness of Ray's lips teased every corner and space available in and around hers drawing a groan from her, melting herself into him. At that moment she lost the struggle with her consciousness and she forgot about the door, the shop or the possibility of anyone walking into the store. Oh how she wanted Ray . . . , her body responded well to him, he said the right things that made her moist all over . . . and it had been a long time . . .

Ray slowly allowed her body to slide down his as he put her down on her feet, creating some space between them. "You allowed society and people dictate to you who to stay with because you were afraid of what they will say, don't let them stop you from what you want because again you are afraid of them." The cold draft that came in from the door which swung shut was the first indication that Ray was gone. Suddenly feeling cold, Ola wrapped her arms around herself as a melancholic mood descended over her. What now, again, Ray was gone.

NOTANABUSER

Poem inspired by the character Ray Johnson

Hands, hands so big
Yet they are not to hit,
They are here to love and nurture you
Guide you to where you want to go
Cover you from the storm
Embrace you when it's cold

Lips, lips so wide
Yet they are not to wound,
They are here to encourage you when you are weak,
Caress you when you are cold
Praise you when you excel

Fist, fist so strong
Yet they are not to pummel
They open out and caress your cheeks
They close up and lift up your head

I am a man, not an abuser,
I am here to love and cherish you

By Ebun Akpoveta

CHAPTER TWENTY SEVEN

"I am a man I am not an abuser,
I am here to love and cherish you"

OLA KNEW, SHE WAS GOING to regret her decision as her harsh words to Ray . . . played over and over in her mind. She wondered what had come over her . . . rejecting his offer of friendship and love. He would never hit her she was almost sure . . . no! . . . almost sure was good enough anymore. Ola realised that was the problem! She didn't want almost sure, she wanted definitely sure, she wanted hundred per cent sure.

"I need to be sure, after Deji . . . , I just need to be sure. I am not a spring chicken any more. What will I say is my excuse this time ehn . . . ? I have two children already so I cannot claim that my biological clock was ticking. I have been there done that and worn the t-shirt. I can't put myself under that emotional stress again. I just can't Ola," muttered aloud as she tried to convince herself she had made the right decision. Even as it tugged at her heart that she was throwing love away, Ola resolutely refused to allow thoughts of what could have been derail her from her plans.

Her business plan was all on course and her store would be opened in two weeks. There was a lot to do so Ola happily allowed herself to be distracted from thinking of Ray Johnson and his delectable lips!

Deciding what to wear has always been a big issue for Ola and that day being her opening day, the pressure was definitely on! So mustering all her strength, Ola got up from the bed where she had been sitting fiddling with her jewellery box, having finally selected yellow pearls which always added elegance to any black dress.

She had been on this long journey of self-discovery and learning to trust and build bridges with her family. It has definitely been a tedious process getting where she was, but looking back now, Ola realised it had been worth it. Starting her own business and getting a space to share with an established business was genius for her. She owed a lot of thanks to the seminar she attended where the speaker told them that there was one small step they could take right now to get to the change they wanted. Ola started baking first at home for her kids' birthdays then for friends and then friends of friends. The results has had been great. The advantage was that it allowed her to work and still be able to control her working hours and be there for the kids when they came back home from school. She was able to still help them with homework and take them for sports and Irish dancing lessons. Alicia loved that and Michael was mad into football.

Ola's cakes had become her unique selling point. In a way, as the saying went *'all things work together for good . . .'* even the bad things—must be true Ola thought. After the developments with Deji and the fight with Michael, Ola became really melancholic, she wanted to disappear, she wanted to run away and hide, but to where? That had been the big question. Who would hide her? It made her so home sick for Nigeria and her birth family she suddenly became Afrocentric as her few remaining friends teased her. She began listening to Nigerian music all the time. Even her African clothes that had gone for years without getting much use suddenly became her comfort clothes.

Ola was happy about it as it became a key to the uniqueness of her business. Her cakes were designed with colourful maps that the celebrant identified with the most. The map of the city they lived in was made into a picture or their favourite activities or group colours. For most of the African Children, she made two maps; one of Ireland and the other from the celebrant's home country then she used the celebrant's face as the connector between the two maps. It was a lot of work but parents were willing to pay extra for the unique design so that had been great for business.

Slipping on her shoes, Ola wearily dragged herself through the door. The kids had been so good and supportive. For a fourteen year old . . . well nearly fifteen, Michael seemed to have matured overnight, becoming more of a model child. Sometimes it felt as if they had robbed him of his youth and youthfulness. He was so serious . . . , so responsible now . . . Sometimes she just wished he would act like the child that he was, but he had taken on the serious responsibility of protecting his family from the very thing Ola was afraid of . . . , the fear of having to face the public alone . . . , one of the reasons she endured years of abuse in silence. The reason she had put up with a lot of Deji's carry on . . . the public masks, the silence, all for what ehn?

"Fifteen years after all that hassle and pain, I am still on my own!" Thoughts of life with Deji and the warm feelings from being with Ray chased each other around Ola's mind leaving her confused as one act of kindness changed over to a different act of cruelty, a caress became a cracking slap . . . a kiss became a curse making Ola shudder.

It had been two weeks since Ola's last encounter with Ray. She couldn't shake the thoughts from her mind. Even thoughts of Deji could not erase the image of his face from her mind—his touch, his words, his kiss, the feel of his warm, hard body against her supple chest . . . and to know that he loved her and actually liked her as a person.

"I wish . . . ," Ola sighed lost in thoughts.

"We are going to be late Mum," shouted Michael as he saw his mum moping around the house as she usually did these days. Ola thought they didn't know that she cried a lot but they heard her in the kitchen after they had done the dishes and presumably gone to bed. Michael felt awful that he did not do more for her, but he had made a solemn promise to himself that when he was older and did not need anyone's permission to work, he would be out there like a shot so he could earn money and ease her pain.

"I will be able to help. At least now I do all that I can" reasoned Michael. *"I make sure all the dishes are done and I wash all of Alicia's school clothes as well. At least that reduces the work for her, even if it's a bit. She won't let me do more, she wants me to enjoy my youth—fat chance of that when I have the image of killing my sister hanging over me all the time. Oh well, that's the price I have to pay for being hot headed."* Michael had been referred to a child psychologist for a short

time as Alicia but he seemed to have managed to suppress a lot of his feelings giving Ola his mum the impression he was coping well after the incident . . .

"Come on Mum, let's go. This is your big day . . . !"

Indeed it was a big day for Ola as she looked around the room with all her friends supporting her. Her guests were having a glass of wine and having a taste of the different cakes and nibbles she was providing for the day. She got the purchasing managers from two hotels to attend as well. So hopefully, they would allow her to prepare nibbles for events at their hotels especially when they had migrant conferences or workshops. Sashaying around, Ola was the perfect hostess, she stopped to say hello to friends, Rita and her husband Ugo were there as well. She made sure her guests had enough to drink. She asked the hostesses helping her for the day to come out with fresh trays of the delicious pastries and cakes as they walked around showcasing her more exotic designs. It was like a dream but Ola felt confident and accomplished. She had come a really long way from the nervous person to the budding entrepreneur. She smiled as she thought about the name of her business 'OlaNibbles.'

Ola suddenly had a prickly burning sensation down her back. She raised her left hand to her throat, running her fingers around her yellow pearl necklace for some assurance. Ola then lifted her head to look around the room, wondering and . . . afraid that Deji might show up to disrupt her event as she had refused him to see the kids unless by the agreed appointment from the courts. It was not beyond him to try and destroy any good thing happening in her life. As her heart began to flutter in panic, Ola looked around the room self-consciously searching for what she didn't know. She believed that it was not possible for good things to happen, not to her! She knew it was too good to be true that she could break through and start a new life, that it was foolish of her, foolish . . . to even think that . . .

"Oh my . . . !" exclaimed Ola as her fear gave way to joy as she fully took in the lovely sight that met her eyes. A big bunch of red roses, probably over thirty! Ola's excitement was heightened by now.

"OMG, who does that these days," exclaimed Ola borrowing from Alicia's girlie vocabulary. It was Ray, her Ray, sweet, loving, caring Ray! He had come back . . . , he had come on her special day.

"Oh God, I am not alone . . . ," Ola realised.

Ray . . . , her Ray was standing at the back of the shop looking at her as if she was the only person in the room.

"OMG," exclaimed Ola again, realising he was making a very public declaration. She found there was nowhere to hide, no need to hide and she didn't want to hide! Looking straight at him, Ola could see the love, respect and value in his eyes, a man who was not afraid or ashamed to show his love

"This is what I need now, enough of the macho, lying cheating men. A man who is happy to wear his heart on his sleeve—and what lovely sleeves he has on," thought Ola as she took in his dashing navy coloured suit and his dark coloured tie with tiny stripes of yellow, sky blue and pink.

"Oh my," Ola couldn't help herself as she looked him over one more time. He looked great and impressive standing with the bunch of flowers and everyone else seemed to have noticed him as well!

Gathering herself together, Ola allowed everyone else fade into the background, the chatter faded, their stares faded, for once she was going to do what she wanted for herself, not what people expected of her. She didn't know where this would lead . . . , she didn't know how it would play out but her mind was made up, she was going to live her life for her.

Ola noticed the promise in Ray's eyes and she allowed herself to be drawn to go and see what they were offering. She was not going to allow her yesterday destroy her tomorrow. Adjusting the collar of his jacket around his neck, Ray and Ola began to move towards each other as their eyes locked across the room and their promise to each other reflected there for all to see . . .

"Maybe . . . ," Ola thought with a smile on her face

Maybe there is life . . .

Contact

To schedule a seminar, workshop or group facilitation session with your group, or to order Ebun Akpoveta's tapes and books please contact
Tel: 00353 87 131 11402, 00353 89 418 5169,
Email: unforgettablewoman.eb@gmail.com
info@tuwn.org
http://www.facebook.com/TUWNIreland
http://www.facebook.com/TRAPPEDprisonwithoutwalls
Web:www.tuwn.org

To attend one of the Unforgettable Women's Network Monthly Seminar you can find us on Facebook to get updates of our meeting dates. We run a three hours session on the 2nd Saturday of every month from 2- 5pm The Unforgettable Women's Network -TUWN believes every woman is important and advocates for the equal valuing of the female person.

For line Editor or Editing

Contact
Growing Words Publishers
Neltah Chadamoyo
Email: growingwordspublishers@gmail.com
Phone: 086 328 7711

Join the women working responsibly campaign - WWR
Support one woman today

If you have been affected by the subject in this book
Please Contact the following if in Ireland

Cosc—The National Office for the Prevention of Domestic, Sexual and Gender-based Violence. Department of Justice and Equality, 2nd Floor, Montague Court, Montague Street, Dublin 2. Tel: 01-4768680, Fax: 01-4768619, Email: cosc@justice.ie, Website: www.cosc.ie

Dolphin House - by referral from the courts

FlacFree Legal Advice Centres, 13 Lower Dorset Street, Dublin 1,

Immigrants Council of Ireland, 2 St Andrew Street, Dublin 2, Ireland, Tel: 01-674 0202, Email: admin@immigrantcouncil.ie

info@akidwa.ie, +353 (018) 34-9851

Information & Referral Line: 1890 350 250, Tel: 01-8745690, Fax: 01-8745320

National Women's Council of Ireland, 4th Floor, 2/3 Parnell Square East, Dublin 1,Rape Crisis Network Ireland, 4 Prospect Hill, Galway, 24 hour helpline—1800 778888, Tel: 091-563676 Fax: 091 563677, Email: info@rcni.ie

Samaritans 24 hour Helpline 1850 60 90 90 (ROI), Email: jo@samaritans.org

Tel: +353 1 8787248, Fax: +353 1 8787301, Website: www.nwci.ie

Tel: 00353 89 418 5169

Akidwa, *Unit 2 Killarney Court, Buckingham Street Dublin 1 Ireland,*

The Integration Centre, 20 Mountjoy Square East, Dublin 1, Ireland; Tel: 01-6453070, Email: ian@integrationcentre.ie, Website: www.integrationcentre.ie

The Unforgettable Women's Network—TUWN, Email: info@tuwn.org

Women's Aid Telephone: By post: Margaret Martin, Director, Women's Aid, 5 Wilton Place, Dublin 2, Tel: 01-6788858, Fax: 01-6788915 Email: info@womensaid.ie

Your Local GP

Around the World

The Samaritans are found in most countries and there are a lot of women's organisations that also give support.

Local Health Centres and GPs can also assist

Acknowledgment

There are so many people who made this book possible.

My sisters Bose Arogundade Aggre and Mae Edmonds who endured with me for two years while I *threatened* to write a book that exposed all the abuse women were enduring behind closed doors.

My two sons Patrick and Alex who were very understanding throughout the summer holiday and long hours where I could not give them a hundred per cent of myself. They encouraged me by asking how far I had gone with my writing and editing, brought me countless cups of tea and breakfast. The best sons ever. Thank you.

My Mum and Dad, Sir, Chief J. S. and Lady Grace Arogundade for bringing me up in love and helping me develop a good sense of self.

Winifred Akinyemi for being a good listening ear for every new thought about Ola and Deji and the madness going on with the Characters' lives.

My dear friend and Editor Neltah Chadamoyo for pushing me the extra mile, your patience and conscientiousness with the plot, dates and names . . . amazing.

I cannot mention you all but you see my heart and gratitude for your love and friendship. Thank you for being my friend.

Also by Ebun Akpoveta

Becoming Unforgettable- Uncovering the Essence of the Woman

This motivational book examines society's attitude toward women and highlights their plight behind closed doors. Becoming Unforgettable encourages women to step out of the box and reach for their personal best and it outlines 12 qualities that can take a woman from an ordinary existence to an unforgettable one. It gives voice to issues such as the following:

- *Martyr syndrome and co-dependency in women*
- *How stereotype compromises women's individuality*
- *12 qualities of an unforgettable woman*
- *What women really want from relationships*
- *Why women feign orgasm and experience low sexual drive*
- *The male and female dysfunctional shopping list for a partner*
- *Being a woman and a person*

Your mind your property—make it work for you

- *Identifying your fear triggers*
- *Why women don't need to be boys to succeed*
- *Submission—is it love or law?*
- *Chitchat—women's Achilles' heel*

For more details go to
Tel: 00353 89 418 5169, 00353 87 131 11402
Email: becomingunforgettable@tuwn.org
http://www.facebook.comTUWNIreland

Join the women working responsibly campaign - WWR

Support one woman today

Printed in Great Britain
by Amazon

10705985R00150